The Organ of Intelligence is as uplifting as it is down and dirty. A comic romp that touches the heart. Goldberg's acerbic and at times disturbing wit is a guilty pleasure, like those things you do behind closed doors that you wouldn't like to tell your friends about.
　　　　　—Stephen Finucan, author of *Foreigners*

Dear Mike Sharp

Celebrate health & Love

if you like this book

give me a call + we

can discuss it further

414-0474

Greg

Goldberg

A portion of the proceeds from the sale of
this book will be donated to the Lower
Mainland Brain Injury Association in Vancouver,
British Columbia, Canada.

The Organ of Intelligence

a novel

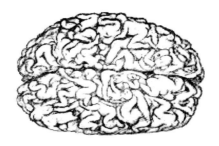

THE QUIRKY AND PERVERSE JOURNEY OF A HEAD INJURY SURVIVOR

GREGORY GOLDBERG

Design and Editing: Mavis Andrews http://peavi.bc.ca/members/MavisAndrews.html

Illustrations: Peggy Capek pbcapek@shaw.ca

The Secret of the Silent Hills © Les Baxter

Note for Librarians: A cataloguing record for this book is available from Library and Archives Canada at www.collectionscanada.ca/amicus/index-e.html

ISBN 1-4120-9513-1

Printed in Victoria, BC, Canada. Printed on paper with minimum 30% recycled fibre.
Trafford's print shop runs on "green energy" from solar, wind and other environmentally-friendly power sources.

Offices in Canada, USA, Ireland and UK

Book sales for North America and international:
Trafford Publishing, 6E–2333 Government St.,
Victoria, BC V8T 4P4 CANADA
phone 250 383 6864 (toll-free 1 888 232 4444)
fax 250 383 6804; email to orders@trafford.com

Book sales in Europe:
Trafford Publishing (UK) Limited, 9 Park End Street, 2nd Floor
Oxford, UK OX1 1HH United Kingdom
phone +44 (0)1865 722 113 (local rate 0845 230 9601)
facsimile +44 (0)1865 722 868; info.uk@trafford.com

Order online at:trafford.com/06-1268

10 9 8 7 6 5 4 3 2 1

To Jenny and my entire rehab team — with love.

This novel is a work of fiction but is deeply inspired by my own experiences and by my family, friends, and colleagues.

A head injury is not the end
of the road. It is the beginning
of a brand new journey.
— *Anonymous*

It is not sex that gives the pleasure,
but the lover.
— *Marge Piercy*

I can't begin to thank my writing coach, Mavis Andrews, enough for steering me through treacherous waters on my journey through shaping and completing this book. Without her expertise and literary navigational skills, I would still be swimming aimlessly in undressed images. Thanks, Mavis.

I would like to begin this book with a preemptive apology. There is a possibility that no matter how fictitiously written, carefully edited and lucidly argued this work is, there may still be people who disagree with my handling of a sensitive and controversial subject matter. For this and any relationship squabbles that I may cause, I would like to extend my sincere regrets.

Personal traumatic brain injury leading to divorce and an unconventional lifestyle has given me excusable reasons to be angry. Happily, my sense of humor didn't die in the accident, although it did come out overly bronzed. My ongoing struggle to manage cognitive problems and sadness was borne in the literal way.

I have revealed through narrative fiction filled with black humor, the inner thoughts and desires of Everyman in relation to the female half of the human race.

With my creative impulses now free of inhibition and flowing, vastly superior to what they were under my pre-accident limitations, I needed to express myself through a medium that would attract the imaginative person. This book has allowed me to get hot and heavy while taking a comical approach. It's nice to think that I may have some ease after releasing what was bottled up inside of me for so long.

I believe that men carry inside them a flask of sexual thoughts and that only mature women know its flavor. It is the "drug cocktail" of testosterone.

G.G.

A POLL OF LOVING COUPLES

From the multitude of trendy cafés and street corners in Victoria, British Columbia, 500 male-female volunteering couples between the ages of 20 and 70, were asked to verbally answer the following questions. Each couple member was interviewed separately and far from within earshot of their partner's inquisitive auditory capabilities. The questions appear below with their results.

Please Note: This poll is not about women's role in the world. It is not about gender equality or women as a whole. It is simply about views of members of a couple who are in a committed heterosexual relationship.

1) When having sex with your present partner, do you think he/she is fantasizing about someone else rather than you?

Women answered: Yes 74%   No 21%   Undecided 5%

Men answered: Yes 41%   No 56%   Undecided 3%

(Quite embarrassed, an elderly woman volunteer asked: "Is my husband around? Is he around? He better not be able to hear this or we are both in deep trouble.")

2) If you decided to remain celibate for the remainder of your life due to personal reasons, would your partner leave the relationship?

Women answered: Yes 81%   No 10%   Undecided 9%

Men answered: Yes 14%   No 73%   Undecided 13%

(One male volunteer asked before contemplating his answer: "If I had affairs would that be considered leaving the relationship?")

3) Are women as a whole gender group in a state of denial in regards to men's one true need for them?

Women answered: Yes 66%   No 44%

Men answered: Yes 89%   No 11%

(A female newlywed asked: "Do you mean the need that I know you mean? You know the basic need and all that other rude stuff?")

4) For men (at least those who can spell) is intimacy just an eight letter word?

Women answered: Yes 91%   No 9%

Men answered: Yes 67%   No 33%

(A middle-aged man covered in tattoos said: "I never heard that word before. Intima…intima…How did you say that?")

When women go wrong, men
go right after them.
— *Mae West*

The Organ of Intelligence

a novel

THE QUIRKY AND PERVERSE JOURNEY OF A HEAD INJURY SURVIVOR

GREGORY GOLDBERG

CONTENTS

P
A
R
T

O October
N
E

EQUITY

A starter home is a good place for couples who want to start things. Maybe life. Maybe children. Maybe dreams. The Cohens had such a house. It was a detached two-storey, wood-frame structure with a green shingled roof and white trim. A porch thrust out from the front door into a small yard. Mrs. Greenberg's drooping old cherry tree, now bare, hung over the sidewalk. "That neighbour of yours—her fucking fruit tree makes a mess of the whole neighborhood," was a mantra of the Cohens' retired (and moderately sane) other neighbor, Herman.

Reuben Cohen was on his way home from the Fresh Deli at the end of the day, a small bag of meats and cheese in one hand and a loaf of French bread in the other. Herman was in his front yard, swearing at the cherry tree again. Reuben quietly approached him from behind.

"Hands up! Gimme your wallet!" he shouted, sticking one end of the French loaf into Herman's spine. Herman pivoted on his newly replaced hip, and hit out at his attacker with a stiff left hook that almost connected with the mock thief's solar plexus. Reuben jumped back. "Holy shit, old man! You're getting faster every day!"

Herman blushed, pride over punching speed mixed with embarrassment. "Sorry, Reuben. You okay?"

Reuben, having regained his stance and composure, laughed. "You still have one hell of a hook, old man. Good thing that one didn't connect."

Herman snorted. "I'll get you next time. Say, did old hag

Greenberg give you more of her mountain ash jelly? That stuff will give you the shits for a week straight. I hate her damn jelly." So did Reuben, but he shrugged. He didn't want to hurt the elderly widow's feelings so he just stored the jelly in his basement cupboard, out of sight, out of mind.

"Take it easy, Herman," he called out as he headed up his front walk. He just had time to whip up a little picnic and have a quick shower before Shelly got home. As the door closed behind him, he knew he was grinning like a love-happy fool.

All around the city, as evening closed in, cars, buses, taxis and subway trains spat out weary workers. Meals were being thrown together or ordered in, and water use soared as people sought to shower away the cares of the day.

POTENT BUT WARM

Shelly Cohen closed her eyes against the luxuriant heat of the shower and let the water soothe her. Think positive, she told herself. *Life is almost perfect and it is just going to get better. So there.*

They had a nice house and plans for a family. She wasn't pregnant yet, but…Shelly smiled to herself at the thought of the fun they would have trying to conceive. On top of that, Reuben was so excited about his new job. As of tomorrow he'd be Chef Reuben at a place so classy it could get away with having "Shack" in its name. Murphy's Seafood Shack. He'd taken her there once. The food was great and you felt like a star sitting there among the *hoi polloi*; they'd blown a month's budget on the meal.

She let the water beat at the tension in her neck and shoulders, and tried not to think about her own job, but the more she tried, the more it beaded up behind her eyes like a headache. *It's just a job*, she told herself, *just eight hours out of a day to finance the rest of my life.* But "just a job" didn't cut it. Eight hours was feeling like a life sentence. Was it so bad to wish for a simple job that didn't involve pandering to client demands day in and day out? She felt overwhelmed—and what did her boss do? Moved her one rung up the ladder. "You're not overwhelmed," he'd said. "You're underchallenged."

As if! Shelly squeezed the soft bar of soap and wrote on the tile: "As if!" Then: "Work sucks!" She wrote it over and over, the almost invisible letters flowing into and over one another in indecipherable whorls.

Water pounded. Her knuckles scraped across the tiles.

Work sucks!

The water had started to run cool. She scooped up the shampoo bottle and tried to flip up the cap. It wouldn't open. She tried with one hand, then the other, then her teeth, and finally slammed it down on the flooded shower floor. Then she kicked it aside and settled for just using conditioner.

Reuben, sprawled out on the carpet wearing nothing but his birthday suit, was scanning the baseball standings in the daily paper when he heard a muffled thud. He leaped up and raced into the en suite bathroom. "Is everything okay, honey?" he yelled over the pounding of the water. "You've been in there quite a while." He edged open the shower curtain just as water-wrinkled fingers turned off the taps. Grabbing a soft cotton bath towel from the rack, he held it wide. "I heard a bang. Did you slip? Are you hurt?"

Shelly flung the curtain aside and stepped into his waiting arms. He enfolded her in the bath towel and she slumped against him. "I'm okay. I couldn't get the damn shampoo bottle open so I whipped it."

Standing wide-legged, he hugged her against him and rocked back and forth until they almost lost their balance and he had to press her up against the wall. Her face had lost its somber look. She leaned back to look into his eyes. "What would I do without you, Reuben? When I need you, you're always there for me."

"And I always will be." He smiled down on her, relishing the smoothness of her skin and the warmth of the smile that crept into her eyes. He slid his hand down to her ass and squeezed. "Want a quickie?"

"Oh, honey, I've gotta vent first."

She looked serious. He frowned. "What's up?"

"My boss, Mr. Raven, what else?"

"Ol' Crowbait? What'd he do?" Reuben perched on the toilet seat and watched as she marshaled her thoughts. A worry line creased her forehead and he wished he could make it go away.

"'You're not overwhelmed, Shelly, you're underchallenged,'" she quoted indignantly. Her voice deepened as she mimicked her boss. "'I want to raise the gates and move you onward and upward, Shelly. And, may I say, my dear, that I feel you are valuable to this organization, a real team player.'" She slumped against the sink, arms crossed, and raised an eyebrow at her spouse. "He says I'm the most attractive financial consultant team member he's ever had the pleasure to work on top of."

Reuben snorted a laugh.

Shelly rolled her eyes. "He's such a jerk. Plus he makes me gag, and I'm not kidding" She pulled a disgusted face. "If there's such a thing as bulk after-shave, he probably buys it. I can't imagine smelling him for another day, let alone another twenty-plus years. It'd be a life sentence — no, it'd be a NO-LIFE sentence." She grabbed the towel and started scrubbing her paintbrush-like hair. Reuben eased the towel from her fingers and took over.

Tension seeped out of her, and finally she moaned, "Oh, Reuben, I want out, I really do. My life is wasting away with every grinding second on my cubicle clock, click by crawling click. Every day seems interchangeable with any other day."

Reuben rubbed her hair soothingly. "I wish I could tell you to quit, but...what choice do we have?"

"I know, I know, it's a must," Shelly interrupted. "It's just that I fell into this job straight out of college and I feel like I'm still falling."

"This job at Murphy's — it's gonna go somewhere, I can feel it, and then you can sit back and look at your options, okay?" Reuben rewrapped her like a fragile gift and sat her on his knee.

She burrowed her head against his neck. "Did I ever mention that ninety percent of my clients are old bags? And that fifty percent of them are mean?"

"Focus on the paycheck."

She sighed. "The highlight of my day is my Caramel Macchiato coffee and blueberry muffin every morning. It's my only way to fuel up and prepare for a wheel-spinning day of clients who are either rude, loud, or bent on maintaining their upper-crust lifestyle, but I'm going to get so fat."

"I'm always happy to help you work off the muffins." Reuben grinned, waggling his eyebrows in an exaggerated leer. "Anyway, you're climbing the corporate ladder and Raven obviously thinks you can handle it. That's something to be proud of."

"I guess."

"It won't be forever."

"Promise?"

"Hey, I'll do the best I can." Reuben leaned forward to rub noses with her.

"I could go back to school. Or be a stay-at-home mom."

"Or hang out with your friends. Gossip and shop."

Shelly stroked the back of his neck, winding a blond curl around her finger, a dreamy look on her face. "That would work."

Their favorite place in the whole house was their spare room. It was large and bright, with a wide bay window and hardwood floors. The thought of transforming it into a baby's room was almost too exciting to visualize.

The eager couple wasn't waiting for Shelly's eventual pregnancy; they had already started decorating. In one corner stood five crooked stacks of children's books topped with *The Complete Tales of Winnie the Pooh, Charlotte's Web, Charlie and the Chocolate Factory, The Adventures of Huckleberry Finn,* and *Treasure Island.* Beside these fragile towers of children's literature sat a covered picnic tray prepared "à la Reuben," with aromatic cheeses, delectable cold cuts, cherry tomatoes and fat Sicilian olives nestled on a plate next to slices of French bread slathered with butter, a bottle of California merlot, and a cluster of candles.

Shelly's damp towel stood in for a mattress; they didn't need anything more. After a while, lovemaking gave way to hunger. Reuben spread out a sleeping bag, and when they were settled with picnic tray at hand, he popped a bright red tomato in Shelly's waiting mouth. Then he reached down and tickled her knees. She squirmed aside, laughing. He passed her a carefully built sandwich and a glass of wine, then settled back with his own. Shelly bit into her sandwich and reached for *Charlotte's Web.* "When I was a kid, I used to read under the covers with a flashlight, when I should have been sleeping," she said. In the soft glow of the candles, she leaned against Reuben and flipped through the pages, the illustrations flitting by like frames of animation. Distant sounds of the night city drifted softly in through the window as they watched the moving images through one book after another until the last book dropped, and then they fell asleep in each other's arms, lulled by thoughts of what the future would bring.

Rays of morning sunlight beamed into their future nursery and drifted over two naked bodies locked in a cocoon of contentment. From outside came the jarring sounds of children's quarreling voices. Reuben groaned: "G'way, kids." He rolled to his feet and stretched wide before padding across the room to a rolling cart on which sat sample cans of paint and a selection of brushes. Sheets of newspaper were spread out under a large unused poster board on the wall. Facing it, he began painting with an impulsive morning vigor.

Murals of Shelly's favorite childhood characters would be painted on the walls. Reuben had already applied an undercoat of white to the huge board and now was testing colors one by one. Shelly stretched lazily and enjoyed the view, watching the way his cute butt wavered with each exquisite stroke, like two soft and very touchable sponges set side by side.

She studied the poster board. "Let's do a wall of virgin white to symbolize our family's new start, with touches of blue to add a calm, imaginative feel. Think Chagall."

"Chagall it is." Rueben's brush splashed streaks of blue and yellow across the poster board. She nodded and, stretching wide, sang out, "Listen up, world! I am so lucky to have a husband who is almost as beautiful as my illusions of him."

He laughed as she danced around the room singing like a high school cheerleader as she bellowed her hurrahs. "He's creative and thoughtful and hot—and, oooh, can this man cook! Look out, world, Reuben Cohen's on his way!"

"Yeah, but now we've got to get a move on." Stepping back, he dropped his brushes in the water bucket, and then headed off, saying over his shoulder, "We'll get back to it tonight—celebrate my new job. Hey, yours too!"

"Okay, okay," she muttered, staring at the poster board. "Oh, Reuben, just think," she called out, "these bright colors will provide a psychological lift for the dreariest of days. That's what my *Interior Design for Expectant Mothers* magazine says." Shelly, dream-driven, danced around, scattering newspaper with her feet. "Just imagine the beauty that will fill us all in this room!"

She raced into the bathroom. With his chin lathered in shaving cream, Reuben stuck his head through the shower curtain. "Shel, honey, we've got to hustle. I can't be late and you won't want to be."

"Oh, I'll be fine—and so will you, honey." She gave a pinch to his bum that made him jump and said, all innocence, "Are you feeling nervous? You shouldn't be. Murphy's Seafood Shack is lucky to get you."

Reuben had graduated at the top of his class as a certified Chef de Cuisine and ended up being a sous chef at the Zum Rhein German Schnitzel House. He'd hated it. No room for creativity, he said, but this new job was a plum. Although Murphy's called itself a shack, it was anything but and had a four-star rating. A few years there and Reuben would be ready to reign in the kitchens of a top hotel.

Shelly took her turn in the shower and got ready in record time, time she spent thinking. "The magazine also said," she told him, slipping into her dress, "that the written word can be a powerful image. Let's put up a saying that motivates and inspires us."

"Let's save it for tonight." Reuben finished cleaning up in the bathroom and headed for his clothes.

"We'll put a slogan as a border around the room." Wiggling her toes into a pair of low-heeled shoes, she cleared her throat. "It's going to be 'The power of now!'" she shouted as he shrugged into his freshly dry-cleaned slacks and sports coat.

"Here's some power of now for you. If we don't get out of here now we'll be late. Can you spell 'unemployment'? You're beautiful, it's late, let's go."

"I'm ready," Shelly smoothed her hair and slung her purse over her shoulder. "What's your panic?"

Reuben urged her forward, wondering what she'd say if he told her how badly his stomach was knotted? She'd probably have them both dropping into the lotus position for a ten-minute meditation. Which wouldn't help. The only thing that would help was succeeding at Murphy's. Finally he was getting to do the kind of work he wanted and excelled at. *Now I can really start to contribute to my family*, he thought. It sounded good.

DIARY

Stiff with nerves, Shelly rode the escalator from the concourse to the main lobby elevator of the Toronto United Plaza. The huge clock with its oversized numerical display read 8:46 a.m. and she was very proud of herself. In her entire financial career, being fourteen minutes early for work was a new record. Into the elevator she went, clutching her *Workaholics thank God it's Monday!* mug in her left hand. As usual, it was brimming with her favorite specialty coffee, Caramel Macchiato. The requisite low-fat blueberry muffin from the main floor bakery rested in her right hand. Shelly Cohen was ready to start her day.

Seconds later she arrived. Mr. Raven was waiting to introduce her to the RRSP team members at the morning meeting. At 10:06 a.m., just as she was coming back from the meeting, the phone rang in her cubicle. *Ugh!* She didn't want to take any calls. Not yet. She felt as if her brain was going around in circles, and she already had the deadly feeling that this new position would turn into just as boring a routine as her old one.

Then she brightened. Reuben had promised to call at his earliest chance to let her know how he was doing at his new job, and Shelly wanted to hear his voice. She wanted to tell him how proud she was of him and that she loved him very much.

She rushed for the phone. Sure enough, the caller ID read "Murphy's Seafood Shack." Resting her half-eaten muffin beside a stack of new client files on her already cluttered desk, Shelly smiled and picked up the phone.

Diary entry of Shelly Cohen — evening of October 4

He's not stabilized yet. At least that's what these doctors who call themselves specialists have said. They only let me catch a glimpse of my husband — thanks, guys!

When I was in there, they were all talking in what sounded like a foreign language: widespread damage, twisting and rebounding, a soft mass surrounded by fluid, traumatic bruising, bleeding of something, bruising to the brain, unresponsive.

Someone started saying something about Glasgow and I lost it. "Glasgow?" I yelled. "We're not taking a fucking trip here."

"Glasgow Coma Scale," a nurse said quickly.

"What are you talking about? I want to know how he is. Is he going to live? Will he wake up? Will he know me?"

The nurse took my hand and led me out of the room murmuring "there there" at me like I'm a kid, but then she explained the scale and how they measure patient responsiveness. My poor Reuben's way down there on the scale, a catastrophic injury, but she says the scale is rising. The doctors think he won't be out for long.

So here I am in the fucking Intensive Care Unit waiting room with nothing to do but wait. I've got my ass on a very uncomfortable chair and an old rerun of *The Mary Tyler Moore Show* is playing on the television up in the corner. No sound, of course. Funny how I can remember some of the lyrics to that stupid show's theme song: "Girl you're gonna make it on your own."

I don't feel like I'm going to. I really need to see Reuben again. I thought what I saw for a moment was him. A man. Same build. Same hairstyle. Same cute lopsided grin. He was walking not very far away so I shouted his name. "Reuben! Reuben!"

The late-night nurses probably thought I was nuts and in the wrong ward. Reuben didn't respond to my yell. He just turned the corner and disappeared. *Gone.* It was scary. Was this a sign that he had died and I was seeing his ghost?

No, it can't be. I just saw him less than an hour ago. He was alive then. I think. All this equipment was attached to him. A catheter, an intravenous board attached with tape on his forearm, electrode pads on his chest and tubes and more tubes coming out of him.

A really kind neurologist, Dr. Somebody-or-other, came out to the waiting room to comfort me and tried to explain why my husband looks like a fucking robot. He wrote it all down for me so I guess I'll have this piece of paper as a souvenir to remember him by. Please God don't let this paper be all I have left of my husband.

Diary entry of Shelly Cohen — morning of October 5

At some point in the night they let me come and sit with him. I was so cold they brought me one of those hospital blankets and told me to rest, but how could I rest when my Reuben's there all full of tubes? I felt frozen. I'm still frozen. I think I should worry but I'm too frozen to worry. This is too big for worry. My mind doesn't want to grasp it, just slips aside.

From the moment I heard a strange voice on the other end of the line yesterday morning — was it only yesterday? — I knew something was wrong. Rueben's boss, I can't remember his name — Sulalman or Soupman or something like that — told me, in a dialect that sounded like it was based on some drunken oral tradition, that there had been an accident involving my husband and a pot. A big pot. A really, really big one.

I started shaking. I still am. Frozen but shaking. My friend Natalie took the phone from my trembling hand, and after moments of silence on her end, I screamed at her: "Is he going to make it? Is he going to make it?"

Natalie didn't say a word, just put her arms around me.

I felt warm and alive but as if I were in a frozen state. I couldn't believe that something could be really seriously wrong with my Reuben. I still can't. What if he dies? I can't comprehend it.

My thoughts went crazy; they're still going crazy. I don't look good in black. I look frumpy in black. I can't look frumpy at my husband's funeral if he dies.

Oh my God, I'm talking nonsense here. I can cope with Reuben being hurt, but what if he dies? No, I can't think that. What if he doesn't die and I have to be his caretaker for the rest of his life?

No, I can't think that. I can't do that. I have to set boundaries. I must learn to say no to things I don't like. Why do I feel compelled to be nice to everyone? Okay, so maybe he won't be able to mow the lawn for a while. I can ask Herman to help, right?

The cab ride to the hospital seemed to take hours. I am so very grateful for Natalie; she is so good to me. I couldn't stop talking about Reuben the whole time we were in the car. She probably got fed up with hearing about him. Poor Natalie is between husbands and she certainly doesn't need to have me going on about how wonderful my Reuben is. She might have got fed up but she didn't show it. I couldn't have made it without her.

Now I'm back in the waiting room with its horrid vinyl chairs and silent television set while they run more tests. I need to try and relax but I couldn't stand to get down on this floor, so I sat in the lotus position for a while and tried to get centered. Did it work? Not so much. My chest isn't as tight as it was but my mind is still racing and I can't help but wonder if I have taken my wonderful man for granted. I swear I never will again. Am I being punished? Is he? Dear God! Reuben has to be alright — he has to! We have so much more to do with our lives.

Please God, don't take my beautiful husband away from me.

THE POT MISHAP

On the first day of his promising career as a chef at the prestigious and misnamed Murphy's Seafood Shack, Reuben was kneeling in front of a granite-topped cabinet, selecting a twelve-inch hard-anodized steel skillet from the carefully stacked supply when the tragedy happened. A large pot rack hung from the ceiling above his head, and from the rack hung a number of bulky stock pots and steamers. One enormous pot—a hundred-quart stainless steel beauty—had not been properly hung from its hook. The slamming of a door on the far side of the kitchen made the pot rack shudder. The hook released its burden, and the pot fell straight down onto Reuben's mandatory Seafood Shack hairnet. He dropped immediately, momentum throwing him against a metal shelf of crockery on his way down and then against the stove. He lay unconscious on the kitchen floor as stacks of plates and crockery toppled and then smashed and rained down upon him.

DOCTOR'S REPORT

Dr. D. K. Ridgley, October 22

Reuben Cohen was a healthy man both physically and emotionally until at the age of twenty-nine he was hit on the left side of his forehead by a very large, heavy pot.

Mr. Cohen was unconscious for three days indicating a severe head injury and was not able to recall anything about the accident or its aftermath. Impairments have occurred as a consequence of a closed-head injury of sufficient severity which have manifested in several and significant cerebral impaired cognitive functions.

The traumatic brain injury sustained by this patient will have few outward physical signs but will be evident in behavior and speech. The injury will impact the ability of this attractive, formerly confident and physically fit man to sustain a normal life.

The type and location of Mr. Cohen's head injury and the resulting period of unconsciousness and amnesia make it likely that he will develop an altered state of consciousness resulting in an increase in one or more of the following:

· delusional behavior
· irrational anger
· heightened fatigue

- impairment of cognitive and physical abilities
- aphasia
- inability to avoid libidinous thoughts
- idle curiosity
- fascination with human sexuality leading to uncharacteristic and/or socially unacceptable acts
- behaving sexually at inappropriate times
- obsessive staring at objects or persons with sexual feelings
- constant attraction to pornographic material and a fascination for thoughts of overt sexuality.

Mr. Cohen will not be able to understand and will certainly be unable to comprehend that an injury of this nature will produce significant life-altering problems.

Cerebral vascular accidents, aneurisms and congenital deficits are specifically excluded from this analysis. These are available upon request with specialist authorization only.

PART TWO

November to March

Duties
1. get cleaning up
2. vegtables wash
3. Nife sharp
4. floor cleansed

Excerpt from diary entry — Shelly Cohen

Aaarghh!

POST-POT PREPARATION

The moon beamed in through the large bay window as Reuben Cohen hunched over the dining room table, clad in his chef's uniform, worn inside out. He was busy scribbling, illegibly, in a small notebook.

He was almost finished writing out a list of duties for his nonexistent kitchen staff. Tightly gripping a blue crayon, he carefully wrote instructions in painstaking, indecipherable letters. Looking up, he squinted at the wall clock. It read 5:08 a.m. and not a single kitchen employee had arrived yet.

"Don't my staff know about showing up on time?" he yelled, glaring at the clock. He jumped up and began pacing, his heavy limp throwing him off balance. "I've got to co...co-or...the work and the staff and the...the...stuff." He couldn't find the words, his mind as uncooperative as his tongue. He sped up, lurching against walls and furniture as he paced. "I've all ended my list and no one is here yet to do the do part. I'll beat them both good when they arrive. These bah...these bast...they're costing me a fortune in not used up time."

Struggling with the pressures of an executive chef, Cohen turned his anger inward. "I am a failure. A no good chef. I can't do this. I'm no well-being." He swung back to the table and limped into the kitchen, frantically searching for his notepad. "I just had it...that thing, that writing...with blue lines...I wrote on lines."

He veered into the living room. "Goddammit anyway...where did you go? Where did I...square paper thing." He slammed against an end table, toppling a lamp.

The crash awoke Shelly. She sat up, still sleep befuddled, to the sound of thuds and crashes from below. "Oh fuck, what's he done now?" she muttered, scrambling out of bed. Reuben had only been home from the hospital for three weeks. *Sounds like he's already gone off his rocker.*

She raced down the stairs. Reaching the bottom step she slowed her pace, deliberately calming herself before approaching the pacing chef. "Good morning, sweetheart," she said in a gentle tone just like the doctors had told her to do. "My, you're up early. Is everything okay?"

"No! No! No! My workers aren't here! My staff! No staff!"

"What staff is that, honey?"

"Cooking helpers, Shelly. You know," he said indignantly. "To preh…preh…get stuff ready for your wonderful meal."

Shelly nodded. "I see." *Doctor's orders,* she reminded herself, *remember the doctor's orders. Show respect no matter what, accept the present. This is just an emotional hump, that's all.* "While you're waiting for your staff, why don't I get you a glass of orange juice?" she said brightly. "A little Vitamin C to start your busy day."

He gave a mechanical smile but remained silent, still agitated, and resumed his pacing. He peered at the wall clock again. "Now it's 5:22, dammit!"

Shelly opened the fridge. To her dismay, beside the orange juice sat a pair of his dirty running shoes. She rested her forehead against the fridge for a moment and closed her eyes. *Okay, so he's delusional. I'm married to a delusional head injury survivor. Okay. The doctors told me to expect this, didn't they? After a serious head injury we get delusions, they said, along with anger, depression, sleep disorder, amnesia, aphasia, use of lewd language, confusion and this and that and this and that. Stay calm. I can handle this. Take a deep breath. I'm not even going to ask about the shoes in the fridge.*

The chef suddenly stopped pacing and swung around. "So you finally got here! Oh, welcome, Carlos and Bruno." He stretched out his arms as if he was grabbing each imaginary employee by the neck and Shelly watched him tangle with nothingness. "You lazy bastards will never be late again or I will set fire…you fire…no job, and you won't have work anymore. Get busy, you stup...you..." he said, ges-turing angrily. "Preparation your...your...stuff and wash those veg ...things."

Shelly approached her angry husband again, and handed him the glass of juice. "Drink up, it's good for you." She watched him take a swallow. *Show respect, even when he's talking to absolutely nobody, show respect. Speak softly.* "I'm sorry to interrupt restaurant business, but I have to get ready for work so that I can be on time, unlike Carlos and Bruno," she said, with a smile. *He didn't get the joke.* "Don't forget to finish your juice." *And take your runners out of the fridge.*

Carefully remaining calm, Shelly escaped to the shower. It was impossible to stay mad at him for any length of time. The accident wasn't his fault; the stages he'd have to go through weren't his fault either. She had to remember that this was just an emotional hump. No matter how strange he was acting, he was still her Reuben. *Keep your sense of humor, Shelly,* she told herself. *Laugh; you've got to remember to laugh.*

Even through the noise of the shower, she could hear him yelling at his imaginary kitchen workers. "Have you washed those veg...vegetables yet? Dammit! Shelly will be coming home soon!"

TESTOSTERONE VS. ESTROGEN

The only tactile experience that Reuben Cohen's manly balls were going to experience tonight was a self-inflicted vicious scratch. For this to happen, Cohen would have to remove one of Shelly's hands that had him locked in the deathly grip that she said was a loving squeeze. She snuggled against his back, intent on demonstrating the conventional lovers' hug, commonly referred to as spooning.

"Doesn't this feel good, honey? So cozy and warm. So together. You smell so sweet, so tasty," Shelly whispered into his ear, gripping him tighter while her small, lush body wriggled against his softening muscles and strands of her short hair prickled his sensitive skin. "Isn't this better than screwing?"

Cohen's unlucky ear, the one that wasn't pressed against the pillowcase, heard the question clearly. Hoping for a sexually positive response, he managed to answer, "Maybe better than screwing but nowhere near as sata…satas…satis…good as making love to the only woman I have ever loved." He squinted at her as he twisted his head around and then lunged at her earlobe with his furry tongue. He missed his target and ended up licking her eye. A sloppy kiss on her forehead would have been a less erotic but better destination.

"Yuck!" Rocketing on a thrust of anger, Shelly vaulted out of bed, breaking the tranquility of the moment. She wiped spit from her face and then leaned against her night table facing him, her arms crossed. The dark parquet floor creaked as she shifted her weight from one foot to another.

Cohen smiled as her hips rolled in fleshy invitation.

"Ever since your accident there's been no difference between screwing and making love," she shouted. "When you think you're making love you're only screwing. And screwing is just a physical act, Reuben. You think it sounds better to say you're 'making love' but for you it's still just a physical act. Well, I am no longer going to be sucked into that psychological bullshit!" Shelly paused for a deep breath and forced her voice into a lower, more normal tone. "You just want to get off and everything nice you do has an ulterior motive, and that motive is always linked to your most basic need. And I'm not talking about the hunger for food! Don't think you're fooling me. You'll say anything to get off, won't you? You're pathetic!"

Cohen, sporting a third-stage bulge as hard as a rock, took the verbal abuse. Like a cautious cobra attacking his prey, he slid his soft belly over the small hills of the duvet towards the iron posts at the head of the bed. Supporting himself on his elbows, he grabbed his new football-shaped accent pillows (deep-plum and embellished with mirrored sequins) and pinned them against his ears. He didn't want to hear a thing. He only wanted to watch the naked woman on the dance floor in front of him. Humming his favorite stripper song from a cherished record album he had purchased at a garage sale, Cohen imagined himself as a strip club manager giving an audition to an inexperienced girl-next-door type nude dancer. The burlesque sounds of "Lonely Little G-String" from the 1950 classic album *Take it Off—Strip Tease Teaser Tunes* filled the space between the pillows and helped tune out everything else.

Pointing at her thick bush of pubic hair, Shelly continued her rant. "You just want in the box, the bush, the love canal. The twat, the pussy. The slit, the snapper." Her lower lip quivered and her voice cracked. "You are pathetic! You're not the caring, and sensitive man I married, that's for sure. He's gone. Gone!"

Arousal was making Cohen's present position uncomfortable. Still holding the pillows to his ears, he shifted until he was squatting on the bed like a catcher behind home plate.

Shelly was not surprised when she saw his engorged penis. It wasn't that large anyway. Tears vanished. The naked dancer crouched down on the bedroom floor to try and escape her husband's objective stare. "You actually think that simply having an erection gives you the license to fuck me, don't you?" she growled, but inside her head a panicked voice was crying, *Oh my God, what's happening? I have to pull myself together. I have to be strong.*

Stretching with feline grace, she squatted to get out of Cohen's field of vision and slowly moved crabwise towards the bedroom door. She had just about made it, moving between two floor lamps with low, beaded shades and a pair of lucky elephant brass candle stands (he had recently been on a shopping spree), when she caught sight of herself. Her naked image, thrown back at her by a dozen mini mirrors he had glued to the back of the bedroom door, brought the ghost of a smile to her lamenting face. She glanced, offering a shallow nod of approval. *Twelve of me isn't so bad*, she told herself.

As for Cohen, Shelly may have told him how awful she thought he was, but at least she had exposed her genitals to him. He liked that.

SCRATCH AND WIN

To be able to take a break without the weight of worry or guilt on her shoulders, Shelly hired Natalie's new boyfriend, Norman ("Pickle") Berofsky, to keep an eye on her husband every Saturday and drive him to doctor appointments. "Babysitting a grown-up man," he called it. In return, Norm was paid the handsome sum of a Scratch 'N Win ticket, a slice of pie, and a few bucks for gas.

The two of them, "Retired Pickle" and "Disabled Reuben," enacted each Saturday just like the previous. Norm would arrive at noon with Natalie for his babysitting duty and as soon as the girls left he would head for the sofa and sit down. Once he was comfortably seated, he would begin to scratch. First his neck, then his Brillo-pad head, then his armpits, and finally his "package."

"Now it's time for the real scratching to begin," he'd announce over a one-handed drum roll on the arm of the sofa. He'd place his wad of lottery tickets on the snack table directly in front of him and remove his lucky nickel from his lint-filled pocket. Then he'd crack his spine with a sound like popping corn, bite his tongue, and begin scratching. This process was simply magical, for every time Norm scratched a ticket, he won money. In all his years of scratching, he had never uncovered any single ticket of great monetary value, but, over time and over thousands upon thousands of tickets, he had accumulated enough money to retire.

On this cold November day, after scratching off excess ticket skin (he referred to it as "pay dirt"), Norm stretched out on the Cohens' sofa to watch reruns of the previous night's sports highlights before taking a well-deserved nap. When Cohen woke up he shook Norm. "Hey, Pickle, wake up."

To help Cohen not feel completely isolated from the outside world, Norm, as usual, rain, shine or frost, took him to a driving range located behind a rundown factory on Lakeshore Boulevard. They got their regular quantity, two small buckets of golf balls, and a left-handed driver for Cohen (who had forgotten where his clubs were), before heading out to their regular driving tees, their routine as mindless as they were.

Norm had mastered the perfect swing but Cohen had lost his. He was trying hard to get good at the game. He had once been great at golf, but now he hated it. His balance was completely askew. The furthest he could hit the ball was a mere fifty feet, and then only if it got a good bounce off a piece of frozen turf, and he often felt terribly frustrated. But, as Norm kept reminding him, at least he was outside, getting some semifresh air and doing something he once loved to do. Cohen drooled as he watched Norm's three wood glide smoothly in his back swing before, in an effortless swish, it launched the awaiting ball. The contact of the club head on the ball made a sweet clicking sound as the small white dot projected into the gray sky. Cohen grimaced. He knew that Norm purposely put a little extra effort into his follow-through for added distance and visual effect. Cohen hated him for that.

Back at home, he returned to his bed for a rest while Norm fetched himself a treat from the fridge and headed to the sofa. By the time Shelly and Natalie got back a few hours later, Cohen was safely tucked away in bed, asleep again, and Norm was stretched out on the sofa in front of the TV.

"Everything okay, Pickle?" Shelly asked.

Norm was busy indulging in a ferocious bout of coughing. When the coughing eased he took a deep breath and launched into a reply that was somewhat slurred and unintelligible. "Same old, same old shit. Same shit, different Saturday. Nothing interesting, nothing hot, nothing so different it would knock your pantyhose off, just the same old. This job is godawful boring and so is your husband. Can't you liven him up?"

"Oh, how I do wish he would perk up, Pickle," Shelly said with a sigh. "How I do wish."

Natalie, meanwhile, had zeroed in on her boyfriend's disrespect for his own health and Shelly's furniture. "Take your shoes off, you idiot," she yelled. "That sofa is no Skylar Peppler but it's nice. And that cough better be from a cigar you smoked outside, not in here."

Excerpt from diary entry — Shelly Cohen

I can't get Reuben to be the person I want him to be, the guy he used to be. Before, he was so beautiful and I got everything I needed. Smiles, encouragement, compliments, little kisses, phone calls for no reason, little treats, questions about my day, dancing, dinner, walks, invitations to lunch, talks till the wee hours and lots of love. Lots of love! He liked to invent recipes for all sorts of food and even cocktails. Now he can't even pour himself a fucking glass of apple juice or stay up after ten o'clock.

I had it all. My Reuben was the closest I've ever come to finding everything I wanted and now he's not. Something is missing.

What am I saying? *Everything* is missing.

CRÈME DE LA CRÈME

On Saturdays, Shelly and Natalie went to the café Crème de la Crème. Its upscale image dripped with an aura of distinction, as if you were *somebody* just by being there. Large oil paintings of flower gardens and colorful portraits of strong, sensuous women adorned the restaurant's strangely lit interior. Ornaments (reddish-colored wrinkled baby elephants) swung gently from the high ceiling. A multitude of colored halogen lights reflected off walls painted in soft blues, greens and lilacs, giving the illusion that the café was much larger than it was. In the center of the room was a low dais edged with plants and a wrought iron railing.

They had a regular table right in the middle of the dais, and felt somewhat superior to people who sat close to the walls. They knew that diners who wanted to appear as sexy as the sensuous paintings were bound to be disappointed, what with the ever-changing colors reflecting on their faces.

Although Shelly couldn't afford to go out for brunch even once a week, the bill was always on Natalie, who rationalized her friend's social and dietary needs by tapping Norm's credit card with a long manicured fingernail and commenting, "Plastic is good for many pleasurable things."

Shelly so appreciated Natalie's generosity that she always ate every scrap. The plate now in front of her was piled with a stack of pancakes that looked like Mickey Mouse ears. They were crowned with whipped cream, coated with syrup, and encircled by an array of fatty bacon slices, smiley peach wedges, and tiny raspberries. Natalie's gasps of feigned embarrassment at the feast on Shelly's side of the table were simply part of their weekly Créme de la Créme ritual.

Natalie was five foot nine and weighed one hundred and twenty pounds, but every time she looked in the mirror all she could see were saddlebag thighs and a hefty waistline. She knew she was fat and got angry at anyone who disagreed with her, but once a week over brunch with Shelly she went wild. In front of her rested a small bowl of fruit — slices of pineapple, banana, apple and strawberries, each wearing a sinful (though light) coating of icing sugar. She nibbled guiltily on a thin slice of banana and sipped her Manhattan while Shelly trolled through the weed-bed strips of syrup on her plate.

Today, like every Saturday, Natalie stuck out her tongue and, as always, asked, "Do you ever think about who in the world is going hungry when you gorge yourself like that?" and, "How can you eat so much? You're like a duck in the park that eats all the time."

And today, like every Saturday, Shelly gave the same response. "Get off my case, this is the highlight of my week." She licked a spot of grease from her lip and scooped up another forkful of bacon.

Natalie shuddered. "How can you stand to eat that?"

Shelly didn't answer the question right away because her mouth was full of bacon. "I don't like the meatless bubble you live in," she finally managed to say. "Look at all the vegetarians out there seeking the texture, flavor and appearance of the very thing you avoid — meat! — and eating the great pretenders out there. Phony baloney, fakin' bacon and Tofurkey — all just pallid imitations of the real thing."

Natalie leaned forward. "Oh yeah? Well, why don't you tell me more, oh wise one!"

"Do you think that bit of protein will help you win the Boston Marathon or something?" Shelly jabbed her fork in the direction of Natalie's lap. "During the race either you'd be passed by stronger, healthier carnivores, or they'd have to carry you to the finish line on their backs!"

Natalie took a quick chomp from the high-protein health bar on her lap, and said, "You're just jealous because everyone's catering to vegetarians now. First it was the fast food chains and now it's men.

That's right, hot red-blooded hunks will be drooling over my body because soon I'm going to have the shape they desire." Natalie cupped her soon-to-be perfect boobs in both hands. "Veggies, fruit and fish and plastic surgery! That's the new me and this is the new wave, Shelly! Jump in, and swim."

Shelly snorted. "And drown with you tofu twits?" she said, a pancake crumb quivering in the corner of her mouth.

This feast was Shelly's orgy for the rest of the week; in fact, it was the extent of her social life. Food had now replaced good sex. She chewed thoughtfully for a while and finally, after a long swallow, declared, "My life has been stolen from me."

Natalie, knowing by heart her friend's declaration from having heard it so many times, joined in to chime, "Tragedy was the thief. Let me console myself in food."

Shelly fell silent. Natalie sipped her dwindling Manhattan and eyed her. "So what if Reuben's not the man he used to be. Think of all the women out there who would kill to get married, and look at you — you've not only got a mate, but he's faithful, and a good man."

"Faithful and good?" cried Shelly. "He used to care about me. He used to be someone I could talk to, someone who listened. Now it's all about him. Not that it's his fault, of course not. But it's hard."

"At least he's good-looking, except for the scars. What do I have?" Natalie answered her own question. "A rich putz of a boyfriend who's always gambling."

"So? He's coughing up for the wedding, isn't he?"

Natalie laughed. "Yeah, but he leaves peanut shells all over the TV room floor. His only talents are burping horses' names in Yiddish, choosing winning Lotto tickets, and he used to get his pug, Scratch, to dance. But his best talent—" Raising her arms as if she had scored a game-winning goal, Natalie quivered like a child on too much chocolate. "—is giving me frequent orgasms. That other stuff is irritating but oh…Oh…OH! A woman who loves orgasms is forever young."

"That's all very well for you, but the closest I come to orgasms is—" Shelly waved her fork at her plate.

"You poor baby." Natalie leaned forward and patted her arm.

"And if that's not enough, at the meeting yesterday morning

Mr. Raven brings in his new temporary assistant, Madeleine. If she keeps baking I'll probably die. What could be worse than dying from indigestion?"

"Working under Mr. Raven?" suggested Natalie.

Shelly groaned. "True, but I have to. That's if Madeleine doesn't kill me first."

Excerpt from diary entry — Shelly Cohen

Oh God, I am so humiliated. Friday's meeting was horrifically halted due to a dangerous stomach heave by yours truly. We're talking belch — the mother of all belches. We're talking heaves. The entire team gasped in disgust. I had to run out of the room and could hardly bring myself to return.

But everybody said it wasn't my fault. Raven's new temporary assistant was to blame for my misbehaving stomach. Madeleine, fresh out of university with a double major in business and psychology, was trying to impress us with her latest late-night baking project.

Apparently she can't stop baking. Not only that, but during the meeting she kept stacking and restacking the piles of paper in front of her, over and over until they were all the exact same height. It's clear to me that she is obsessive-compulsive. I just read about this mental disorder in an article entitled "Over and Over Again" in the latest issue of *Cosmopolitan* magazine.

Madeleine wasn't there when I got back from the washroom. People were talking — and it wasn't about me! — and everyone agrees she's sick. Apparently she spends hours in the kitchen, experimenting with recipes for the perfect pie. The one she'd brought in that morning was rhubarb, unfortunately for me. Some of the team said she probably baked with the acidic rhubarb they used to use for cleaning dirty pots and pans. Can you believe it?

But we didn't know that at first, of course, and we didn't want to hurt Madeleine's feelings, what with her being so well-intentioned. And a treat is a treat after all! I was the first to volunteer my taste buds, but muffins, coffee, and suspect rhubarb pie were an explosive mix. Everyone was so understanding, but I still feel humiliated.

NATALIE'S BOND

Shelly grabbed the remote and curled up on the couch. "It's show time, Reuben. Are you all set?"

"Oh, yes," Reuben said in a muffled voice. He was in his favorite chair, anchored by bowls of popcorn, jelly beans, and frozen banana slices that Shelly had prepared in anticipation of tonight's screening. Spraying bits of popcorn with every word he said, "Movies just aren't good unless you're armed with your favorite snacks."

Shelly laughed. "And you are certainly armed, dear."

"What's the movie? A horror, I hope."

"Not this time. It's Natalie and Pickle's wedding. Remember, I told you about it?" Natalie had made copies of her big day for everyone who wanted a memento of this unforgettable display of affection and charged only five dollars per DVD. Shelly aimed the remote and hit Play. "This is it, Reuben," she warned. "No intermission breaks and no pee breaks."

"What about drinks, Shelly?"

"Just enjoy your snacks." In a minute he would forget he'd been thirsty.

A bright flower-laden chapel appeared on the screen with the caption "The Ties that Bind — the Wedding of Natalie and Norm."

"Who's Norm?" asked Reuben.

"Pickle."

"Holy shit! Pickle is married? To Natalie?" Spraying popcorn and jelly beans as he spoke, Reuben was almost bouncing in place.

"When did that happen? And where?"

"Shhh—it's starting. A Las Vegas wedding, can you believe it?"

The walls of the Little White Chapel were festooned with white wedding balloons. Arrays of plastic candles were wreathed by plastic flowers. Shelly hit Fast Forward as the camera panned the chapel like an advertorial. As a tuxedo with plaid vest slipped by, she hit Stop. "Oh my God, I've got to rewind. Did you see that?"

Reuben, busy eating, didn't answer. When she hit Play again, she looked closely, and hit Pause. "Pickle looks like a fucking gangster in that rented tux, doesn't he? And look at the banner up there behind the Chaplain: 'LUCKY IN LOVE IN SIN CITY.'"

Reuben started to laugh. "Where's the strippers? Where's Elvis?" he shouted.

The next image made Shelly laugh too. It was a close-up of the proud bride in all her shining glory. "Oh my God, now I've seen it all. Talk about the ties that bind! Her wedding dress looks like it's made out of duct tape. This third marriage was supposed to be the lucky one, the one that was going to stick." Shelly giggled. "Nothing sticks like duct tape! Do you like Natalie's dress, Reuben?"

"Las Vegas," yelled Reuben spraying more popcorn across the floor.

Shelly shook her head. "She looks like an alien. They didn't take a limo to the chapel, they took a UFO."

"Where's the strippers?" Reuben yelled again. "Where's Elvis?"

"What was she using for brains? Her hair looks like a lava lamp. And what's with the music?" Natalie was slithering up the aisle not to a bridal march, but to the tune of *Beth* by the rock group KISS.

"Beth, I hear you callin'," sang KISS.

"Beth?" asked Reuben. "I thought she was Natalie."

"I can't take it anymore," Shelly muttered, and hit Stop. "Reuben, show's over, put your dishes in the sink."

Later, in bed, she spread out like a snow angel and mentally reviewed, in a state of disbelief, what she had witnessed. *Natalie never ceases to amaze me, that crazy lady!* Exhausted from laughing so hard, Shelly closed her eyes and drifted off into a nightmare about Natalie's wedding that kept playing over and over.

Beneath layers of pancake makeup and a fantastic light silver gown (close cut and flattering to her plastic body), Natalie, choking on depression, started to suffocate. Shelly, sensing her friend's trouble, stuffed cherries and ten-dollar bills down her throat, trying to help. Natalie kept asphyxiating and her green face spun round and round as she squealed for air and one more cherry.

Shelly awoke in a swelter of confusion, her heart pounding. She knew she was truly back in reality when she heard the rumble of Reuben's snores saturating the room.

SIDE SHOW

Sleet battered the windows of the Crème de la Crème and turned sidewalks into slushy trails. Natalie and Shelly settled at their table, glad to be out of the weather. Manhattans first, then "the usual." They had a lot to catch up on now that Natalie was devoting herself full time to being Norm's pride and joy.

Shelly forked a mouthful of pancake. After a moment she said, "Let's not talk about me anymore, it's too depressing. Let's talk about you. How's married life?"

Nibbling an apple slice, Natalie said, "It's good. I do love my Pickle. I hated his dog though," she confessed, holding her fork like a weapon. "I said I loved Scratch but when Pickle wasn't looking, I kicked him."

"If Scratch had been a greyhound racer, Reuben would adore him," inserted Shelly. "He loves those fast fuckers."

"And I hear greyhounds are great with kids," Natalie said. Shelly's face fell and Natalie quickly added, "I'm so sorry, dear. I didn't mean to mention kids."

Shelly just kept chewing in dejected silence as Natalie went on. "Pickle's got money, lots of it, and remember that money is the greatest gift in life. The next greatest is looks. Well, his looks aren't that great but you can buy physical beauty. If you've got the money you can even buy talent and intelligence." Natalie stroked her new perfect boobs, then dug in her purse for her compact and contentedly patted powder on her cheeks. The telltale creases of her facial flesh were now only a memory, surgically erased.

Natalie had quit her job right before getting married in Nevada. "I love to do things just a touch out of the ordinary." She smoothed on her lipstick. "You know me. I hate 'regular.' But," she added, pouting at Shelly, "you didn't even come to my wedding."

Shelly tried to look sympathetic but was too busy eating.

"I went to yours, that casual little get-together in your back yard." Natalie snorted. "It was so casual it was more like a picnic than a real wedding." Not getting a rise from her friend, she sipped at her cocktail for a moment before continuing. "Anyway, I witnessed you and Reuben tying yourselves into the matrimonial knot you are presently enjoying so much."

Shelly eyed her narrowly. "That's mean."

"And let's not forget that delicious picnic Reuben prepared. Must have taken him hours: coffee, eggs and toast."

"That wasn't all," Shelly said, stung. "Anyway, it was a wedding brunch."

Natalie ignored her. "And let's not forget that Burberry plaid blouse you wore on your special day, so unique. You know what they say, 'Dress British, think Yiddish!'"

Shelly smirked. "You don't know classy when you see it."

"Oy Vey!" Natalie said, raising her glass. Then she slumped in her seat and poked at her fruit bowl. "In fact, nobody came to my wedding. Pickle was so hurt. He organized the whole thing and he knows how to save money, my Pickle. You could have saved, too, while having a blast. Cheap stand-by flights, a discount Travel 'N Save Motel to stay in just a couple of miles from the strip. And the nightly entertainment in the motel lounge was quite naughty!" She ran her tongue over her teeth. "All-you-can-eat breakfast buffets for your entire stay and twenty dollars of slot machine money to play with." Slipping lipstick and compact back into her purse, she cried, "You missed the whole thing. Everything, Shelly! How could you!"

After her second divorce, it was time for Natalie to learn about a new breed of companion. She chose a female tiny teacup poodle to keep her company. Natalie's shopping friends loved Kyle-Bob (named after her two previous husbands). "Her blue and dark chocolate coat looks so delicious," they told her. But, living with her owner in a ritzy, all-expenses-paid condominium high above Toronto's suave Yorkville neighborhood, Kyle-Bob did not settle in very well. To relieve the boredom, loneliness and frustration of living in a one-bedroom condo, Kyle-Bob resorted to several destructive behaviors. But Natalie just couldn't get rid of her. It would be like a third divorce.

The most common activity among puppies, and definitely one of Kyle-Bob's favorites, was chewing. But Kyle-Bob's feasting upon the Skylar Peppler sofa was not her most abhorent feat; it was her constant urinating on Natalie's new kitchen floor that sent her to the Four Paws Puppy School.

Ironically, a well-mannered pug named Scratch helped her meet her third and present husband. Norm Berofsky was the only male dog owner at the Four Paws Puppy School's "Bark N' Greet." A throng of Chihuahuas, dachshunds, Maltese terriers and toy poodles pulled on their owners' arms while making a terrible racket of excited barks. The owners of these untrained little beasts made faces reminiscent of Picasso's *Guernica*. They yearned for help, frustrated by the never-ending turmoil caused by their beloved pets.

Green chinos, black Club Monaco T-shirt (two sizes too small), lemon-colored socks and sporty Ralph Lauren deck shoes all helped accentuate Norm's prize possession: a Ralph Lauren leather bomber jacket with lambskin collar that he'd bought on eBay. It even made several non-canine bitches turn their heads. One was Natalie.

Norm wasn't at the Bark N' Greet because his little pug was behaving poorly; he was there to meet women. Chubby, single, and financially very comfortable, Norm was lonely. He was so lonely that he had adopted a disabled, but still cute, male dog from a dog rescue society. Scratch, a ten-month old pug, suffered from hip dysplasia which had required surgical repair. This disorder developed one evening when one Toryip Rawbeateng, age 68, spotted the stray pup. Toryip was extremely drunk and highly aroused but couldn't afford a prostitute. The puppy was "wagging his tail and acting sexy" so Toryip pulled it into the bushes and tried to have his way with the little dog. After a brief scuffle, the puppy bit Toryip's penis, sending him staggering off, dripping blood. The inhumane sexual assault twisted the pug's body and caused physical damage to his rear end.

Holding Scratch in his arms (and making sure the Polo logo on his jacket was still in full view), Norm opened his bloodshot brown eyes as wide as he could and smiled his jack-o'-lantern smile. Above the noise of yapping dogs, Norm, attracted to Natalie's scent and tight ass, said one of the most distinguished and enchanting lines ever heard at a puppy school. "You and your dog are very much alike. You both have tiny bodies hiding a large heart."

Natalie was being wooed. She batted her eyes. "You're such a discerning gentleman," she said, "and so cute. Your nose reminds me of a pickle except that it's not green." She playfully tapped his arm. "That's what I'll call you—Pickle."

As soon as Natalie's and Norm's dogs met for their first one-on-one meeting, there were several things that Kyle-Bob did not like about Scratch. The pug's Chinese background gave him a certain dignity which, combined with a poor sense of humor, a terrible dance routine, and the desire to always be the center of attention, annoyed the tiny poodle. Barking continuously while standing his ground in Kyle-Bob's personal cuddle basket, Scratch was to blame for his own death.

In Natalie's kitchen, Norm, a.k.a. Pickle, was busy fondling Natalie and removing her gold toreador pants which looked as if they had been painted on, her small embroidered jacket and skimpy silk blouse. He was molding her not-yet-monumental breasts and howling "Si, senorita, si, si!" when the tragedy occurred.

With the amount of information Kyle-Bob had acquired in Puppy School, she knew Scratch would be easy prey. Pugs were not bred for fighting. Scratch might not back down from a fight and might defend himself to the death if necessary, but his soft, round mouth would be no good to him now. The dangerous teacup poodle tried to appear bigger by carrying her pompom tail higher. She added a slow wag, then, like a matador taunting the bull before stabbing him, Kyle-Bob taunted Scratch by chomping on her Fun Toy squeaker. Scratch barked and wanted to play.

But no games were being played here.

Pouncing on the pug, Kyle-Bob stabbed him with her sharp blades-for-teeth. Scratch yelped but, with his injured back, the poor pug couldn't escape. Their owners, frolicking on the kitchen floor, were unaware of the bloody fight transpiring in the living room.

Kyle-Bob tore at Scratch's body, chewing and ripping until he was near death. Initially aiming for the pug's vital organs, but missing, this out-of-control tiny teacup poodle still managed to cause fatal tissue damage and massive blood loss. Even though Scratch did retain consciousness for a brief time, Kyle-Bob left him to die in agony alone. Then she returned to carve off pieces of the lifeless body with her sharp teeth and distributed them on the kitchen floor as trophies for the otherwise-occupied and soon-to-be-mourning owners to see. Once they stopped making out.

PART THREE

March to April

DIAMOND HILLS SPA

To give herself a belated Valentine's Day treat that was just a little out of the ordinary, Shelly booked two nights at the luxurious Diamond Hills Spa Village for the two of them. She deserved it. Being married to Reuben since The Pot Mishap was quite an accomplishment.

During his first dinner at the resort, Cohen often smiled. "I love eating dinner with my robe on. It's kind of lug...lugsy...luxo—"

"Luxurious, the word is luxurious," she said.

That whole day, including all meals in the dining room, Cohen had stayed in the white cotton robe and pool sandals provided for guests of the spa. The Spa's theme was "It's All About Your Comfort." He loved that.

Their assigned waitress in the dining room sported the name "Trainee." At lunch Cohen asked her about the specials. She recited them and left. He stared at the menu, frowning, then finally called, "Trainee, Trainee!"

"It's not her name," Shelly hissed.

"What are the specials, Trainee?" Cohen asked when she returned.

The first time she repeated them patiently. The ensuing times her tension was almost palpable as she attempted to exercise courtesy and discretion while dealing with him. Finally, Trainee, who was on the tail end of her first double shift, had had enough. "If you keep asking me over and over, I won't be able to submit your damned order before we close, you fool!"

"Number four," said Cohen. "No, wait — number five."

"Reuben, be quiet." Shelly scowled at the waitress. "How dare you speak to my husband like that?"

"Four," snapped Trainee, and stalked away.

Shelly glared after her. "I've a good mind to complain to the manager. The Diamond Hills Spa staff should have been trained to be friendly and patient with the customers. Especially customers in your condition."

Cohen shrugged. "I really don't care, Shelly. I just want to eat. My stomach is lonely and I've stolen tons of soap from the room." Like most people, he felt quite virtuous about filching hotel stuff, which he felt was provided for the purpose of being stolen. "Hotel toiltes… toilets…toilet stuff is worth stealing from posh places. The soaps at Murphy's Seafood Shack were no thicker than a bank card. But the soap bars here are thick and even engraved with the initials 'DHS,' and they are wrapped so nicely," he enthused. "Guests to our house will think we're rich."

"Oh, Reuben, what am I going to do with you?" Shelly peeled the tightly wrapped foil off a chocolate heart she had lifted from the hostess bowl on the way in and regarded him thoughtfully as she chewed. "I do love you but you're so strange now. You look the same and everything, except for the scars," she waved a hand at the bandage on his forehead. "Well, you do limp and talk a little funny, but you're the same guy, more or less. At least, I think you are. But if you're in the mood to be a kleptomaniac, why don't you get some hotel pens. The maid keeps a load of them on her wagon. Next morning when she's cleaning other rooms, you could take some. Pens, Reuben." She paused while Trainee set down a basket of bread and left again. "No more 'Do Not Disturb' signs or towels or mini soap bars, okay? Pens!"

That night Cohen climbed into the king-sized bed, leaving his bedside lamp on, and rolled onto his side, his back to Shelly. "Wasn't that a delicious meal tonight, Shelly? That Curried Coconut Tofu was incredible," he said. "Firm tofu, coated with curry and pan-seared; set on a bed of coconut rice noodles with a black bean and caramelized leek salsa. It was so delicious."

Shelly stared at her husband, blinking back tears at this sign of his memory. "Oh my God! Your short-term memory is working again." She leaped out of bed and danced around in circles, her hands clamped against her temples. "It's going to be all right. You remembered all that detailed information? Oh wow!"

She paused for a moment to stare at him, tears forming. "Oh Reuben, I'm so proud of you. Oh, thank God, thank God! This is a miracle," she exclaimed, jumping up and down like a jackrabbit. "Oh, the doctors won't believe this. You're healing much faster than they anticipated!"

He had rolled over to watch her, grinning. "What? What mira... miracle are you talking about? I just read it, just this minute, from the menu I stole from the dining room. See?" He held up the menu that he had concealed from her view and burst into laughter. "Pretty good gag, huh? I'm going to keep it here on the floor beside me for bedtime reading. It will help me dream of food."

Cohen, as usual, didn't notice the stricken look on Shelly's face or the clenching of her jaw. He just, as usual, switched to another topic that pleased him. "My massage was so terrific. The massage lady even gave my numb right calf a little extra rubbing. It feels not so bad," he said, prodding at his still-numb calf. "I can almost feel it. Gee, I'll have to tell kiss...Cass...my therapist about this."

"You do that," said Shelly, sinking to the floor.

What guests wore beneath their spa robes was their individual choice. Some people chose to wear a swimsuit; others wore undergarments, and some wore nothing at all. Cohen had chosen the latter.

"I told my hot mass...mass...massage—"

"Masseuse," said Shelly.

"Told her I'm gonna wear what I feel comfortable wearing. I'm not wearing anything but I am wearing something. It's like nothing under something." He rubbed his whale belly. "I even asked my hot massager to stay in the room while I un...dis...disrobed, but she said that she had to protect my right to privacy. 'I must ensure discretion,' she told me." He sighed. "I told her not to worry about that rule and discretion stuff. But she still left the room. I guess she didn't know what she was missing."

Shelly snorted. "I guess not. You're definitely proof that high fashion just isn't what it used to be."

Cohen took a bow. "Come back to bed, honey," he told his wife, who was now lying face down on the floor. "You can be a spoon for me for as long as you like. We'll make love or just be cozy or warm or together...sweetheart?"

From the floor she looked over at him. "I'm so very sorry, Reuben. I just think that most men are pigs. Most men, of course, not you. You're not a pig, I swear it. Not really. I just get crazy sometimes. That's all."

"Apology accepted," Cohen said, and then, speaking softly in an attempt to cheer her up, added, "This holiday is a very special surprise and I appreciate everything that you're doing for me. Our room is so cozy, warm like. I love this old Grand Victory look, Shelly, and the—"

"Victorian grandeur, Reuben."

He flopped back onto his pillow. "Oh, Shelly, stop killing me with that seaman...man words...seaman—"

"The word is semantics, Reuben, as I have told you before," Shelly quickly corrected her confused husband. "The science of words, Reuben. Semantics, Reuben," she repeated forcibly, her voice getting louder, her face turning red. "Semantics!"

"I'm doing the best I can. Be patient, please!" Cohen snapped at her. He yanked up the covers and rolled onto his side again. He couldn't ignore her tone, and his fragile confidence was shaken. "I was like a happy flea bug rug. Like a small happy flea rug or something like that. A bug rug...bug rug," he shouted, thumping his fists against the scars on his head. "Rug bug! The fucking words are so fucking difficult sometimes."

"As snug as a bug in a rug, Reuben," she said wearily. "It's a simple, childish rhyme. As snug as a bug in a rug."

Excerpt from Speech–Language Pathology
Assessment and Progress Report
Compiled by Yanna Harrington, April 20

After repeated analysis, Reuben Cohen has speech
problems which are consistent to his head injury.
They include:

- difficulties with awareness
- attention to detail
- handling larger volumes of information and
  short-term memory
- word finding
- verbal fluency
- lucid explanations
- exaggeration.

Reuben has also been observed to be somewhat
impulsive in conversation, with his intonation suggesting
assumption of listener's knowledge.

One visit per week will aim towards specific
long-term goals, as follows:

Long-term Goals

1. Improve word finding and vocabulary
   comprehension skills.
2. Improve clarity of expression in conversation.
3. Improve comprehension in conversation.

WHAT?

As a result of Reuben Cohen's traumatic accident, his brain was severely bruised. Swelling placed pressure on the delicate structure of the brain, causing damage to his speech and communication skills. Aphasia was the diagnosis.

Aphasia, a language disorder that results from damage to the part of the brain responsible for language, usually occurs suddenly, often resulting from a severe blow to the head that causes damage to the frontal lobe of the brain. Individuals suffering from this language disorder frequently speak in short phrases that are produced with great effort, and have varying degrees of ability to comprehend the speech of others. As a result, they are often aware of their difficulties and become easily frustrated by their communication problems.

Even after several months of speech therapy, Cohen's deficit was still quite frustrating for listeners. His ability to name things was affected, so that he was often unable to remember the specific nouns or verbs he wished to use and had difficulty naming things when he tried to speak or write. Initially, when words finally escaped the cage of his aphasia, they lacked sense.

"When you speak to me I feel like a foreign prisoner in a strange land standing trial without a translator," his friend Pickle once told him. "Actually, you sound like a Porky Pig imitator sometimes." Pickle had laughed.

Cohen's biggest challenge was finding the courage to accept and then learn how to deal with this permanent linguistic disability. He showed tremendous determination with speech therapy rehabilitation and learned new strategies to improve his speech impairment.

He read simple large-print books, repeated the names of objects, over and over. He copied headlines of newspapers, learned to add adjectives and pronouns to his vocabulary, and talked excessively about anything. These were all approaches Cohen took to lessen the impact of his aphasia. He was an air traffic controller for linguistics, maneuvering the flying words where they needed to go.

He even had a favorite book now. It was that synonym thing... the soras...thesasars...thesaurus. Yes, the thesaurus.

Those who were familiar with his impairment eventually grew accustomed to his snarled language.

YANNA

Cohen's promise to deliver himself every Wednesday to his speech therapy session was recited out loud, like a postman's creed. As soon as he stepped out of his door, he faced the crocuses peeking through the tangle of dead plants in his yard and shouted a pledge that was always some version of:

> *Neither rain nor fog nor dark of night*
> *Nor sleet nor even a hot babe*
> *Shall stay this courier*
> *From his speech therapy appointment!*

Then he headed down his front walk, past new shoots fighting their way to the surface on either side, none of which he noticed, and marched to his first stop: the Fresh Deli. This pilgrimage consisted of a brisk stroll down old streets and narrow sidewalks, a three-block obstacle course of haphazardly parked vehicles, clusters of gabbing housewives, and class-cutting teens.

Then he turned the corner into the Perry Sawlor subdivision. On each side of the cement path, stood a forest of carbon-copy houses with one of two exterior designs: limestone grey with Cape Cod cornerstone trim, or Sparkle Red brick with nine-foot pillars at the front entry. *Boring, boring, boring,* thought Cohen. They didn't just need paint or pretty plants; they were in desperate need of an extreme makeover. He zoned out, preferring to pretend he was walking through the flat, cold tundra of Winnipeg—which he was sure he'd seen once on a nature show—with polar bears fishing in the distance and the northern lights flashing all around.

Number 223 Desantris Street featured something quite ugly, yet very different from any other house in the Perry Sawlor subdivision. Orange letters across a fire-engine-red, double-wide garage door announced:

LEARNING TO COMMUNICATE
EMPOWERS US TO ACHIEVE OUR POTENTIAL

Once a week, ready to receive "The Cohen Package," was Yanna Harrington, a South African speech therapist who loved horses and was so passionate about gambling that she traveled to famous casinos throughout Europe, when things were going well, that is. But eventually her "fun pot" would run dry and she would return to her trained profession. This well-spoken woman, with an accent that Cohen thought of as exotic, led him through the intricate maze of language. He followed willingly and admiringly.

Today, as always, Yanna wore fluffy sheepskin slippers and a flowered silk dress. She was fair skinned with gray hair that was dyed bright red. She had a smile the size of a horse's mouth, though it was hard to see past the dipping brow of her ceremonial Zulu hat. It was made of woven animal hair, also dyed bright red, and was adorned with an extravagant arrangement of peacock feathers.

Cohen was still on the doorstep when Yanna began to talk in a carefully paced manner. "You have made it for another memorable occasion," she told Cohen, throwing her arms up in excitement. "Today we will celebrate the Ceremony of Articulation—the production of speech sounds. Aren't you excited?"

"Yes, I am!" Cohen responded in an effortless flow of speech. In truth, he just wanted to go inside; her house was something to behold.

"Now listen here, Reuben." Yanna shook a disciplinary finger in front of his face. Cohen stared at the finger. *It looks delicious. I'd like to suck on it.*

"Pay attention to where you are."

"I am at your house," he said obediently. "South Africa."

"We keep having this problem, don't we? Maybe your doctor should check your meds." Yanna eyed him and shook her head. "I am South African but I live here in Toronto, in a concrete jungle, not a South African one." Cohen was shaking his head. She gripped his shoulders firmly. "Listen, Reuben. Look at me. We are going to enter my home. It is a two-bedroom bungalow, not a jungle. You will not find elephants or crocodiles, nor even an ocean in my bungalow. Do you understand?"

Cohen nodded as if he understood. He didn't. He stepped through the door—

> *...and stomped up to the first rung of a rustic step ladder, which led to a stainless steel bridge running across the entire length of the house. This was Cohen's first step into a tropical paradise. Below the bridge lay a pool of ocean blue enclosed by natural granite rocks planted with tropical trees and filled with aggressive crocodiles that awaited the day's first deep-sea diver. Above his head, a forest of elephants, trunks held high, marched beneath arching clouds.*

—and into a front room arrayed with South African memorabilia. A big papier mâché crocodile lurked in the corner. A large painting on one wall showed a herd of elephants marching across the veldt beneath thunderclouds. Natural light was flowing in through large skylights. Yanna set her amazing hat on a table. The feathers quivered.

"You can see that my home is just a house, with memories of the picturesque town of Knysna, in the western part of Cape Province where I'm from," she reminded him, as she did each time.

Cohen nodded, stepping carefully to avoid the deadly crocodiles, as he did each time.

Yanna led Cohen to her immense all-marble bathroom with its ceiling dotted by numerous small skylights shaped like Ping-Pong balls. To Cohen, the room seemed as large as a basketball court with its beige marble walls, and it was full of mirrors—oval, round, square, hanging and free standing—all reflecting numerous Reuben Cohens.

"It's like a fuc...fuh...fun house in here," he exclaimed. "Why the need to see so many of me?" He didn't know which one of her reflections to look at when posing the question.

Yanna's many reflections answered, "We have talked about this before. Due to their reflective nature, mirrors not only make a great design accessory to enhance the room, and God only knows that the greatest room for accessories is the washroom, but mirrors are also a crucial tool in effective speech therapy work.

"As I keep telling you, mirrors help you learn how to properly enunciate certain sounds and control your larynx, your voice box, by watching your own mouth move. Every one of my mirrors in here is strategically placed to create many viewing angles so that I am able to see every inch of your mouth, my dear. Every inch! I know that your main problem is aphasia, but your functional speech also needs to be clearer. This will increase your ability to be understood," she assured him. "I want to watch the movement of your tongue and lips, Reuben. We are going to build your muscles."

Cohen raised his arm and flexed.

"No, no. Your muscles of articulation—the tongue, the palate, and the lips will all get stronger. Wow! Bang! and Presto!" Yanna was excited to begin.

Cohen, meanwhile, had already been distracted, and was busy playing with his favorite mind-boggling gadget: the revolving toilet seat. Remote control in hand, he sat on the toilet like a child on a merry-go-round, spinning around, first in one direction and then the other, over and over again. "In my bathroom in my house, I've got stuff like a Goofy toothbrush," he shouted as he spun, "shaving cream, a razor, tons of thick soap bars and a few towels from the Diamond Hills Spa. You got crazy stuff in here like smell-good sponges, all kinds of lotions and creams and even clean magazines. Plus all the mirrors. So many mirrors!"

Yanna thwarted his childish giggles by hiding the remote under a magazine and announcing that it was time to get started.

She stood behind him. "Today you will practice speech sounds with such intensity and vigor that you will feel it. Watch my lips.

Watch my tongue. Wow!" An enthusiastic Yanna urged Cohen on: "Wow, Bang! and Presto! Feel this." She grabbed Cohen's forefinger and touched it to her red lips. "Wow! Bang! and Presto!" she articulated, then moved Cohen's finger to his own lips. "Try it yourself. You will feel a small orgasmic surge washing over your lips, washing over your mouth, and the sensual feelings will begin to arouse your awareness."

Yanna firmly believed that speech skills had to be practiced until they became automatic or so overlearned that the person in need of help could do it in their sleep. One technique that Cohen loved was Visual Feedback. For this practice he sat beside Yanna, like a pubescent Bonzo ventriloquist's dummy on his master's lap, in front of a large standing mirror, and waited for her to pull his strings. Here he watched her tongue, lips, and jaw move as she pronounced different sounds.

"Watch and listen to me first before you try," she ordered, and slowly pronounced, "The Rascal of a Rabbit Raced the Turtle Through Turkey."

Then it was his turn. Cohen tried to get his muscles to move in the way hers did when trying to pronounce the sounds; however, he did not hear anything about a turtle in Turkey. *I open my blouse, pull down my bra, place a thick nipple in your mouth, and thrust my clitoris against your Adam's apple. AHH...AAHH...PLEASE...PLEASE...OH MY GO-O-OD!* The aroused student began to pronounce aloud what he thought he heard: "Oh My Go-o-o-od! My first earth-shattering orgasm."

Yanna gave her head a shake and patted his arm. "Don't worry. Although what you said was quite exhilarating, it was not what I was expecting nor, for that matter, have ever experienced. Proper pronunciation takes time, and so do earth-shattering orgasms."

Over the next hour they went through one exercise after another. By the end of the session, significant condensation had built up on the mirrors reflecting the trembling lips, jaws, and tongue of pupil and teacher, so that Yanna and Cohen had disappeared behind an ashen mirror-cloud. Cohen ran a finger through the cloud and snickered. *Yanna's sex sounds with deep moist breath must have radiated extreme heat.*

"Look at that rain," said Yanna, rotating her neck to unwind. Cohen followed her gaze as she looked up at the skylights; fat teardrops of rain bounced against the glass. Yanna waved her hand at the sight. "Those clouds are black, like herds of dirty elephants gathering together, and I don't want you to get wet."

Cohen smiled. He already was.

"So even though we have completed our assignment for today, I think we should do a little more work. You could use it and I could use a little more money from your insurance company. Repeat after me: April showers bring May flowers—FLAU-ers," she articulated carefully, and then shook her head and sighed as Cohen mumbled incomprehensibly. "Do you have any feeling in your mouth or lips today?"

Cohen smiled and shook his head. Sometimes when his mouth was misbehaving, Yanna had to rub or pat his lips or tongue or the roof of his mouth. She offered him tactile experiences with various textures, such as cotton balls, feathers or swabs to help him become aware of these areas. But, as usual, truth had absolutely no bearing on his response.

He smiled again and said, "No feelings. I need stimulation to wake up all my mouth parts."

On hearing that, Yanna, as always, brought out a tray of her many weapons for sensory feedback. She chose a feather and leaned forward. "Open your mouth."

Before his accident, Cohen had been aware of the conscious difference between reality and fiction, but he was no longer hampered by that distraction. Now fantasy presented itself as a sideshow and Cohen was the star.

> *Yannaphrodite, the pearly-skinned goddess of speech*
> *therapy love, sprang from the sea on an oyster shell and*
> *gave birth to Coheneros, a working speech-impaired*
> *aphrodisiac. Each morning she bathed her client and fed*
> *him oysters in the bath. Coheneros, drawn to the oysters*
> *because they resembled a woman's vulva, quested for*
> *more seafood, but Yannaphrodite gave him slender slices*

of carrot, cucumber, celery and tender stalks of
asparagus which evoked erotic images in the minds of
both Yannaphrodite and Coheneros. After the delicious
dinner another sensual ritual began.

Naughty-looking fruit in the form of figs and
bananas stimulated the sex organs of Coheneros once
again as he rubbed whipped cream up and down
Yannaphrodite's spine, behind her ears and down her
neck, around her nipples and breasts and along the
insides of her thighs. Yannaphrodite swelled up,
oblivious to reality.

"Wow! Bang! and Presto!" said Yanna. "This tactile technique is really increasing your sensitivity. We're getting some great results — I'm so proud of you, Reuben!"

Excerpt from Physiotherapy Assessment
Compiled by Cassandra Baker, April 10

On a once-per-week home visit basis, Reuben Cohen will undergo Neuro-Developmental training in order to inhibit abnormal reflexes, postures and movements, and encourage normal muscular action. The patient will be guided to unlearn the faulty motor patterns that have arisen as a result of his traumatic brain injury.

During initial physiotherapy sessions, changes in the patient's patterns and movements caused by muscles not responding properly to the brain's signals were easily noticeable.

Over the course of scheduled treatments, Reuben Cohen will be properly positioned in prone and seated positions. Work will be targeted to prevent contractions or further tightening of the muscles due to improper positioning of the limbs.

Stiffened muscles have inhibited Mr. Cohen when doing his own self-care routines such as dressing and grooming. With proper and continuing therapy and help in performance of daily functions, these will be significantly improved.

MIDNIGHT MAZZALMA

The following Saturday, Shelly woke up, tangled in rumpled bed sheets (that no longer smelled of her Reuben's Old Spice after-shave), to the frenetic sounds of cartoons rumbling up the stairs. With no pressure to get ready for work, she tuned them out and spared a thought for her week. The routine, the blessed sameness of it. Dealing with the old bags that came in for advice, with their reedy, querulous voices and their wrinkled fingers heavy with old money. Dealing with her boss, Mr. Raven, and the way he kept leaning over her with his hand on her shoulder, standing close as if trying to remind her what it was like to be close to a man, a real man, one who was all there. But he wasn't Reuben.

Tears of self-pity rolled down her cheek. Reuben wasn't Reuben anymore, either. Why couldn't things be like they used to be?

Saturday mornings used to be special. She'd wake up to Reuben all warm and sweet-smelling beside her. Sex was as inevitable as breathing, all hot and wild; afterwards, after the postcoital cuddle, their playtime in the shower would start it all over again. Then she'd trail after him down to the kitchen, where he'd whip up a feast just for her. Not that she ate much then, not like now. Back then it was all about heat and passion and being wild for one another. Why couldn't they be wild anymore? It wasn't fair. Not fair at all.

Now Saturday mornings were a kind of survival test. Sometimes the desire to reverse time was so strong she had to scream. An inside, bottled-up scream when people were around. At home in the shower, though, she would let go, soap-writing on the walls and screaming until the water went cold.

Unless Reuben was home. If she screamed he'd come shambling in. "Shelly, Shelly, what's wrong?" he'd say. "Rub my back, it'll make you feel better," he'd say, as if rubbing his back could even begin to touch the magic they once had.

The unvoiced cries sometimes so filled her chest that they threatened to choke her. At those times, she imagined a place where screams could be released unheard. In her mind's eye she saw a wide blue sky and, below it, a vast expanse of white. Snow. The purity of snow. She imagined herself sailing above it, soaring through crisp air that would draw the screams from her. They would dissipate around her and fall like snowflakes to the ground. And she, weightless, would fly.

Head against the pillows, Shelly turned to gaze at the photo of her and Reuben on the dresser. It had been taken on their first date by a roving photographer, five bucks a shot.

Throughout high school and even in college, Reuben had been too shy to have any luck with girls. Then, one bright fall day, Shelly went to the Culinary Arts wing at Georgian College and entered the classroom of Professional Food Garnishing and Presentation 101 to fetch two hundred cucumber sandwiches for her Personal Finance Management class's Friday lunch. That was when she got her first glance at her future sweetheart. She fell in love.

So did Reuben. He used to say that the sight of her long, smooth legs escaping from beneath a leather miniskirt and her pert nipples straining against the "Hotel California" crest on her muscle shirt were enough to inspire him. He gathered up his courage and, without even knowing her name, asked her on a date. He asked her to the track: "Everyone loves horses, right?"

Her first glance at Reuben made Shelly's heart flutter. His invitation to the racetrack surprised but also pleased her. *That lopsided smile of yours is so hypnotizing in a strange sort of way — you have potential,* she thought, smiling at his handsome, earnest face. *I'd go anywhere with you, stud,* she thought, and she had.

The next day at the track, they chose a homely long shot called Just Passin' Bye. As the horses paraded to the post, the heavens opened up and turned the track into a sea of mud. Rain quickly soaked the horses' coats, but not the spirits of Reuben and Shelly. Mascara streaked down Shelly's face, zigzagging as she opened her wide mouth to whinny at the horses that were set to leave the starting gate.

The gate sprang open. Like a fireworks display, vibrant colors exploded into space: skyblue with blue and cerise jockey cap and pink with lime and red cap ran stride for stride with peacock blue with green cap, and white with orange flashes ran beside tangerine flares with strawberry circles. All galloped far ahead of the mud-spattered Just Passin' Bye. He was dead last.

"Use the crop, jock," Shelly screamed at Ray Hartatack, his jockey. "The crop! Whip that maiden!"

The term "maiden" meant any horse that had yet to win a race and Shelly's use of it was a good sign. Reuben smiled. "You know your horse racing."

"You bet I do," she said. Through Reuben's binoculars, she witnessed something remarkable. The ugly mud color was starting to streak past the gay tints of jockey silks, one by one. In just a few moments, Just Passin' Bye passed tired bays, grays and chestnuts. His jockey rated him patiently behind the leaders and maneuvered the nimble colt, picking up horses down the backstretch and getting into contention at the turn for home.

The mud packed in his hooves and the sticky clods thrown back at him did not discourage Just Passin' Bye. He swung wide to the outside and passed horse after horse, but, though the brave gray tried valiantly to catch the race leader, he never did, never coming any closer than one and a half lengths.

After he finished a respectable second, Shelly cashed out – he had returned a handsome sum of $5.60 to show, just enough to purchase two small hot chocolates for the shivering couple. Chocolate-tinged lips kissed to celebrate their newfound romantic success. They smiled into each others' eyes. Reuben touched his nose to hers. "Wanna go somewhere private?"

"Are you going to show me your etchings?" she asked coyly.

"Hmm…how about a bunch of jockey silks? Just give me a sec. I know a couple of the jockeys — be right back," he said, and took off. A few minutes later he was back to escort her to the silk trailer at the back of the track's parking lot. He opened the combination lock on the door and ushered her in. Once inside, hard bales of hay scratched stud Cohen's bare ass while his female jockey, clad in bright red, rode him bareback until the trailer echoed with their conjoined sighs of release.

He took her home for a bottle of wine and mutual rubdowns. Shelly, cuddling her stud in his well-sprung bed, had looked into his bloodshot eyes and said, "Let's forget about all the courting bullshit and just get married. I love you."

The morning passed. Natalie was going downtown early and couldn't pick her up, so, for a change, Shelly was meeting her at the restaurant. She took a few minutes to whiz through a couple of yoga positions and promised herself, *tomorrow I'm going to start doing this regularly.* Then she whisked through the housework and headed off. So eager was she for escape that the lunch hour had hardly begun when she stepped off the subway and joined the parade of Saturday shoppers that rushed and pushed and jostled around her, vying for space like racehorses just out of the starting gate.

Natalie hadn't yet arrived when Shelly reached the restaurant. She slid into her accustomed seat and soon was sipping her drink, pretending that she, too, was a Saturday shopper exhausted from her rounds of chic boutiques. She smiled, the way she imagined a wealthy woman might smile after a morning of successful shopping.

The restaurant door opened and Natalie entered, lit from behind by a blaze of sunlight, her high heels *clip-clopping* across the floor. A moment later the waiter arrived with her Manhattan and a fresh one for Shelly. After the initial pleasantries, Shelly returned to her train of thought. "I was thinking about shopping. Reuben and I used to love browsing through stores, buying gifts for us or our friends. Now he has no idea how to shop and he doesn't have any friends."

"He has Pickle."

"His social circles have diminished to a pinhole," Shelly went on morosely. "He doesn't take care of himself anymore. He expresses himself in strange ways and that fucking aphasia thing drives me batty." She covered her face in a display of shame. "I should be stronger than this..."

Natalie was silent.

Shelly dropped her hands and sighed. "Why is life so unfair?" At a nearby table a baby laughed. Sad-eyed, Shelly turned to watch it: a pink-clad girl waving a multihued rattle. "Reuben has turned into a child who needs to nap every day."

She sat back as the waiter brought their food, then picked up her fork. "Do you hear me? My husband is now a child who pisses the bed. And have you ever shaved a child? That's what I do now. I shave a child with whiskers. I have to clean out his dirty ears, too. He can't do it himself because he might do something stupid with the tip. I'm my husband's babysitter!" Shelly cried, stabbing a pancake. "He used to take care of me—now I have to take care of him. Without me, he wouldn't survive."

"That's true, dear," said Natalie. "But at least you have a good job you can escape to."

Shelly snorted. "Good job. Right. My work life is boring too. You're lucky you don't have to work anymore."

"Is Raven still on your case?"

"Ol' Crowbait, Reuben used to call him." Shelly rolled her eyes. "Oh yes. And that assistant of his, that Madeleine, she makes my life miserable, always in my face. I don't want to talk about it."

Natalie daintily dabbed at her mouth with the corner of her table napkin. "Perhaps you want to talk about Reuben. Just for a change, of course."

Shelly swallowed hastily. "You can joke, but you're not in my shoes. My marriage is..." her voice trailed off as she stared wistfully at a young couple at a table nearby. The young man stroked his companion's arm, touched her cheek, smoothed her hair. Shelly sighed again. "Well, I've thought about having an affair but I'm not a cheater, I couldn't live with myself. Never. It's not only the sex, although that's important. I need someone to make love to me in so many different ways, like my Reuben used to. I miss him. I miss my healthy Reuben."

She fell silent, involved in her brunch, enjoying Natalie's shivers of disgust as she chewed her bacon. But she couldn't remain silent for long. "Does Pickle look at you when you make love?"

"Of course." Natalie preened. "Why wouldn't he?"

Shelly shrugged. "Reuben used to look at me when we made love but he doesn't anymore. Not that sex these days could be called lovemaking. And he always has his eyes closed like he's thinking of someone else. Ha! Can you believe he'd think about someone else?"

"You know, Shel, everyone is entitled to have their own fantasies and private thoughts, no matter how bizarre they may seem to someone else."

"Oh, just shut up and let me talk," Shelly snapped. She stabbed a forkful and downed it before saying contritely, "Sorry, Nat, but I'm really frustrated. I don't mean to take it out on you."

Natalie shrugged. "Whatever."

After a moment Shelly went on, calmly, rationally. "I went to the doctor last week and got checked out because of my heavy flow. He put me on the pill to help with the flow. 'Listen, doctor, I don't need contraceptives,' I told him, 'my husband is my contraceptive,' but I don't think the good doctor got the joke. Anyway, he also told me the heavy bleeding's probably stress related. I was going through an old *Cosmopolitan* the other day, and read an article about 'the need to bleed.' It said that women who experience radical changes in diet, environment, stress levels, career and family expectations often have heavy bleeding due to the accumulated effect of all these factors on their hormonal cycles which, in turn, affects their menstrual cycles."

Natalie was occupied watching the multitasking young man at the next table play footsies with his date while dipping bits of lobster into a bowl of butter bubbling over a spirit flame. She licked her lips.

Shelly went on. "Since the accident, Rueben's sexual technique is like a gorilla trying to play a violin: he just can't get me to carry a tune. When we do have sex —" she played a drum roll on the tabletop. " —first, he wraps himself in penis plastic because God forbid we have a child now, and then the action begins. Up and down, up and down, side to side, one more up and down, followed by release and then sleep. Then he snores. That's it, the whole thing."

Natalie gave a grunt of sympathy.

Shelly acknowledged her friend's sympathetic noise with a nod of her head, and carried on. "I came across something about how chemicals and hormones are released from the brain, prompting blood to fill the tissues of the chambers inside the penis, thus erecting it."

Natalie chuckled. "Came across?"

Shelly ignored her. "My stallion's brain is so injured, it probably doesn't even recognize erectile tissue anymore. I tell him, enjoy fore-play, it will make us both feel much better. It's supposed to be fun — fore-PLAY, Reuben!" She shook her head. "He does it like it's work, like washing the dishes or something — fuck! There's no spontaneity with him anymore…yet I've caught him masturbating, so he obviously gets the urge."

"It's not his dick then?" Natalie asked.

Shelly shook her head. "No, that's the same little thing, but his imagination has shrunk. Before the accident my clit was such a highly charged zone it could've boosted a car battery!"

She sighed as a thrill of memory coursed through her. "I need sex that will challenge my mind and touch my emotion, and if I can't have that I'd settle for closeness. If he'd only cuddle me sometimes, I'd be happy."

"Well, you'd never know just to look at him. He's still a good looking guy. Minus the scars and weight, of course," said Natalie.

Shelly slumped back in her seat. "That's the problem. You're not the only one who thinks that. A head injury is called the invisible disability, did you know that? Poor Reuben is messed up on the inside." Shelly chewed on her freshly manicured nails. "He keeps repeating everything, and his ideas are way out there."

"Maybe he just has a great imagination, Shel. Have you ever thought of that?"

"And I don't? You've known me for years; don't I have a wild imagination? Remember the column I wrote for the Georgian College paper? 'Girlfriend: Do You Have A Problem?'" She dug through a bunch of papers in her purse and came out with two pages stapled together, which she thrust at Natalie. "I found this the other day —

remember? My pen name was Midnight Mazzalma. I was wild," she added as Natalie scanned the pages.

Dear Midnight Mazzalma,

The last piece to my romantic jigsaw puzzle has been discovered. I have found my perfect match in church today. My yin, my yang or yinyang was in the confessional. While I was there (yet again) to confess my sins for masturbation, my intuitive side took over.

Without a doubt I have not mistaken this. In the matter of spirituality and religion I have recognized my soul mate by voice alone. It soothes me. I'm flattered by his words of punishment. I am so hot for Father Montgomery. Oh, what do I do? What can I do to express my lust for such a religious man? Will I be considered a slut in the House of the Lord?
Yours truly,
Catholic Slut

Dear Slut,

Don't you worry about a simple sexual sin. This is your opportunity to be as close to a heavenly experience as you will ever get. My friend Zelda had sex with a priest, dozens of times. In a confessional, during high mass, and at Sunday-school snack time. Oh, what spirituality she must have experienced. Zelda told me that he even wore his cassock.

Just collect as many rosaries as you can and next time you trot into that little booth, kick down the wall and tie him up good! What do you think private school skirts are for? Let Father Montgomery see your shrine of spiritual distraction! Let him focus his mind, body and spirit on another great calling, if only for a confessional session. Like rules, celibacy was made to be broken. Go get him, Catholic Slut! And keep this wee limerick in mind, lass — it may just do ye well:

There was a young girl in a cast
Who had an unsavory past,
When the neighborhood pastor
Tried fucking through plaster,
His very first fuck was his last.

"I was wild," cried Shelly. "Oh, so wild! Why did they fire me? Was I that bad?" Her breath was harsh and shallow. "Do I really have to wear blinkers for the rest of my life? They make it so easy to turn a blind eye but they're hurting my head. I can't bear the pain of being alone but I can't stand the pain of living with this stranger either. I need to escape but his accident has clipped my fucking wings." Her chair screeched backwards as she leaned over the table, gasping. Natalie reached across and dabbed at Shelly's running nose with a table napkin.

After a moment Shelly sat up and dried her eyes. "Nat, do you remember Reuben back in the good old days during our first year at college?"

"Yes, I most certainly do."

"The guy I met in college was strong, brave and smart. And gorgeous," said Shelly. "Especially with that crooked smile."

"He was just a guy training to be a cook," said Natalie.

"A chef!"

"Yeah, well, it's not like you met a fucking scientist or anything."

"Oh, Nat," Shelly cried, "he could put things together. He could slice, he could dice, he could boil, he could fry, he could bake. Now look at him! A man who graduated at the top of his class and he can't even turn a stove on."

Excerpt from Progressive Doctor Report
Compiled by Dr. C. F. Stephan

> It is difficult for Reuben Cohen to keep focused and
> involved in discussions, particularly those relating to his
> disability and the resultant symptoms and limitations he
> is experiencing. Such discussions frequently precipitate
> heightened anger and loss of impulse control.

RED MEANS STOP

Lying naked in bed, Cohen took a deep breath. "I'm fine with it. Really," he told Shelly. Since his accident, she had been experiencing extremely heavy and irregular periods and didn't seem to understand why. She was also suffering from vulvodynia, a pain in the external female genitals, the vulva. This condition was not caused by irritants or infections but by emotional distress, and Shelly had been suffering from it since The Pot Mishap.

Professional medical advice said she needed to reduce the risk of vulvar irritation by wearing pure cotton underwear during the day and no underwear at night. The first night she followed the advice she happened to bend over, and when Cohen saw that she wasn't wearing underwear, he got turned on. Turned on and happy. He thought her lack was an invitation, but when he moved in she slapped him down. "Sorry, Reuben," she said sternly. "My privates need to breathe, get some air, you know?"

And then there were the red times. "Sorry, Reuben. My privates need privacy, get some peace, you know?"

This was one such occasion. Cohen just nodded, gasping like an asthmatic in desperate need of a puffer. "You have no control over your body." (Deep breath.) "I understand."(Deep breath.) "Really, I do. Like that Picasso guy. He had a rose period and you always seem to have a red one." (Deep breath.)

As usual when he couldn't contain his need to explode and didn't have the patience to wait for his copilot's dry period, he slid out of bed and went on automatic pilot to whack off in his chilly basement hanger. It was his place and his alone. Shelly had disdained the basement since the day they moved in for fear of spiders and other creepy crawlies. "Besides," she told him, "it's so gloomy."

Safe in his hidey-hole, a naked Cohen stumbled to the basement washroom and turned on the bathtub taps. As the water rose up to meet the black ring a few inches from the top, he poured in generous capfuls of Diamond Hills Spa peppermint bath oil. Then, like a well-behaved dog trained to anticipate his master's touch, he waited. Sitting on the side of the tub, he watched bubbles being born and dissipating, watched the swirling of the receptive water, the plunging of the flow as he delayed his pleasure.

Then the water rose. It was time. He started with a leisurely stroke. His breath quickened. His hand quickened. His moans of self-gratification intensified. His grimy washroom mirror (which he had installed after his first trip to Yanna's) witnessed intense blasts of warm sperm squirting into a hairy potbelly.

Immediately after base eruption, Cohen wiped his belly with a Diamond Hills Spa hand towel and turned off the water. Then he held his breath and plunged into the bath. Oily water drifted over layers of fat, unexercised flesh that he rubbed with a small rubber ducky, his favorite childhood toy.

Today, however, a surprise visitor interrupted his postblastoff session. "Oh fuck!" Cohen shrieked under his breath when he heard footsteps. The washroom door banged open. He felt a wave of embarrassment. "No-o-o...no-o-o-o!" he shrieked. "When the door is closed that means something is going on in here, something private."

Trying to regain some composure, he stood up in the bathtub, dripping with mint-scented oily water, his buttocks jiggling in the cold air as he searched for something to cover his privates. He didn't need anything very big.

Shelly stood in the doorway laughing at him. The thought of telling his wife that his little wet worm was so small because he had just masturbated did not sit well with Cohen, so he remained silent; so did the rubber ducky, who had seen everything. Shelly's eyes held a disturbing glint that made him nervous. She grabbed a crinkled towel from the shelf and snapped it.

"Well, it's just not fair," Cohen blustered. "You never can do it. At least you say that. And I need an outlet. I have never been more displ...disjun...disgu...disgustingly dirty with myself and happier, calm and ex...ex plus a hill...ex-hill...exhilarated since I started to really get serious about pleasure...pleasing myself." Cohen lifted his chin and gave a smug smile. "If you're not going to please me, I have to please myself."

She twisted the towel into a whip and turned on the hot water at the sink. Waiting for the water to heat to scalding, she just smiled. Then she wet the towel. To Cohen it became a stinging serpent.

"I wondered why you came down here all the time, but I wonder no more." Her voice started off low and calm but within a few words had risen to a shriek. She began snapping the serpent, grazing Cohen's fat, tender buttocks. "So this is what you do down here! You whack off!" she shrieked, cracking Cohen's ass with the hot tip. *Whack! Whack! Whack!* "My nightmare is now a reality."

"Holy fuck, that stings!" he shrieked, hopping to get away from the hot snake.

"You're a bastard! A pervy maggot bastard with a teeny-tiny dingaling." *Whack!* "That's what you are and that's what you have! A teeny-tiny dingaling!" *Whack!* "Have fun with what's left of yourself — if you can find it!" Shelly took a deep breath, then another. Then she threw the towel on the floor and left, slamming the door behind her.

SETTLE THIS

Shelly's Burberry purse was sitting on the bedroom floor when it started to buzz. It was not her vibrator (which was a piece of semi-rigid rubber that looked like a real penis, with veins and everything, except that it was lime green and very long), which had been dormant for a while. Because of her irregular cycle since Cohen's accident, Shelly didn't bother charging the batteries anymore.

The buzzing was her cell phone. She flipped it open, and there was her dear friend Carrie on the other end, conversing in a rapid squeal about how she and her husband, Pete, a helicopter pilot, had found a home to buy near the lake.

Listening to the squeals, Cohen counted his wife's insincere murmurs of happiness for her friend. He lost track after eight, and gave up. Settling back against the pillows, he confidently reminded himself of the recent letter from his highly regarded lawyer which indicated his lawsuit from The Pot Mishap would be concluded in about six to eight months, likely in the fall.

With his life so devastated because of his injuries, Cohen was counting on a large settlement to get back on his feet. After months of uncertainty, things were starting to look good, financially speaking.

Personally, however, Cohen was living in a hell of confusion, exhaustion and helplessness. He was bitterly disappointed to be living in limbo, and finding things to do was every bit as important to him as getting compensation. He had no one to empathize with him while he waited for his settlement. Local head injury support groups were available, but Cohen wanted nothing to do with them because he believed that attending those meetings would be admitting defeat. And Cohen would not take his defeat gracefully.

Shelly got off the phone and sighed. Cohen told her not to worry. "Once I get my settlement, Pete and Carrie's house will fit into our garage," he said, his voice rising with every word. "I'll be rich!"

"We sure will," said Shelly. "Like Pickle says, you have been wrong done by."

"Wrong done by!" echoed Cohen.

PART FOUR

May to July

WILD GAME HUNTER

One humid morning in May, Cohen went to surprise Shelly by picking her up at the airport on her return from a banking conference in Cancun, Mexico. Three weeks before, at six in the morning, a black sedan had carried Cohen's wife away, wheeling down the blossom-lined street to the airport, leaving him alone.

Unable to store much information in his memory, Cohen had written Shelly's flight number and time of arrival on a blank recipe card and stuck it on the fridge. Now, to be safe, he printed the information on the back of his hand with black felt marker. Then he folded the card into his back pocket.

He left home hours early to face the challenge of deciphering buses and routes, and made it to the terminal with fifteen minutes to spare. Sitting as close as he could to the departure and arrival monitors, he watched people come and go, periodically looking back and forth from the notes on his hand to the monitors.

Finally the flight was in. While he waited for Shelly, his imagination worked in full gear. Every golden tanned man who looked like a stud and every priggishly pink male who looked like a bank consultant, Cohen hated. *It's not me she wants,* he thought glumly. *After what I put her through by no fault of my own, she needs someone else. Probably a real handsome business fancy pants who knows about money and stuff.*

Every male face seemed to wear an expression of sexual satisfaction. *Is my wife one of their sexually satisfieds? Did any of these guys pay for her services? Is my Shelly a prostitute now?*

Every male with a sly grin or a happy-to-see you smile as he greeted some woman (who had to be his lover who he cheated on with Shelly), Cohen hated. *Shelly let other men bathe her back in suntan lotion, and did the same for them. How much sex can a woman have at a three-week bank conference in Cancun anyway?*

He was afraid of the answer.

Even with his poor eyesight, Cohen easily spotted Shelly. Her outfit consisted of a brightly patterned sundress wrapped around widened buttocks. On her feet, pink flip-flops were rhythmically *flip-flapping*, making her look touristy and, he thought, quite annoying.

"Shelly, Shelly," Cohen hollered, shuffling through the others waiting at the arrival gate. Open arms and a slanted smile surged towards Shelly. The smile was unattractively lopsided, curving up the left side of his lips. His newly acquired physical quirks came with an added sound effect: a *clinking* in his pants pocket that gave him as vociferous a presence as his spouse.

"You look great! I missed you," Cohen confessed. "All of you!"

Shelly, embarrassed, turned her cheek away from her husband's scruffy face and patted his shoulder. "Thanks for picking me up. Didn't you shave when I was gone?"

"I kinda forgot how. And I was a little fra...fry...scared of cutting myself. Plus you do it for me now anyways. Remember? I thought I could wait."

"Since I'm home, I'll do the best I can," Shelly said with the least sincere smile she'd ever given. She sighed and, with a tiny touch of optimism, added, "My conference in Cancun is over and I'm back to you. Lucky me."

"Lucky you? Lucky me!" said Cohen. "Damn beard patches are itchy. They gotta go! I love it when you lather me up!"

"Back to me now. Notice, please—I'm a new girl, refreshed, tanned and, of course, more knowledgeable about RRSP contributions. Do you see my beautiful tan?"

He couldn't see any difference in her skin tone but something told him he'd better say something positive. "Yes, you look like...like south of the border."

Shelly rolled her eyes. "I'm energetic, a little fuller in the face — and elsewhere," she said, turning around to shake her proud and heavy ass in front of Cohen's face.

He was not smiling. "What happened?"

"The All You Can Eat Banker's Buffet is what happened. It was open twenty-four hours a day, every single day!"

Oink, he said, but he could tell he hadn't said it out loud because she didn't respond.

"I figure now there's more of me to love. I feel good. I'm ready for new and exciting things."

She feels good? This was the best yet. He didn't know what went on in three-week banking conferences in Mexico, but Shelly feeling good was great news. Unable to contain his excitement, Cohen reached into his pants pocket. "I've got a little wall…well…welcome home treat for you," he said.

A tinkling, silver-plated charm bracelet danced in his hand like a trained cobra.

"So that's what was making the noise. It's beautiful, dear." Shelly winced, eying the bracelet. "But I'm a little confused. What exactly are those charms supposed to be?"

"Can't you tell?" Cohen asked sadly. "If it's not a fork it's a knife, and if it's not a knife it's a spoon. One day we will laugh at kitchen you…util…uten…stuff," he said proudly.

"Oh, I see."

"At the pawnshop they called this 'The Cook's Charm' and I'm a cook, right? It's silver and the pawn shop told me it's nothing short of breathe…a breath and a take…breathtaking."

"Well, it does take my breath away, Reuben. In fact, I'm feeling a little light-headed," said Shelly, turning it over in her hand. "It's as classic as classic can't be."

"You will look like Cleopatra with it on. Put it on. Put it on!"

"Not here in the airport, Reuben. Someone might steal it right off of my wrist. I'll be sure to put it on at home when nobody is around."

Cohen almost danced with glee. "And to think that me, dis… disabull…disabled Reuben Cohen, got a unique piece of jewelry for a great price. It has a total of fifty-seven charms on it. Fifty-seven forks, spoons and knives!"

"Yes, I see," Shelly said, again examining the twisted silver utensils, and added, "Watch your money, Reuben. Your settlement hasn't come through yet."

"And when it does—boy oh boy!" Cohen laughed.

"Then I can afford to quit my damn job and take real trips," Shelly dreamed aloud as she headed for the luggage pickup with Cohen trailing behind. *Have more adventures. Meet new people.* After a minute she added, "I was married at such a young age and never really had any other experiences with other men or even women. Perhaps I missed out on something. When your settlement comes—"

"I'll be rich," chorused Cohen.

Shelly smiled and gave him a sideways glance. "Last night at the cocktail bar, a very large Hispanic lady—who, ironically, was also an RRSP specialist just like me—ordered a martini for me and then just sat there and watched me drink it. In the nightclub later she asked if I wanted to go to her room with her and cha-cha the night away. I said no. Do you think that was a mistake?" she asked her stunned spouse. "I might want to live the life of a liberated woman now."

Astonishment faded as Cohen thought of Shelly wanting to experience other women. Especially fat, foreign ones. He smiled.

She was saying, "That's not the kind of new exciting thing I'm interested in, though. Liberation isn't about sex, not really. It took me nineteen years to work up the nerve to do something risky—winter parachuting. What a rush! I don't think I'm too old to go winter parachuting again, do you? Or maybe I just need another thrill every bit as big. Only in the present moment can I free myself to reach my potential. Remember what I've always said: The Power of Now!"

She paused to point out her luggage. "My man is strong like bull," she said. *At least he used to be.* She grabbed the suitcase she had borrowed from Natalie (it had well-oiled wheels), and resumed her musings. "Oh, don't get me wrong or anything, I love you, of course, and being married to you these days is quite a thrill but I think it's time to change a few things about myself." She patted Cohen's arm. He hung two weighty bags over his shoulder, grimacing as the extra weight was added to his frame, and followed in her wake, moving like a dehydrated camel climbing a steep mountainside with two overweight sheiks riding between his weathered humps.

"You had time to crystallize your life. But mine?" Shelly tossed her hair away from her eyes. "My life is loose particles of dust taking no shape at all."

"What do you mean, Shelly?" he asked anxiously.

"Oh, nothing. Go get in line." She pushed him towards the taxi passenger pick-up sign. Full of anxiety, he dropped her bags and limped heavy-footed to get a good spot in the line that was forming.

Shelly sighed. "I've been taking care of you for so long, Reuben, that I forgot who I was. Your accident scattered my brains, too, you know," she said, lifting her face to the sun.

Cohen thought that once Shelly was home, everything would return to normal. He was wrong. Ever since his accident he had become used to being alone. Even with Shelly home, he was alone, but he was not afraid of being by himself anymore. In fact, he was never lonely; his imagination had become his most intimate friend.

POLISH KISHKA QUEEN

If Reuben Cohen's very own wife did not want to caress what he thought of as his rocklike physique, didn't want to get her fingers lost in his wild forest of winding (albeit receding) blond curls, and wasn't interested in being the receiver of his sexual treats, he knew someone who would. Or, at least, someone he hoped would. First, he just had to properly introduce himself to the cute foreign bundle of possible rebound love down the street.

A three-block stroll from his front door was where his innocent fantasy could be found, at the Fresh Deli. Cohen loved the slogan on the store's front window: "If it's fresher than our deli, it's still runnin'."

Cohen knew there had to be more to his Polish Kishka Queen than just being a simple meat slicer and counter clerk. She dressed like a hot blue-collar worker on an assembly line, in tight jeans and a thin blue T-shirt that nicely showed her firm nipples as she sweated at the meat slicer on a hot summer's day. Her complexion was pale and she wore not even a blotch of makeup, but Cohen's imagination painted her in high style. Her gray running shoes looked as if they had been on many pairs of feet before hers. Cohen listened and learned things about her. What he didn't learn, he made up. She was Polish and she was independent. Her family was very prosperous and lived in a posh district in Toronto's West End and had owned the deli for twenty-two years.

Cohen knew she was a smart woman who did not want to work at the deli anymore. He knew she had big dreams. He knew she wanted to please Reuben Cohen.

He went to the Fresh Deli at the same time every day, and every day she greeted him the same way. "Roast beef and cheese on a poppy seed bagel with hot tea to stay, as always. Right?" she asked, then answered herself, "Yes."

"Yes!" he said. What he really wanted to say was: *You're lying on my basement floor with your pale, exotic skin, and your foreign ass waggling just for me and my mind's camera — that's what I really want, thank you.* Instead, he said, "I had Polish mountain cake last night."

"You did? How did you like it?"

She seemed to be waiting for his answer. When he was nervous, it was hard to find words. His mouth moved, but finding the correct words to describe the texture of the cake seemed unattainable, so he finally just handed over his money.

The guy waiting in line behind Cohen was a regular, a rude veteran truck driver, aged sixty-something. Dusty Cowboy, Cohen named him. With thumbs hooked behind his overall straps, he yelled his food order over Cohen's shoulder: "Cold ginger ale and a fatty ham with tissue-thin slices on rye to go — don't forget the mustard! I'm running the road and racking up miles. I gotta get going!"

"Where did you have Polish mountain cake?" asked the Polish Kishka Queen. She counted out change in rhythmic Polish dialect.

"At...I...at the...I don't know."

"You don't know?"

"I was so busy eating I forgot to ask," he finally managed to say.

"C'mon people," bellowed Dusty Cowboy. "If you can't serve me, there's a dynamite Waffle House just across the border and I'm Yankee-land bound."

Other customers were also mumbling in discontent and the door was now being held open by several human door stops.

Hunched over so that nobody could see him, Cohen carried his bagel sandwich and warm tea to his regular table, where he sat down, flinching from sideways glances and cold stares. He removed his gloves and leaned them up against his cup to provide a black leather wall that helped to hide his ugly visible impairment. His left hand bore a long lumpy scar that to Cohen looked like a dried splotch of cum. It matched what was hidden by a wide brown bandage: three deep scars that looked like pieces of knotted cum stretched across Cohen's forehead, so freakish that they could rapidly transform innocent looks to stares of disgust. When the pot missile struck Reuben, his arms had flown up as if he'd been shot. One flailing arm struck a teetering pile of dinner places which fell, shattered, and then ricocheted off stoves and counters, exploding into sharp chunks which stabbed his face. Other small body wounds were nowhere near as ghastly. Only "The Three" garnered all the unwanted attention. Cohen wanted to keep all his scars hidden. He was ashamed.

Head down, he started eating his sandwich. The vibrating drag of chair legs being shoved across the floor caught Cohen's attention. Nearby, a man was shoving his chair away from his table, a compactly built bully of a man with a grain-colored goatee beneath his stitched lower lip. He approached Cohen. Black leather-clad fingers reached over and gave Cohen's shoulders an athletic squeeze. The stranger offered a gap-toothed smile. "Hey man," he said.

Cohen just smiled back, not betraying the pain he was in, not wanting to upset this unknown person. Once the grip was released and the hurt subsided, he stood up, jarring the table in the process, and leaned across his spilled tea to shake a proffered hand.

"Neat scar, man," the intruder complimented, peering at Cohen's left hand. "Don't tell me you cut your head open, too? Must have been an awesome fight, eh?"

After Cohen's quick grip and longer stare, the stranger offered an inept introduction. "It's me. It's me, Steam Engine, remember? You know — Jeremy Gollar. I was your left-winger when we played together on the Coolers. Tuesday night hockey is still rockin'," Jeremy added, "but the Coolers are now the Stubbs. We got some new guys but you haven't been around."

Cohen nodded. He didn't know what to say; he remembered only a little. He had probably passed the puck to this man many times, or seen him naked in the dressing room shower, but he just could not recall him. He smiled at Jeremy with the clear, blank eyes of a man who couldn't remember much of the past.

Jeremy didn't seem to notice. "Me and some guys on the team

heard you were in some kind of freak accident at work. Well, shit, you look pretty good to me except for that bandage plastered across your head." He snorted a laugh. "Why not come out and tie up the laces this week? Are you still as fast as you used to be?"

Cohen was silent. Steam Engine sucked a breath in through the gaps in his teeth and puffed, "We still play at the Lions Club Arena and we still start at ten-thirty every Tuesday night. All of us would be thrilled to see you there, man."

Thrilled? Cohen laughed to himself. Here he was, a guy who used to be able to work hard in the corners and skate really fast and now he could not even stay up after ten o'clock. It would seem likely that teammates who once called themselves friends would have visited or at least shown some concern, but Cohen could not recall seeing any-one from the team near his home at any time after The Pot Mishap. Did they even send him a gift?

As far as Cohen was concerned, Jeremy's display of false com-passion indicated that he wished Cohen had not survived. And in truth, the Reuben Cohen that Steam Engine had known had not sur-vived. Meanwhile, there was this brand-new Sherwood hockey stick, signed by every past and present Stubbs and Coolers teammate, hid-den in the back of Shelly's closet. Shelly had received it just two days after Cohen's return home, but she had worried that if he saw the stick he would be emotionally torn apart. He had loved playing hockey. The stick was hidden out of sight until she thought he was ready for such a thoughtful gift, and, as far as Shelly was concerned, he wasn't ready yet. His teammates really did care, but he didn't know it.

"You still seem as rock solid as when we played together," said Jeremy, giving Cohen a stiff shot to his bicep. Cohen barely contained his wince. He had spent his time since the accident trying to hide from others and keep them from the truth. It was almost impossible for Cohen to be honest with himself, and admitting weakness was one of the most difficult things he would ever have to learn to do.

What a sucky baby, a sucky baby with a lack of toughness that would shame the whole team, Cohen thought. He stared at Steam Engine with a noncommittal smile, all the while imagining a return to the smoke-filled, beer-stinking dressing room.

After absorbing the initial barrage of postgame snide remarks about how bad a player he now was, and "what a fucking ankle glider" he had turned into, a new target would be made visible when he undressed. On seeing his fat belly as he made his way to the shower, the Stubbs would erupt in a roar of laughter. Tightly wrapped balls of tape would be whipped at Cohen's pockmarked ass cheeks while assholes screamed shit remarks about his snowman physique.

Cohen would get his revenge. Blinking through the thick shower steam like the shutter of a film camera, he would visually record an exciting and vicious murder scene. The victims would be the entire Stubbs hockey team who paraded around as if they were professional hockey players, little knowing that Cohen would kill them all.

He would smash each player's skull with the thick, taped butt of his stick. The petrified look in the eyes of any surviving Stubbs would reflect their fear of Cohen's misconduct. He could just see his teammates on the slippery dressing room floor, scurrying around like wild boars and tripping over other players who had been high-sticked.

"...and I bet you still have that wicked wrist shot, right?" Jeremy was saying. "And I bet you can still skate circles around all of us, am I right?" His smile seemed as genuine as a newborn baby's involuntary grin.

But Cohen felt alienated because the other players just didn't know how drastically their sports buddy had changed or the impact these changes would have on the rest of his life. And he wasn't about to let them know. "I'm so busy with work and my wife and other stuff but I would like to come out and retie...untie...get with..." he said. "See them see me... some of the guys..." Cohen took a deep breath.

"That's on Thursdays at ten-thirty, right?"

Jeremy eyed him carefully, and finally answered with a cruel lie: "Always a spot on the bench for you, Conlan. Especially on Thursday nights."

"It's Cohen," Cohen said under his breath, but Steam Engine was no longer paying any attention to Conlan. *Now what am I reduced to?* Cohen asked himself as he watched his former teammate walk away. *A husk, a living shell of what I used to be. I lost my strength. Look at me – look at me!*

Steam Engine headed out the door. Before long he had become a dull blur in Cohen's eyes.

Cohen sat down and attacked the rest of his roast beef and cheese on bagel, with an image building in his mind of Jeremy returning home to wifely hugs and his kids' kisses. *Heck*, he thought, savagely biting into his sandwich, *all of the players on the hockey team I used to play for are probably happy family men by now.* Now divided from him forever.

Excerpt from diary entry — Shelly Cohen

The doctors told us that Reuben was likely to experience high levels of anxiety and depression during the years following his head injury, and that having children would simply exacerbate these emotions.

But I don't want the grown-up child I've got. I want a real one. One I don't have to shave. One who smells like baby powder instead of sweat. One who smiles when he — no, she! — sees me.

I think about the dreams we had, picnicking in the spare room that was supposed to be a nursery and isn't, and will never be. Because we'll never have kids.

That splotch on the paper is just me crying. My tears are all that's left of our dreams.

I have had numerous meetings with concerned physicians and therapists. They have made me understand that children of a head-injured parent often experience emotional problems because their own needs are often neglected, which can impair their performance at school and in social circles. On top of that both the kids and the noninjured parent have to cope with the difficult behavior of the head-injured parent. I'd have to be mommy to the kid, and both me and the kid would end up parenting Reuben.

"Your husband is already so much work for you, Shelly," they told me, over and over. "You say your house is in a mess because of him. That is only one of the many problems you're dealing with now."

My house being a mess is not my fault. Reuben's a lot of work. A huge lot of work. First I can't have children and now I can't even have a nice house? That isn't fair! "If I can't have a beautiful and tidy house like my friends Pete and Carrie have," I told them, "I at least deserve a baby."

But they were adamant. "A new child could cause you serious emotional problems. We can only suggest that parenting be forgotten about, Mrs. Cohen. We know you want children and this is horrible news to hear, but it would not be fair to the child."

Oh, sure, Reuben's rehab team got all sad over telling me the bad news, but their tears didn't change their message: "Please remember that there are not just head-injured individuals but head-injured families as well, Shelly."

Yeah, no shit.

Tell me about it.

DREAMER

Since one of Cohen's impairments from The Pot Mishap was fatigue, naps were his greatest ally. Being on full-time disability offered him numerous opportunities to hit the hay, but he had to keep on a regular schedule. Lately, before Cohen shut his heavy lids for his daily nap in an unmade bed, he focused on escaping to one place and one place only — via dreams. It was his cold basement, and its occupants were himself, a mental camera, and a naked Polish Kishka Queen.

Eyes closed, Cohen concentrated on creating a vision of his basement before turning his attention to the heat of one of its occupants.

> Walls of pale brick with cracked mortar encircled the cement floor, reminding him of an old outdoor skating rink behind his public school. The lighting was dim and the place looked like a wet and slippery dungeon.
> In contrast, there was the warmth of his foreign guest. Her naked, meaty body glided over the cold floor, reminding him of a fat and frantic seal in search of her safe home under the ice. Cohen was the hunter, his camera was the club, and he desperately wanted her pelt.

On this day, however, a loud squeak rudely interrupted Cohen's entrance into REM sleep. He frowned in protest, only to realize that the disturbance was his own fault — the front door hinge, which he constantly forgot to oil, had become piercing. It fleetingly crossed his mind that Shelly could never surprise him with her arrival as long as that hinge still squeaked. It would be convenient for him, had he been the type of man to take a real lover—the idea was faintly, and ironically, amusing.

Following the opening of the front door, the would-be hunter heard another sharp noise. A human squawk sounded: "Reuben? Honey? I got off work early."

The voice and the accompanying tap-tapping of heels drew closer. "Today is so strange. No flooding, no spotting, no cramps. My flow has tapered off, at least for the moment." A vision appeared in the doorway, a Shelly-vision lounging against the doorjamb like a wannabe sex goddess. "So I took off early and I thought we'd take advantage of the time to peck and cuddle and have sex," Shelly cooed. "Actual penetration, Reuben. Isn't that exciting?"

Cohen wasn't dreaming; he hadn't even dreamed himself into the basement. He also wasn't even horny yet. He sat up in the rumpled bed and sighed—he needed his basement time. "Can't we wait, honey buns?" He tried for a winsome smile. "You know how important it is for me to stay in a routine. Spontaneity is fun and all but no good for me, even for pecking and cuddling. Besides, I'll have more energy for you when I'm finished my nap, okay?"

Shelly froze in the doorway, only the darkening of her eyes betraying her hurt.

"Just kidding," Cohen said hurriedly, and patted the bed as he regretfully relinquished his sought after fantasy. His dear wife needed his attention.

Since his accident, Cohen's nap time and sex with Shelly had fallen into specific time slots. Sex was not on a routine in accordance with the custom of young lovers, but it did happen at least once a month. On a rare night when she was not having her period, Shelly would say, "Hey, there, stud. Wanna have good a time?" That always meant she wanted real sex.

Leaving the en suite clad in attire she seemed to think was sexy, Shelly would spin around and jump into his arms, rub her rotund chin against his nose, and then order him to touch her softly before removing her cartoon-figured pink flannel pj's.

Out of pure frustration, Cohen usually just ripped the pajamas from her body and went to work, concerned solely with geology: her once proud twin mountains, her vast glaciers creeping upwards towards a forest of pubic hair that offered the clumsy surveyor entry into a warm and waiting cave.

But this was the cruel and glaring light of day, with no darkness to shelter Cohen's eyes as Shelly disrobed. Her hormonal imbalance had led to catastrophic changes in body temperature which, unfortunately, had affected her entire outer surface. Her snowy mountains had begun to sag, and sag they did. Her glacial expanses had begun to melt, and melt they did. Cohen slumped in bed, watching in grim fascination. Shelly's external beauty was dying out. He could tell that she couldn't see it or maybe she just didn't care, but it was glaringly obvious to him.

Since The Pot Mishap, Mother Nature seemed to be working quickly to make Shelly extinct, and she wasn't fighting back. Her hormones had slowed to a crawl before tilting completely off balance. Ever since the accident, she'd been on a steady downhill course of well-being. Her diet was atrocious, she had no strength to exercise and her stress management skills would have had her on the unemployment line long ago if she wasn't so good with clients.

Cohen, meanwhile, had also been living an unhealthy lifestyle since The Pot Mishap. What was left of his physical beauty was in a state of rapid decline. Little did he know that Shelly was not overly impressed with his present appearance, either. He was now a large whale beached on the rumpled sands of bed sheets.

He could stand his own changes but not his partner's. Definitely not. When it came to sex, this dewy animal had to mentally escape to a more comfortable location, and escape it did. As Shelly stretched out beside him he reached for her, and as he reached, Cohen journeyed beyond the bedroom; in fact, his sex drive hustled him down to the cold basement to screw someone else.

REVENGE

With every thrust of Cohen's hips against her ass, the Polish Kishka Queen screamed in ecstasy. She was screaming for forgiveness, and with every thrust of his hips, his father, Aaron, smiled proudly at his boy from the heavens.

In his healthy years, Aaron had been a man who dressed with impeccable taste. He always proudly announced the *vilder metziah* (bargain of the year) to his appreciative customers at his hat shop, and, when the occasion seemed to call for it, would often jump out from behind the cashier's table and triumphantly click the heels of his handsome shoes together .

Aaron was a manufacturer of mourning hats and Cohen was forever being told by his entire neighborhood all about what a wonderful and kind person Aaron was. Even his present neighbor, Hilda Greenberg had known him.

"Your father was quite handsome, too, Reuben. For a Jewish man, of course," Mrs. Greenberg liked to tell him. She had married an Irish Catholic man and was now an eighty-year-old widow (cute for her age, even when covered in mosquito bites). Cohen figured it was a good thing Mrs. Greenberg lived two houses away from his other neighbor, Herman, because they hated each other. Herman idealized the Indianapolis Colts while Mrs. Greenberg was a Green Bay Packers fan. She was convinced that her husband was named after Bart

Starr, the iconic football quarterback.

"I used to call him 'Dark Starr, the four-eyed fat man,'" Herman told Hilda one summer day, taunting her with a megaphone liberated from the high school's athletic department during his freshman year. (In Herman's high school days, if you wanted to be considered a *cool niner* you had to steal a piece of school property or kiss a grade twelve girl. Stealing the megaphone was the easier task for him back then. He'd been an ugly teenager.)

Sitting in a lawn chair in the shade of her sprawling cherry tree, Hilda ignored the old man. "I think it was Aaron's eyes," she mused, fanning her face with a fly swatter. "His eyes were so green, so environmentally friendly, just like my Bart's, just like the grass in Ireland." She took a sip of her Chinese mint tea from a white ceramic mug with "Packers Rule" printed with the color of Irish clover. "Do you remember your father's eyes, Reuben?"

"Of course I remember my father's eyes," Cohen lied. What he really remembered were his father's stories.

Hilda Greenberg smiled at him over the rim of her mug. "When you have more time I will show you all my photo albums showing Bart and me on our travels through the U.K. and Ireland. I created them to celebrate the things I love most in life, not the least being my dear Bart." She bared her teeth at Herman in a semblence of a smile. "My darling Dark Starr. He and the entire Green Bay Packers team," she said with a sigh, and popped a Smartie in her mouth as she reminisced. "Anyway, just because my Bart is dead and gone doesn't mean you can't come in and drink from his favorite mug and have some of my homemade cookies. Gingerbread men with green Smarties for eyes. Oh, how he loved to crunch those eyes. His mug is the same as mine, except that his says 'Packers #1.'"

Cohen shook his head firmly. "I can't come in." Dead Dark Starr was creepy and Cohen didn't want to have to drink from his mug. "I have to go but you can give me cookies if you want. I like cookies."

"Alright," said Hilda. "But one of these days you'll have to come and see my photos."

"Sure," he said, but, in truth, he was tired of hearing how handsome his father and Hilda's husband had been and how much better

102

the Packers would be this year, and he hated looking at other people's vacation photos. *I'd rather die*, he'd grumble to himself.

In his better years, whenever Reuben's father heard of a passing in their tightly-knit Jewish community, he would make a nightly visit to sit Shiva with the mourning family and offer his condolences, a bag full of freshly baked twisters, and a few extra mourning hats in case they were needed. Aaron's supportive presence was appreciated by the immediate family. His attention shifted their sadness a little, and he always told Reuben that his smile, hugs and fresh treats eased the mourners' difficult time.

After he was diagnosed with an enlarged heart and irregular heartbeat due to high blood pressure, Aaron spent many days and hours attached to mechanical breathing apparatuses on constant duty by his hospital bed, but he still found enough breath and the quiet effort needed to remove the mask, and tell his son the stories told to him by his own father. Reuben clung to every word of Aaron's stories. Fairy tales about the witch in *Hansel and Gretel* who put the children in the oven, or the wolf who gobbled up the pigs, were not heard here. Aaron's tales were of true horror and the worst degradation known to mankind, about the most inhumane living conditions and individuals being condemned to death en masse. He recounted the frightful tragedies and horrors of his ancestors and their struggle to live as proud Jews in times of war.

"Why do you tell him so much of our long past, Aaron?" Reuben's mother would ask. "Why do you tell him of such *farpeynikn* — such torture?"

"He must understand the troubled times we came from. It is so important that our future generations never forget the past. Mine is his first eyewitness testimony," Aaron thundered back, speaking as strongly as a weak and dying man could.

"I want him to understand that there will never be a happy ending. Never! He must understand to be proud. To be strong, and never trust a goy. I lost two brothers and my mother's family was totally exterminated. If my stories can leave images in Reuben's mind that will never go away, something has been accomplished. I am the *Yiddisher Kop* — the smart person."

Aaron fought hard and proud. He passed away when Reuben was only seventeen. His tales of horror made the young Reuben feel desperate and neurotic, and inspired intense emotions within him and a once deeply hidden desire for vengeance.

Down on all fours, her fingers clenched into weak fists, her head thrown back, eyes dilated with horror and knees trembling on the basement floor, the Kishka Queen screamed as historic revenge was taken out on her naked body. He pounded his meat into her, shouting, "You need to shut up and respect my father's right to silence. Because of your people he is terrified of loud noises and especially people screaming. So shut up! Shut up!

"The day of reckoning has come, my dear," he shouted into his victim's ear. "Your people amused themselves with our deaths. I am going to amuse myself with your body. Oh, what pleasure I will have on your pure sweet flesh. So smooth, so warm and so guilty. My blood is on fire.

"You shall suffer now in this frozen expanse of concrete, suffer in this dark room, just like my people suffered in the concentration camps."

Cohen grasped a handful of her hair and snapped her head back towards his potbelly. "Here's for your myth that we are responsible for Stalin's persecution of the Poles," he cried. "Here's for all who stood watching the destruction of Jewish communities and took wrongful inheritance of our properties," he roared, slapping her meaty ass. "Here's for everyone who actively helped the Germans by denouncing the Jews who hid under Polish identity. Even Polish school children, my father told me again and again, turned on their Jewish friends and became informers."

Then all at once the scene changed and he was an artiste, a photographer with his zoom lens camera. "Pose for me," he instructed the model standing in front of his mind's eye.

"Give me a look that is correct for the role you are playing. Give me the look of a tragic prisoner, a confused recipient of hate with a pencil-thin figure and big boobs," Cohen demanded. "C'mon, your face must reveal the inner character I imagine you to be. I want your body to be the main attraction, a beautiful work of revenge. Display it!" he shouted. "Display it!"

"That face of yours, it looks too innocent. I need a confused and scared look in the prisoner's eyes. Give it to me!" the photographer demanded, forcefully taming his prey. "Work with me and make confused yet passionate love to the camera! Give me a smile of terrified confusion."

To capture this emotion from his subject, Cohen abandoned normal handheld camera techniques and switched to a more versatile piece of photographic equipment. Leaning against the basement's back wall, a tool stood idle, one that could be used, with a little ingenuity, for taking steadier mental photos and rendering quick exposure shifts. Two leg thrusts away and his battered old hockey stick was in his hands. This piece of taped timber was easy to move around. In fact, it offered photo opportunities that had never before existed as it transformed itself into a powerful camera. Tilting and bending and panning were movements so easily conducted with this homemade device that Cohen's mind soon created a wonderful idea.

He decided to use the "deke" method to confuse his slave model and get the look he desired. He moved the hockey stick laterally and the Polish Kishka Queen went with the move. Then he skated across the basement floor and moved the stick in another direction, away from his subject.

The technique, moving in one direction while looking in another, momentarily distracted the Kishka Queen,

*and that lapse of concentration allowed the artiste to
capture her confusion.*

*The most convincing move the photographer had in
his offensive repertoire was the fake shot. Cohen started
to shoot and, at the last instant, stopped, spun around
and moved wide while continuing to click away. The
whirling antics of Cohen, wrapped in a skintight Coolers
jersey, offered the only clue to his whereabouts. Moves of
this nature showed his expertise at forward and
backward skating and his mastery at stickhandling.*

*"You're giving me fits!" cried the Kishka Queen.
"Fits! You are too tricky. I don't understand what is
going on." Cohen had taken so long capturing the
images that her forced smile collapsed. Her mouth stayed
open and uneasy.*

*"Exactly. That's it!" Cohen shouted. The more
photos he took, the merrier his mind was!*

*"What are you going to do with the photographs?"
his subject asked.*

*"Like the ocean beats upon the shore, life beats upon
my mind's photos," he answered. Thin columns of
intense summer sunlight seeped in, between the metal
bars of the basement's only window, and flashed on his
face, forcing him to shut his eyes for relief.*

Opening his eyes, Cohen was in a state of shock. No longer was
he in the basement with his victim. No longer was he the swift and
talented photographer. He was in his bedroom, straddled by his wife.

"Oh, honey, that was nice. Wasn't that nice?" She rotated her
pelvis like a hula dancer. "I love it when I'm not bleeding and we can
have sex. Even if it's only once in a blue moon. And you're not even
wearing Old Spice!"

He was silent.

Shelly planted a kiss on his forehead and dismounted. Giggling,
she squirmed happily on the rumpled bed sheets. "This is very strange
for us lately. Twice in one month—wow! And I hardly even had to

get you going, you were so into it. Whatever you're doing to turn yourself on, keep doing it."

He did not respond, just rolled onto his side with his back to Shelly and then curled up like a child afraid of thunder.

"Hello? Hello, husband. Do you hear me?" Shelly leaned over and smacked his butt cheeks.

His mouth curved into a smirk. "Time spent with you is very good, Shelly," he said. "Very good indeed."

Excerpt from Progressive Physiotherapy Report
Compiled by Cassandra Baker

At the commencement of treatment, Mr. Cohen was able to write almost legibly and move his fingers, albeit slowly and with effort due to fine motor difficulties. He has shown moderate improvement. Further improvement in his dexterity will come with time and practice.

CASSANDRA

A refreshing breeze filled the air on Thursday afternoon and brushed a hot, bright sky. Cohen curled up on his tomato red (and crumblined) sofa and waited for his tardy physiotherapist to arrive.

His full-time disability had been approved almost four months earlier. Since then, on Wednesdays he had speech therapy sessions with Yanna and in-house rehabilitation with Cassandra on Thursdays. Luckily, Cassandra had other clients who lived nearby, so coming to his house was convenient for her. She worked on specific physical and cognitive impairments resulting from The Pot Mishap.

The only thing Cohen really worried about during his time of rehabilitation and "life of leisure," as he called it, was when, and if, his therapy sessions would begin. They were the starting blocks to his stimulating world of continuous fantasies.

Footsteps sounded on the front walk, then Cohen heard a knock on the door. Stiff and limping, he went to answer it, feeling weighed down by the extra poundage encasing his fatigued body. The rapid drumming of his heartbeat almost drowned out the squeal of the door hinges as Cassandra poked her head in.

"When are you going to fix that, Reuben?" she asked.

"I'll get to it," he mumbled. "I keep forgetting. That, and...and remembering to...to do it."

Cassandra was only twenty-five and, at five foot eleven, she was all legs. The sight of her always put Cohen in a sports frame of mind. Her firm black skin covered continuous hills of appealing muscle. Her rump reminded Cohen of two basketballs and her curves were so tight that the most skilled race-car driver could not have negotiated them.

Today her hair was all askew. "Yes, my hair's a mess," she told a gawking Cohen. "It is very windy today. W-I-N-D. Haven't you noticed?"

"I was waiting for you on my nice red sofa. I haven't been out-doors yet," Cohen admitted, "so I have not seen any wind."

Cassandra brushed her hair out of her eyes as she entered. "Today I want to work specifically on your upper body. I believe you will be able to concentrate better on cognitive tasks if you are feeling comfortable."

"Yes. Yes," the happy client agreed.

Cassandra's beautiful bosom almost touched Cohen's forehead as she pulled upward on his arms and stretched them out during their warm-up. Her breasts reminded him of plump softballs.

After his arm stretch came his neck. Cassandra stood behind him and carefully guided his head back against her bicycle rack of a torso, rotating it clockwise, then counterclockwise.

> *His masseuse's thin veil drifted over a permanent smile now engraved on Cohen's face. She began to move sinuously around the living room to the thump of rapid drumbeats. Now clad in traditional Zulu/Tonga regalia and covered with animal skins, she twirled an ivory-headed spear around her body. Singing in full cry while acting out the part of the brave Ntombinde in the Congolese legend, "The Girl Who Loved Danger," Cassandra pulled Cohen from the sofa to join in the festivities. While this brave beauty twirled her spear, Cohen began to sweat.*
>
> *Nearing the climax of the folkloric story, a naked Ntombinde bathes in the river looking for the Snake Man of the Forest who resides there. Although she is scared of the beast, Ntombinde knows she can conquer him*

through kindness, cunning and nudity. She insists upon finding the legendary Snake Man and making passionate love to him. He is actually a handsome young man who has been placed under a spell.

Her courage and intelligence are rewarded with the breaking of the curse. Sweaty Reuben Cohen, the Snake Man of the Forest, showers Ntombinde with tender love bites while she, in response, sprinkles red powder on his body in hope that, by restoring to his pallid skin the color that symbolizes life, the great sexual powers he had lost would be restored to him. The two lovers trade sensuous bites for hours.

"I'm so proud of you, Reuben," Cassandra said. "Your flexibility is really improving. It will keep improving and I sense that you are now able to bend your arms enough to start applying deodorant like I asked you to. You smell better now. I like that! After these sessions you will feel so much looser, and you must keep deodorizing—every single day," she encouraged him. It had taken her months to get up the courage to do so.

"Didn't I smell tasty before?" Cohen asked. "My wife told me I smelled tasty. She loved my smell without any additives. I was all natural!"

Cassandra wrinkled her nose. "According to my sense of smell, up until now you smelled like a plate of curdled milk. Your fresh, clean smell is so much better."

Cohen gave her a slanted and somewhat sexy smile. "When I'm with a woman I enjoy, I always put a little splash of Old Spice behind my soft and crazy earlobes, okay? And now I'm feeling and smelling so much better than I used to. Time spent with you is very good," he told his therapist. "Very good indeed."

GREGORY GOLDBERG

Excerpt from diary entry—Reuben Cohen, July 5

Dear Therapists—The following is what I lost because of the accident. I would like them back <u>please</u>

· I would like back my original left hand and face. The ones without the long ugly scars that I always try to hide

· I want back my original right calf. The one without the soreness and stiffness that makes me limp and be sloppy

· I want my active sex life back. The one that I'm too tired to enjoy now.

· I want my organizations and words back.

· I want my balance back

· I want to be independent again

· I want to play hockey

· I want to have hopes and plans again

· I don't want to be angry anymore

· I want me back

HIDE AND SCRATCH

A mechanical device awoke Cohen one Wednesday morning. It was not the alarm clock, but the telephone jangling him out of an abyss of sleep. Through a viscous lethargy he fumbled for the receiver.

"Hello," he cracked in a phlegm-filled voice.

"Hey buddy, it's me, Norm. I'm taking you with me today. Get ready for the most arousing experience of your life."

Cohen scratched his head. "The only place you take me is to the driving range. That's on Saturday."

"I want to see more of you, Reuben. We're buddies. Put on some loose clothing. I'll be there shortly, buddy. Be ready!"

"I can't be ready until 11:30. I've got my speech therapist Yanna today. I'll be home after my a…a…a and a point…appointment."

"I'll drive you there and pick you up," Norm hurriedly suggested.

"No!" Cohen shouted into the receiver. "I need to walk there. It's good for me." *Also good for me*, he thought as he headed off, *will be my usual roast beef and cheese on poppy seed bagel to go from the Fresh Deli.* He always stopped there on his way to Yanna's, needing fuel for his journey and the chance to see his Polish Kishka Queen. He now always ordered his sandwich to go because the thought of sitting at one of the tables in full public view made him uncomfortable.

Cohen loved opening the tightly wrapped foil that protected his sandwich from external elements and softened it up a little. Gooey processed cheese overflowed from the bagel halves, between which was nestled one thin piece of roast beef. For every order to go, the Polish Kishka Queen included a single dill pickle in a small, tightly tied plastic bag that looked as if it was suffocating the already wheezing vegetable. This was a fine last touch to his grub bag.

He always thanked her for her efforts which allowed him to have a delicious Fresh Deli experience on his way to speech therapy, and gave her a sexy wink, after checking to make sure that she hadn't forgotten the dill pickle. She usually returned his wink with a foreign word and a giggle.

He was just leaving Yanna's place when Norm pulled up (sporting the same spiffy duds he had worn to the "Bark N' Greet" where he'd met Natalie). Cohen waved good-bye to Yanna, and climbed in the car, pausing to finger-comb his hair, using Norm's large reflective sunglasses as a mirror.

"In appreciation for you being my shuff...show...chauffeur, I got you a little gift." Cohen slanted his smile towards his pants pocket where he was concealing the gift. Then he reached in and, like a magician with his hat, pulled it out: a rainbow-colored, battery-charged, blinking dog collar.

"Holy shit! Where did you get that?" Norm cried. He reached out and eyed the tag. "It even says 'In memory of Scratch.'"

"I'm gonna be rich after my settlement, so I went all out. The engraving on the tag costs twenty-five cents a letter, and that's no chump change right there, I'll bet." Cohen grinned at Norm's fondling of the collar and said proudly, "You go to a pawn shop 'cause you think you're gonna find something really rare, and most of the time it's a total waste but once in a while you find something that'll make you shit your pants. Pickle, I gotta tell ya — in just two days I shit my pants twice. Once when I saw Shelly's cal...cun...canarily ...kitchen charm bracelet, and the next day when I saw this dog collar for Scratch. And I put it somewhere safe, but then I found it again."

"Don't go shitting your pants in this car, Reuben," Norm said as he pulled away from the curb. "Natalie gets crazy if the BMW smells or has any trace of dirt in it. I always have to stop and clean up my peanut shells before I get home. I love the smell of peanuts. I'll get a car of my own one day," he cried.

Cohen cranked around and nodded at the chocolate-coated health bars scattered on the back seat. "That's not a Pickle mess, is it?"

Norm shrugged. "I don't know where Natalie gets so many health bars — there must be a sale on or something. She loves those things."

Cohen settled back in his seat. "When you get another dog of your own, he can be a boy or a girl. The pawn shop told me this classic dog charm is unisex, which means boys and girls. And if he's being mor...mur...mur...killed, you can detect it quicker. Listen to this." Cohen pressed a plastic button on the plastic collar, which sparkled as it spoke. "I'm being attacked. I'm being attacked. Help! Help!" an electric voice screamed from the collar's mini-speaker.

"That voice sounds like you. Is that your voice, Reuben?"

"Yeah, isn't that fantastic!" Cohen beamed. "There's a little recorder inside that records your voice. You can say anything, but you only have ten seconds. I tried my best to sound like Scratch would in such a dilly...dillyma...dilemma. But, as you know, dogs can't talk."

"Gee thanks, Reuben, I never knew that," said Norm.

"And if your dog falls on his side while his attacker has him pinned down," Cohen continued, "the button automatically engages."

"It's really great and useful too. I'll cherish it forever," Norm gloated, tossing the dog collar over his shoulder to land on the health bars. "You know, Reuben, I think we're gonna start to become good friends. When Natalie first introduced me to you, I didn't think we had so much in common, but, come to think of it, we do!" Norm banged his hands against the steering wheel in excitement. "We both have crazy wives, we both love our independence, and we both like looking at women, and...and..." he stumbled, trying to find more commonalities between them. "Well, that's a start. It's a start."

A few minutes later they pulled into a parking lot behind an old concrete building. "What we're about to enjoy is a two-hour class of Hot Yoga," he said with a lascivious smile. He licked his lips. "Hot Yoga!"

Then, in language culled from the bluest of the blue, Norm

painted a picture of a classroom filled with overheated, sex-starved women, all in porn positions: sitting, standing, lying down, beads of sweat flying off their nearly naked bodies. He grinned. "They have to concentrate and can't be disturbed so we get to watch everything from a little room with one-way glass. They can't see out and they can't see us lookin' in." He snorted with glee. "My wife doesn't even know I'm lookin' at better-lookin' babes."

"Doesn't anyone ask who you are?" asked Cohen.

"Not yet, my friend, not yet! I go in through the back entrance." Norm slipped on his sunglasses and laughed with the bubbling promise of all things bright in the very near future. "Sometimes seeing the unattainable can only be accomplished by going undercover." He scrambled out of the car and strutted towards the building, Cohen at his heels, as he exclaimed, "Oh, I love Wednesdays. Fuck golf! I stole Natalie's yoga schedule and there are also classes on Saturday when our wives are always out to lunch. We'll come then, too, and they'll think we're golfing," he chortled, swinging open the door to the viewing room, happily vacant. "Fuck golf!"

On the other side of the one-way mirror, a gasping heater blew hot air around the yoga studio, regulating its temperature at 105°F. Thirty-two women and one topless gay man began to sweat. Then the instructor entered.

"Look at her," gasped Norm, his pickle nose pressed up against the one-way glass. "That's Valerie, the goddess of Hot Yoga. Just look at that woman!"

Valerie, clad in a black spandex bodysuit, moved like a brave and naked native woman walking into a bar full of racist cowboys. Her face was as inviting as her magnificent body, with well-proportioned lips, high cheekbones, skin without a trace of blemish. Shamelessly, both Cohen and Norm drooled.

As the class rested in the stillness of Shavasana, the corpse pose, Norm fixated on the beautiful Valerie, filled with the glowing feeling that she secretly fancied him. She didn't. She didn't even know he existed.

Cohen had moved on and was gawking at the rest of the scene beyond the glass. He elbowed Norm. "Look at that babe!" he said, pointing to a luscious dark-haired creature. "Magical, just magical, and look how well built she is. They gotta be phony, those big, tippy tits. Look how still and firm those things are!" He watched in silence and then burst out, "I'd love to meet her."

Norm reached out and thwacked Cohen on the back of the neck. "Your short-term memory sucks and so does your long-term. You've met her a million times, and I've given her a thousand orgasms." He snickered. "That's Natalie, you idiot! Get your eyes off my wife — we're here for other women."

"Well, you're one lucky man. She looks good, sexy," Cohen said wistfully, rubbing his neck.

"Yeah, sure." Norm flicked her a glance. "She's not getting any younger but she still turns my crank when it needs crankin' and I turn hers too. But look at that instructor! That's something special, very special indeed."

Valerie, tall, fit and ripped, moved through pose after pose in exquisite detail, her taut and sleek limbs working gradually towards a single ideal shape: the Bow, the Triangle, the Cobra. "What I would like to do to that!" Norm gasped, licking his lips again. "Listen to those sweet sounds." Beyond the glass Valerie was calling out instructions over the background buzzing of the heater, but the one-way glass turned her clear voice into throaty moans. Norm poked Cohen with his elbow. "Doesn't it sound like she's having sex?"

Cohen just grunted, being occupied in wondering if Shelly would exhibit her body for him in skimpy clothes the way Valerie the Yoga Goddess was doing. "She's fat but I bet she might even look half good in a getup like that," he muttered to himself.

"Oh, Reuben! Tons of wet women and an instructor molded by God." Norm jumped in place, his eyes moving back and forth, like a spectator at a tennis match.

Cohen started jumping with him. "I feel so loose, so free. I'm as free as an ast...ast..."

"Astronaut?" guessed Pickle.

"Yes! astronaut, like I'm dancing on cushions of air," cried Cohen. "Fuck golf!"

After the class they raced out to the car. Fifteen minutes later,

Natalie, a soft white towel wrapped around her shoulders like a bleached boa, greeted her husband with a peck on the cheek. "For once I didn't have to wait."

He grabbed her heavy gym bag from her hand and swung the driver's door open for her with a grand gesture. She slid into the driver's seat and froze, glaring at Cohen who was in the back. "Why are you here? Pickle, why is he here? You aren't getting my leather seats dirty are you, Reuben? And where are all my health bars?" She swung around to glare at Norm. "What have you done with them?"

"We put them in the trunk," Norm told her, slinging her bags into the back seat. "Hey, and there's a wooden box in there, looks like a coffin. Did someone die or something? And there's a fucking air tank in there as well."

"You didn't touch anything, did you?" Natalie asked sharply. "The box is…was a promotional gadget. You know, 'Eat Healthy or Die.' I won it. Yeah, there's just more health bars in there, of course."

"I figured it was something like that; I'm not as dumb as I look, y'know. But what's with the pump? You going deep-sea diving or something?"

Natalie was on a roll. "Don't be stupid, Pickle—you never heard of a flat tire? You want me to be safe, don't you?"

He nodded vigorously. "Of course."

Natalie started the car. "What are you standing around for? Get in. I don't want to be late for my pedicure." She eyed Cohen in the rearview mirror as Norm raced around to the passenger seat. "And what the hell are you doing here anyway, Reuben?"

Cohen shriveled up against the seat cushions. "Just out for an air-conditioned car ride in this hot weather, that's all," he croaked.

"Y'know," Natalie said as she peeled out of the parking lot, "if you boys enjoy hanging out with each other so much, you should go golfing on Wednesdays as well as Saturdays and pick me up after."

"We could probably do that," said Norm. "Yes, indeed." He turned around and winked at his silenced partner in crime.

P
A
R
T

August to September

F
I
V
E

DON'T BE A BOOB

The following Saturday at Crème de la Crème, Shelly and Natalie decided to change their routine. Instead of cocktails with brunch they set aside the menus and polished off several liquid appetizers. Over the first Manhattan, they caught up on Natalie's week, and over the second it was Shelly's turn. Her boss, Mr. Raven, and his harebrained assistant Madeleine, came under attack, as did Madeleine's incessant passion for baking.

Now nearing the end of their third drink it was Natalie's turn and she was well into one of her favorite topics: Pickle. "The man can fucking scratch, Shel. Tickets, not me. In fact without touching me, my Pickle makes me itchy. He used to be such a clothes horse but now he wears the same sweater all the time."

"Like Einstein," said Shelly, taking a dainty sip of her drink.

Natalie mulled it over and gave a satisfied nod. "Einstein, sure, that's what I got. And have I mentioned that my Pickle has the perfect cock? I feel like Goldilocks did when she found the perfect-sized bed in that bear place. Not too short, not too long. Not too wide and not too narrow." Shifting in her seat, Natalie uttered a noise that to Shelly sounded distinctly like a preorgasmic moan.

"Reuben's penis is perfect, too."

"I thought it was small." Natalie shrugged and tried to coax another drop out of her Manhattan glass before reaching for its replacement. "I could go for a man like Reuben, minus the scars and small cock, of course. And the added weight. Mind you, he'd be even more attractive if he had money. Has his settlement fight ended yet?"

Shelly had drained her third glass and was now in mid-swallow from her fourth, so she frowned and just shook her head.

Natalie went on. "My friend Nanu the cosmetics queen could fix him up good. Why is Reuben so shy about wearing a little makeup over those scars? He would be so pretty." Natalie laughed, then she tapped a highly polished nail against the menu. "If you keep eating so much he'll soon be screwing Mrs. Dumpy the Elephant," she said, tact not being her strong point. "Do you think that Mrs. Dumpy is brave enough to take a really good look at herself in a full-length mirror? Do you really want to have a body that will turn Reuben off sex for the rest of his life? You'll lose that husband of yours if you don't watch out."

"I read something the other day about penis size. Let me see…" Shelly interrupted, rummaging in her purse. She hauled out a page torn from a magazine, and read aloud: "'Fear of the Spear. Women widely believe a man's penis size is irrelevant. Being attentive to a woman's sexual and emotional needs is a far more important factor than how well-endowed a man is.'"

"Well, that's two strikes against you," Natalie declared. "He can't please you sexually or emotionally. What a lucky girl you are."

"Lucky. Right," Shelly said flatly. She gazed into her drink and after a moment confessed, "I don't really screw my husband, Nat, he screws me. He's just happy getting off." She stared blankly into the distance, until her attention was caught by the sight of a stranger at another table, a man flirting with his waitress. Her jaw tightened. "There's no romance, no fun, but now that my hormones and all have settled down we have sex pretty regularly. I spread my legs and let him in. I don't even care if he leaves the lights on — I just keep my eyes closed and in a few minutes the job is done. He gets off, I put my pj's back on and go downstairs to defrost the chicken or whatever's for supper the next day. Then I go to sleep."

She squeezed the tablecloth as if choking the poor linen. "When he needs to get off, I am there for him. That's what men really want. We're just humping chattel. Men are just pigs," she snapped.

For a moment she just sat, breathing hard, then her fingers

relaxed their grip. Pushing back her chair, she stood up, posed like a drama queen, one hand pressed against her breasts. She raised her Manhattan high in the air and announced, "Men are fucking pigs!"

Around them, voices stilled and faces turned as Natalie rose, almost gracefully, her drink teetering high in her outstretched hand, and warbled, "You said it, girl. Pigs!"

Shelly looked at the crowd of silent faces. Through the glow that came with having downed several cocktails, from her position on the dais she had the sense of being on an intimate Shakespearian thrust stage. Her hidden talent bubbled to the fore (as it regularly did these days). "Life is a stage and we but poor players," she misquoted, gesturing dramatically.

"Not so poor," said Natalie.

"Speak for yourself!" Shelly assumed a statuesque pose. "Oh, Reuben, what a lover you are! You give me evenings of unforgettable ecstasy!" She lowered her glass. "I deserve an Academy Award for my performance."

Natalie played the role of Oscar presenter, with her fist as the microphone. She drained her Manhattan (and called for another) and then, turning the glass upside down, held it out to the adoring audience and reverently said, "The Oscar."

Then she spoke into the impromptu mike. "The other nominees in this category were pretty good but, hands down, the most convincing performance in a supporting actress role was by Shelly Cohen, wife of a man suffering from a traumatic head injury. A fantastic portrayal of a woman pretending to be sexually satisfied."

Natalie stumbled around the table and grabbed the winner's hand. Holding it high, she looked at the blurred crowd. "And now accepting the Oscar for Best Supporting Actress in her role as Miss Representing in *Helping Husband Get Off*, here is a winner whose poison is her passion, Shelly 'I'll Satisfy You' Cohen!" With a flourish she presented the trophy. "Just for you, babe—a strong, erect and brazen man."

Shelly grabbed it. "Oooh, just what I always wanted."

"You've got him by the genitals, dear."

"Oooh, just what I always wanted." Shelly clutched the trophy to her breasts and faced the audience. "I want to thank my husband, Reuben, for all his support. This award would not have been possible without him. I love you, Reuben. Thank you for being...well, just for being."

Their audience burst into a smattering of applause for the rather creative improvisation. Both presenter and award winner bowed and sat down. Nervous waiters returned to their duties.

"I need more, Natalie," said Shelly.

"And Reuben will be hanging onto more before too long, honey. Your gorging habits are those of a pig at the trough and if you're not careful, he'll leave the farm. What do you weigh now?"

Hunching over in embarrassment, Shelly leaned close to Natalie's waiting ear and whispered. "It hasn't been easy since the accident. I'm up to a size sixteen."

"Oh my God!" shrieked Natalie. "Sixteen!"

"Shhh." Shelly grimaced.

Natalie shrugged by way of apology. "You need to go on a diet and start doing what a real woman does."

"And that is?" Shelly asked, squeezing her arms tight against her body.

"Lie about your weight."

Shelly snorted a laugh and shook her head. "Anyway, let's forget my weight for a moment—what about ME? I need more, Natalie. More than you. Your husband keeps winning those Scratch 'N Win tickets. He won you with a few scratches of his lucky nickel." Shelly said with a giggle. Subsiding, she toyed with the erstwhile statue for a moment and then blurted, "Does Pickle really give you all you need? Or are you only using him for your wants?"

Natalie simply smiled.

Shelly moaned, sounding something like a drone from an old bagpipe. Her face tightened. "You're such a bitch. Doesn't marriage mean more to you? More than money for you and your rat of a Chihuahua? Pickle gives you money and in return you give him big fake boobs. You went from desert molehills to mountain peaks in eight hours for Gawdsakes!" Her scowl wavered, then cleared. She burst out laughing. "Mountain peaks! Isn't technology incredible?"

"It is!" They paused for a moment to admire the new perky peaks, then Natalie said, "After my two previous marriages, I realized three things, Shel. One: all the good-looking men are married. Two: all the interesting ones are gay. And three: smart girls with big boobs finish first. Pickle is not good-looking but with his beautiful cock I thank my lucky stars that he's not gay either."

Their waiter approached with their fresh drinks. Natalie ignored him as he placed them on the table and hurriedly left. "But Pickle is rich and I landed him. I've got big boobs and I'll never have to work another day in my life." She cupped her almost perfect fake breasts in both hands. "I have two things that are true symbols of femininity, and which also sustain my Pickle's lust."

Shelly shook her head. "Oh, Nat, your reasoning is flawed. You are not allowing for what is natural to occur. First of all," she flipped through her notebook and brought out a clipping. "I cut this out to show you; it's about fakery in the media." She cleared her throat and read: "'Don't be a Boob. The film and advertising industries are the main drivers of the modern idealized body image.' It also says the reason so many actresses and models look so good is because their photographs have been airbrushed and computer enhanced. Don't you read? Don't be stupid, woman!"

"I'm not stupid and I don't have to read." Natalie rested her arms on the table and leaned forward until she was almost nose to nose with her accuser. "I have the money to travel now and I see it all. Plastic surgery has been taken up with amazing enthusiasm in places like China, South Korea and Japan. Did I mention that Japanese men have very small penises? Reuben is not alone." She patted Shelly's hand while Shelly stared at her, astounded. "Of course, he isn't Japanese," she continued, "but Jewish men have little penises too. So he really isn't alone now, is he?"

"Little penises?" Shelly muttered into her drink. "Everyone but Pickle, I suppose."

Natalie ignored her. "And those Japanese people, they're always getting their pictures taken. In fact, they love photography. They love the way they look. Everyone is always taking pictures of each other, think about it!"

Shelly rubbed her forehead in confusion. "I have never heard such shit in my entire life. There is simply nothing to think about, Natalie. We were talking about breast enhancement, remember?" She tapped the magazine clipping. "It says that there is no biological need for larger breasts on a woman. Breast implantation is simply self-mutilation aimed at the male's lowest impulse."

"Where do you get that horseshit?" Natalie shot back, her arms waving like a windmill on drugs as she added, "Why don't you tell me, Shelly, why millions of people who cannot stand their own faces, or even their whole bodies, use plastic surgery to change their appearance? Can you tell me, Shelly, why is it now such a booming industry around the world?"

Natalie smirked, then swiveled to survey the audience. Some watched them, unabashed, but one handsome diner, eating alone, was solely occupied with his food. She eyed him thoughtfully. "I think," she said, "that there should be a Miss Ugly contest where thousands of unattractive women—and God only knows there are many—would compete for a top prize of, say, a hundred thousand dollars' worth of plastic surgery." Her gaze returned to Shelly. "What do you think?"

"There already is something like that. Well, not a contest, maybe, but shows where people who can't accept themselves and are desperate to change go and get themselves remade."

"Ugliness is a woman's worst fear, and old age is a beautiful woman's worst nightmare." Natalie paused to adjust her shirt and pat her hair. "If money can stop my new upward curves from resolving themselves into an unattractive series of troughs and valleys—show me who to pay! I'll be the first to tell you that the emotional trauma, reduced nipple sensation and scarring of breast implant surgery are nothing when you consider the end result. It's well worth every penny. Bring it on, girl!"

Natalie waved her arms as if she was a boxer waiting for the bell. A busboy approached. She just missed slugging him in the ribs. Ducking to avoid a catastrophe, he sent a full tray of dirty dishes crashing down as he hit the floor. The other diners fell silent.

Natalie didn't even flinch at the near collision. Planting her hands on the edge of the table, she leaned forward again, her excellent new cleavage displayed to a nicety. "Tuck in my droopy chin, straighten my jaw, widen my eyes, lengthen my legs, tighten my butt, boost my bust size. I don't give a shit. Just make me attractive! A truly fulfilled woman is one who is happy with the way others see her. Love or approval from others is more important than self-esteem any day." Straightening, she again smoothed her shirt over her boobs and said sternly, "Look here, my friend—I'm sorry if the truth hurts you, but you need to get your priorities straight. You need to take care of your body or you can't keep a man."

"It's not fair," said Shelly. "Why do women feel that something is missing from our lives if we don't have a man?"

"Because there just is." Natalie pressed a hand to her bosom. "Women find ultimate fulfillment through the love of a man. A knight in shining armor on a white horse who will come and rescue each of us from the gutters of life. The success of a woman in the adult world can only be had indirectly through her relationships with men," she said forcefully, waving her arms in emphasis. "Why do you think that the princess was happy to be kissed by a frog?"

Shelly just shrugged.

"By the way, my dog is a rat of a poodle not a Chihuahua."

"A rat is a rat! You never had to work for more than a few months at a time between marriages. Your last two husbands supported you fairly well, didn't they?" Shelly snorted. "Of course they did, but only after signing a prenup that included clauses like 'Having sex as and when it suits the husband.'"

"Is that what you think of me?" Natalie's voice cracked with emotion. "You didn't always."

Shelly, cast in the shadow of Natalie's bright new life, did not hesitate to answer. "When we first met, I thought you were boring."

"Boring? Me?" Natalie was shocked.

"And a bit of a phony."

"And now?"

Shelly sniffed. "I don't like to repeat myself!"

"Then why," cried the lovely one, "are you my friend?" Tears of self-pity welled up. Shelly shoved a table napkin into her hand. Breasts heaving, Natalie sobbed.

"I think it's because we're there for each other," Shelly said thoughtfully. "When I need you, you always seem to be there for me. But I don't need you all the time, just part-time."

Natalie nodded and dabbed at her eyes.

Their waiter reappeared. "Ladies, are you finished your liquid appetizers? I suggest ordering something to eat before you forget how," he said with a softly sarcastic laugh. "Of course, you could just wait until you come again next Saturday, but you'll probably be dead from hunger."

"Or from digesting too much gossip," murmured a deadpan voice from the floor as the busboy finished picking up the mess and reloaded his tray.

Excerpt from diary entry — Shelly Cohen

I am getting so scared. Reuben is switching so quickly from real life to fantasy to real life to fantasy again. He seems confused about who people are.

He also completely misunderstands what is required to please me as a woman. He comprehends so little and is getting violent. He throws things and shouts. I know it's frustration, I really do, but his anger scares me sometimes even though it's not directed at me.

Then there's work. Sometimes I actually find myself envying Reuben for not having to go to work day in, day out. Not that I'd want his problems, but still…he slops around the house while I get to work my butt off. Oh yeah, and this extra weight means my boobs are bigger, and doesn't Raven just love to lean over my shoulder like a horny boy and grab an eyeful of cleavage.

Not what I imagined my life would be. No.

Plus I need some excitement, something to look forward to and make me feel like getting up every day. I keep thinking back to the winter I tried parachuting. The clear blue sky above me, the clear white snow below. I wonder if I can get up enough nerve to try it again. Winter's only a few months away.

A DOE AND A DEAR

The next Wednesday, Cohen's schedule put the visit to Hot Yoga on hold. After his trip to Yanna, it was time to see Dr. Stephan, who had been Cohen's family doctor since The Pot Mishap.

"He's a thin man and small, kinda like a boy, but a guy with one heck of a mah…mah….massive brain. In my sea of confusion he knows the way up," Cohen told Norm as they exited the elevator. "He looks like a kind of scared and retarded grade nine student lost in a hallway on his first day of school, but I'll tell you, Pickle," Cohen said as they entered the waiting room, "I got a doctor here that went from grade nine straight into University. I'll guarantee it. His fucking office is wallpapered with degrees. He looks like a dork but his wife is hot."

Norm slumped into a vinyl-covered chair. "How come you've seen his wife?"

Cohen perched beside him, rubbing his clammy palms together. "Well, on his desk he's got this picture of his wife and she's so hot! I don't know her name but that really isn't important, is it?"

"Not at all, not at all!"

Cohen leaned closer and hissed. "In the picture she's reclah… reclih…lying on this inflated rubber mattress wearing this sleh…slih…flih bike…biki…" Cohen slammed the heel of his hand against his forehead, "sexy swim thing."

Norm offered a guess. "A slender, slim and flimsy bikini?"

"Yes, that's it! She's an older woman but she looks so good in it, almost completely naked."

"And she's got the body to boost your balls," Norm said with a snicker. He grinned his slippery grin and grabbed an old *National Geographic* from the magazine rack by the door. It fell open to a well-thumbed photo of a group of almost naked Native Amazonian women. Cohen smirked.

Norm held it up, staring in puzzlement. "These natives have the weirdest tits. I mean, compared to what I've seen." Norm shook his head. "Perhaps if my mother had let me look at *National Geographic* when I was younger, I'd have a more geographical view of the female breast."

"Gee-o-graph-i-cal?" echoed Cohen.

"Y'know, tits as just a normal piece of nature. Fatty tissue. Fatty tissue with milk producing glands and that's it," Norm murmured. "That's what breasts are. How could seeing the natural female body as a child have harmed me? But almost everything 'natural' is 'immoral' — at least, that's what my mother told me. Really, how could Mom have believed in such stupidity? Isn't the body completely natural? Of course it is!" Norm tapped the photo in emphasis, and blinked, unable to hold back his tears. "My mother subjected me to the Playboy Channel every Friday night. She wanted me to appreciate perfection of the surgically modified female body and said I had to learn to discriminate against women who refused to be artificially enhanced or I wouldn't get any dessert or pop or any of her special high-calorie dinners."

"Jesus, Pickle," Cohen breathed in awe.

"Yeah, can you believe it? As a kid, I got fat because I learned to hate imperfection." Norm groaned with the anguished memories of his mispent youth. "Being nurtured and comforted within the haven of my mother's succulent chest didn't help me lose any weight, did it?" He took a few deep breaths and rubbed a knuckle over his teary eyes. "Look at me, I told you I hate doctors' offices. Shit, I shoulda stayed outside."

Cohen's appointment that afternoon was for a routine B_{12} shot to aid in his struggle with fatigue, but first came an apology from his doctor. "Good thing I didn't send you to a gynecologist," laughed Dr. Stephan, feathering his backcombed bush of hair with his fingers. Dr. Stephan stood no more than five foot four, but his classic Jewish nose and big hair gave him the illusion of heightened stature.

"There are two doctors, a neurologist and a neuropsychiatrist. You were supposed to see Dr. Snai*dear*man the neuro*psychiatrist,* first, before seeing Dr. Snai*doe*man the neuro*logist*. That secretary of mine sent the right person to the wrong doctor at the wrong time; it has happened before. Their names sound similar. In fact, both are the same type of animal—you've heard that song, 'a doe, a dear, a female dear,'" he paraphrased, singing out of tune.

Only a couple of weeks earlier, on a heavily humid day, Cohen and Norm had taken a cab to see Dr. Snai*doe*man the neurologist instead of Dr. Snai*dear*man the neuropsychiatrist.

"I may be kinda responsible, but Natalie's got the Beamer today," Norm had yelled from the back seat as the cab headed down the street with a complaining cough. "But I agreed to go with ya and here I am! I even let you sit in the front seat but I am not going in. I hate the smell of those joints," Norm told Cohen and then waited none too patiently for a thank-you for his endless efforts of kindness. True to form, or at least to Cohen's new form, nothing was heard from him because he was busy ogling women as they passed on the sidewalk. Norm gave up and joined in.

When they arrived at the medical building, Norm stayed outside to enjoy a cigar in the designated smoking area, scratch a few lottery tickets and socialize with the four other smokers who had braved the oppressive summer heat to get their nicotine fix: a couple who seemed to be intent on public copulation, a teen filling out a job application form, and an elderly man attached to an IV drip.

In the empty waiting room Cohen sat his fat ass on a wooden chair and had just started to read a *Curious George* picture book when Dr. Snaidoeman came out to usher him into the examining room. The doctor was an obese, harsh-faced man of about forty, his face tarnished and his meaty nose freckled from the sun.

The walls of his office were bare, with no records of personal medical achievements to be seen. This did not impress Cohen in the slightest. Dr. Snaidoeman looked like a fairly intelligent guy who Cohen figured must have at least gone to medical school—but, on second thought, where was the proof?

"Did you leave your degrees at home?"

"What?" barked the doctor.

"Nothing, nothing at all. Let's get started." Cohen sat down. His gaze wandered over the bleakness of the examining room. He jiggled his foot, unable to sit still while answering questions, the same ones he had answered again and again for other doctors and therapists over many months now.

Then Dr. Snaidoeman's questions became different; Cohen thought they were idiotic.

"What is this?" the doctor asked, pointing to his necktie.

Something I'd like to choke you with, Cohen said under his breath, then answered out loud, "It's a tie, man."

"And this?" the doctor asked, pointing to a pen.

Something I'd love to stab you with, Cohen wanted to say but answered, "A pen."

"And this?" he asked, showing Cohen a calculator.

The patient was getting angry. "I haven't lost my marbles, you know, only my proper voice; word stuff sometimes, doc!"

"How is your ability to taste? Your ability to smell? Your sex life? Are your scars healing? I mean your inner ones, not your outer ones. External scars are not my job," said Dr. Snaidoeman, flinching as he looked at Cohen's face. "But those are indeed nasty, aren't they?" He leaned forward and dug his fingernails into the scars. "And so is that," he said, and gently giggled as he indicated the long scar on Cohen's left hand.

Cohen frowned. "Why are you laughing?"

"Well, I just realized, Reuben, that your scars look like tampons. Little tiny tampons." The doctor snickered.

Cohen scowled. Then he answered the doctor's questions with as much vigor as he could muster. "I can't smell nothin' but I can taste stuff." Dr. Snaidoeman looked confused as Cohen went on. "My marriage is hanging by a thin gown thread and my sex life by a frayed underwear one. My wife's heat used to send me to bed in a sweat, now I go to bed and wake up with chills but I'm still always horny. I'm horny every day, not for Shelly anymore but for someone or something that's firmer and tighter and harder." Cohen leaned forward, his scarred forehead knotted in an anxious frown. "You know what I mean, don't you?"

Dr. Snaidoeman licked his lips and almost imperceptibly nodded his head. "I know how you feel as a man, but you've got to remember a few things. Women enter various periods of hormonal, health and life changes that can affect sexual passion. The pleasurable hot spots that used to turn up your wife's sexual thermostat aren't reacting the same way now. Also, to rekindle that connection I'm sure you and your wife once had, I suggest you take a little more care of yourself, Reuben. I think the sparks you once had are being weighed down." The doctor poked a stubby index finger into Cohen's midriff.

"You're not what you used to be. Well, nobody is. I'm not, you're not, and your wife is not. In fact," said Dr. Snaidoeman, shaking his head in regret, "neither is mine! She's nowhere near what she used to be! She was a hot and sexy piece of work that I used to rush home to! Ah, those were good days."

The doctor sighed as he yanked opened the bottom drawer of a dusty cabinet where mouthwash, deodorant, extra-strength Tums and flavored condoms were jumbled across one very special memory. The items tumbled aside as he picked up a wooden picture frame. He blew the dust off the glass, looked at the photograph and, with another sigh, turned it towards Cohen.

Cohen gasped at what he saw: a black and white photo of an obviously oiled woman with Incredible Hulk thighs and arms that resembled two slabs of hardened cottage cheese. She wore a horizontally striped bathing suit and was licking a melting snow cone.

"That's my Gloria at her finest," Dr. Snaidoeman said wistfully. "If I keep it out I'll go crazy, so I hide the past in a drawer but never lock it."

At her finest? In Cohen's opinion, such a muscular cheese ball was ugly, but he had learned how it felt to look strange to others, so he just bit his lip and smiled.

"Getting older is often a terrible thing, especially when it comes to sex." Dr. Snaidoeman sighed again. "The enemy is time and it is invading us everywhere. We are all traveling downhill to impotence, to infirmities, and then to death."

"Imp...imp...if I can't get it up, I might as well be dead,"said Cohen. "They're both pretty damn bad and I couldn't choose one over the other and stay a happy man."

The doctor reluctantly looked up from his Gloria. "Do you realize that you may be changing too? You're still more or less young, but even the young can be in midlife crisis, or, as we professionals call it, male menopause. It is not uncommon for a man of your age to be experiencing increased fantasies about sexual activity with others. But be strong. Find other ways to make your fantasies come true, ways that won't hurt your marriage. Be sure to share what turns you on with your wife."

Cohen nodded vigorously. "I fantasize about other women. And I play with myself quite often. Oh, yeah, and I limp."

"That's fine! Play with yourself as often as you like, but never, and I mean never, mistake fantasy for reality," Dr. Snaidoeman said as he slowly returned the photo to the cabinet. "They are two completely different kettles of fish; one will sink and one will swim."

Having to focus during the long appointment was making Cohen tired, which made him frustrated, which increased his heart rate. He started to sweat. Happily, when Dr. Snaidoeman finally concluded his questionnaire, he ordered the patient to go into an examining room and strip down to his underpants. Cohen obediently stripped down to his white button-buster boxer shorts.

The wait in the gadget-filled examination room felt interminable. He tested his own reflexes with a nifty little hammer, tried to hear his heartbeat with a "microphone thing," shadowboxed in front of a full-length mirror, and even took a stab at taking his temperature with a rectal thermometer. He eventually stretched out on the table and waited for the doctor to enter.

He woke up when Dr. Snaidoeman eventually bustled in and began testing for reflexes, balance, heart rate, weight and eyesight.

The test results concluded that Cohen was slow, uncoordinated, over-weight, out of shape, and nearsighted.

The doctor then asked for a urine sample. Unfortunately, amongst all his other problems, Cohen had another disabling condition: he was "pee shy." For years he pretended his disinclination for rushed or public urination was by choice. Of late he'd found a more convincing reason. "It's not me after all," he'd tell himself. "I am pee shy because of Cynthia Bloomdale."

Three months before meeting Shelly, Reuben had been invited to Cynthia Bloomdale's apartment for what he was sure would be his first intimate encounter. They both had a lot to drink and Reuben had to pee. Even though the country music on the stereo was turned up loud, and even though Reuben removed his jeans and cowboy boots, he couldn't urinate in her bathroom, afraid that Cynthia might hear his tinkle tickling the water in the toilet bowl.

He could not pee and he could not hold it. His only option was to inadvertently soil himself. Nothing would be heard but plenty was to be seen. Although he tried desperately to conceal his crotch pond, it was no use. Once Cynthia witnessed the immaturity between his legs she ordered him to leave. "I thought you'd at least be toilet trained. Outside, boy!" She had laughed before slamming the door.

Thirty minutes after being sent away to supply a urine sample, Cohen returned with a sprinkle of tinkle in the jar. "I'm sorry it took so long," he told the neurologist once he'd tracked him down. "It's because of that bitch Cynthia Bloomdale."

Dr. Snaidoeman just grunted. "Get dressed and meet me in my office," he instructed, "and don't take so long this time!" He ushered Cohen back into the examination room and left, turning off the lights as he went as if forgetting Cohen was there.

Cohen fumbled with his clothes, trying to get his pants and T-shirt to untangle and go the right way around as he dressed in the dark. Then he grabbed his shoes and sprinted as best he could down the carpeted hall, muttering broken obscenities. In the office doorway he stopped, stunned by the sight of Dr. Snaidoeman spinning in his fake leather swivel chair with a finger blatantly rammed up his nose.

"What the fuck?" gasped Cohen.

The doctor stopped swiveling and wiped his finger on his sleeve. "What?" he snapped.

"Nothing." Cohen shook his head, all at once feeling calmly intelligent. "Sorry for my stupidity but your psych…head stuff methods are bizarre, you know. They really don't make sense. Why does a psych…you want to know so much about my outsides, about reflexes and stuff like that? It's my insides that are screwy, right? But what about the red sofa? Why don't you have one? Or even green? I thought I was going to be lying down when you talked to me."

"Sofa?" The doctor scowled. "Do you think I'm Snai*dear*man? Hah! I am a neur*ologist*, not a neuro*psychiatrist*, don't you know the difference? I treat neurological disorders." Angry blood rushed to his fat nose until he looked like Rudolph the red-nosed reindeer as he began listing body and mental mayhem, counting on his fingers as he recited. "Bell's palsy, Lyme disease, meningitis, vertigo. Those types of disorders, get it?"

"No," said Cohen.

"A neuropsychiatrist employs standard and objective assessments of intellectual, cognitive and psychological functioning. Do you understand?"

"No, I don't," Cohen said again.

"You were supposed to see Snai*dear*man first. Neuro*psychiatrist* first, then neur*ologist*, but you have not seen him yet, have you?"

Cohen swallowed nervously. "No. I have not."

"Damn it anyway!" the doctor screamed, pounding his fist on the desk. "It makes my job so much easier when people get it right." He paused, breathing hard, eyes narrowed, nose still red. "I bet Stephan's secretary has messed up again. You would think that she would learn from her mistakes after making so many." The doctor slammed his fist on his desk again. "It is the *Dear* before the *Doe*. Not the *Doe* before the *Dear*. A doe is not a dear. Stupid woman."

"You're damn right!" Cohen almost bounced with relief that the problem wasn't his fault, not this time. "Stupid woman! You'd think she'd learn."

"I will call Dr. Stephan and get him to sort this whole thing out," Dr. Snaidoeman said with exaggerated patience. "You'll have to wait awhile for an appointment but at least Snai*dear*man's the right guy."

"What will he do?" asked Cohen.

"Oh, that's simple. Dr. Snaidearman will consider the inclusions of enough neuroanatomy and neurophysiology to make the organic neurological syndromes much more comprehensible. He will then provide a background for the functional disorders."

Cohen had nodded as if he understood. He hadn't.

"'A doe, a dear, a female dear,'" Dr. Stephan now sang again, and then sighed. "Please accept my apologies, Reuben. I am truly sorry, but it couldn't have been that bad, right? And at least you got a free cab ride," he said with a laugh. The insurance company was paying all Cohen's transportation expenses.

"Not that bad?" Cohen echoed. "I had to get up at eight in the fucking morning because my cigar-smoking chicken of a friend couldn't drive me. The cabbie stunk of Aqua Velva, we were caught in cars, lots of cars and I was sent to the…no….to the…mistaking… unproper…" He slammed his palm against his forehead and went on, his voice rising in frustration. "You know what I mean. What are you guys doing to me? Don't I see enough doctors already? What do you want from me?"

"You know what I want you to do, Reuben?" Dr. Stephan said calmly. "I want you to take a break. Have you ever thought of taking a holiday? I'd like you to give Shelly a little holiday by going some-where alone."

"On my own?" Cohen stared at him in disbelief.

Dr. Stephan nodded. "You have reached a plateau in your heal-ing. You really are doing very well and it's time to do some things on your own, something just for Reuben Cohen." The doctor drummed his thin fingers on the desktop. "Do you have any friends you might be able to stay with, who would love to spend time with you, kind of keep an eye on you? Only for a little while. Maybe a week or two?"

"Well," Cohen said slowly, "I have a friend in Europe. England is Europe right?"

Dr. Stephan nodded his bushy head. "If you can afford it. It will be expensive and your insurance company will certainly not pay for a holiday, but you will be rich enough soon. Just put the whole darn thing on your credit card or ask someone to lend you a few bucks. You might even get a deal; it's almost the end of the summer. Ease your burdens, ease your burdens. A trip will be good for you. This head injury has taken so much out of you for so long and I think it would be great for you to get away for a bit." Dr. Stephan pulled a prescription pad towards him, scrawled out a prescription for Pindol and handed it to a curious Cohen. "I've written you a prescription for a simple beta-blocker. Be sure to get it filled before you go."

"What does this do?"

"Oh," Dr. Stephan said breezily, "it will affect the response to some of the nerve pulses in certain parts of your body."

Cohen nodded his head as if he understood. He didn't.

"Dr. Snai*dear*man the neuro*psychiatrist* will be available by the time you get back." Dr. Stephan's voice held the dismissive tone that always signaled the end of an appointment, and Cohen rose to go. He had his hand on the doorknob when Dr. Stephan cried out, "Oh my gosh, Reuben, I almost forgot why you were here."

Cohen turned to see Dr. Stephan waving a syringe in the air, the B$_{12}$ shot. "Excuse my negligence, please; I'm just not thinking straight," Dr. Stephan's hair bobbed as he shook his head in disappointment. "My wife and I are going out on the town tonight and she promised to wear her low-cut black velvet dress for me. It's my favorite! And, like all men, my mind sometimes wanders away from responsibility when I think of the hourglass figure under the clothes of a beautiful woman," he said, injecting the B$_{12}$ into Cohen's arm.

Cohen could almost feel it entering his bloodstream. This serum helped fight his fatigue. His body was getting heavier every day.

Excerpt from diary entry — Shelly Cohen

I told Reuben he was the captain of his own ship and that I would make sure that he got what he needed. But my life can't just be all about him. I have needs too — I will do everything possible to put the wind back into his sails, but I need to save a little breeze for myself. I hope this is not too selfish. Is it? No.

SOAP

"Every single Saturday you're crying about something and this week is no different. Where the fuck is my drink?" Natalie complained, swiveling around, snapping her fingers at the waiter who was no-where in sight. "You've got to learn to accept the damn pot mishap, Shelly. Think about what your therapist told you: never get angry at kitchen utensils that you can't control."

All around them the Crème de la Crème was silent, as though the individual breaths and swallows of intrigued diners rested on each word of the two performers.

"Remember how quickly those personal injury lawyers came to the hospital? They must live there, just waiting to take advantage of others' misfortunes." Natalie rose to her feet and took an orator's stance. "When a wolf takes down a deer, then the ravens, eagles, wol-verines and bears all share in the feast. When a stainless steel pot takes down a promising chef, then the lawyers, lawyers and more lawyers all want to be the first in line at the buffet table."

"It's true," murmured Shelly. "Those fucking scoundrels, they'd better get Reuben and me a fair settlement." Hands clasped against her breast and eyes squeezed shut, she offered a quick prayer to the Almighty .

Natalie sighed. "It was traumatic for me too. I told the lawyers about the effect of Reuben's tragedy on me. I've been through hell. Why do you think I've put on so much weight? It'll be just as good for me as for you when we have closure on this. Pain buys money, baby!"

"Maybe pain buys money, but it hasn't made you put on any weight!" Shelly got to her feet and slowly pirouetted, displaying her bounteous form. "I'm the one who's been through hell. Look what this has done to me!"

Scenes like this had become common for the other regulars of Crème de la Crème who loved the Saturday melodramatics these two offered. People who settled in for a lunchtime cocktail or two, a few bites to eat, got to take in the show. Natalie and Shelly's melodramatic dialogue was such a popular attraction that reservations were made far in advance and rarely did a chair become available because of a cancellation. Missing a Saturday at Crème de la Crème was like missing a sharp plot twist in an ongoing soap.

Soap Plot Lines
THE TRAPPED AND THE MEATLESS
Natalie becomes suspicious of Shelly's eating habits and an angry confrontation takes place. A bizarre tale takes yet another strange turn. Shelly is concerned about her friend's strange visions.

The curtain dropped each week when Shelly and Natalie left the restaurant, nearly oblivious of the other patrons and wholly oblivious of the applause that gently erupted once the restaurant door had closed behind them.

ARTIFICIAL SWEETENER

Outside the restaurant, Natalie whispered in Shelly's ear, "You want something new? Something to awaken your depleted sensory system? What about a woman?"

Shelly stiffened. "I'm not a lesbian. Why would I want a woman?"

Natalie laughed. "You can't know what you like until you try it. You're fed up with Reuben. Fed up with being unsatisfied. You need someone gentle, someone to listen. You need someone who doesn't make demands on you."

Shelly shook her head. "I don't want an affair."

"That's what's so good about it. You'll have a beautiful woman who will challenge that hot imagination of yours, all without having an affair."

Shelly looked at her, confused.

Natalie linked her arm through Shelly's as they headed to the car. "You think I'm happy with just my Pickle?" She shook her head. "Sure he's a good guy and all, but I need diversity once in a while. I have this morbid fear of one day running out of sexual excitement. I've tried lots of other men. I've tried herbal aphrodisiacs from prickly asparagus to periwinkle to parsley and got nothing but a green tongue. I thought there'd be no limit to where I would go for thrills, but since being with a woman, I've come to my senses. I'm hooked for life."

"You're cheating on Pickle!"

With a smirk, Natalie articulated her defense. "You can't call it cheating, you can't even call it an affair. This third husband of mine really turns me on, and it's just not his antler of a penis, it's everything. I'm not shy to tell him what makes me feel good. We're doing it at least ten to twelve times a week now—that's almost a baker's dozen! I'm even a little sore!" As they reached the car she opened the trunk and pulled a wooden box from its depths. "I've been driving around with this for a while now, waiting for the perfect time to give it to you."

Shelly eyed the box dubiously. "It looks like a cheap coffin."

"Trust me. It's no coffin." Natalie smoothed her hand lovingly over the box and chuckled, then looked sternly at Shelly. "Perfection doesn't have to be real to be enjoyed, Shel. Come to think of it, neither does love. Remember what I'm telling you: plastic is fantastic. No risk, no threat, no disease—no pregnancy, coercion or violence."

Shelly eyed her friend. "I'm so confused. What's in there?"

"Nurturing, fulfilling and sincere men just don't exist anymore—in fact, they never did! Even my Pickle is full of faults, though I never forget that his pockets are full of money!" She leaned forward to open the box.

Shelly immediately slammed her hands on it to keep it closed. "I can't look, Natalie!" she hissed, looking around to see if anyone was watching. "Don't open the box, please. Please!"

With a great show of reluctance, Natalie obliged. "You don't have to feel guilty, and don't worry about this box. I promise you it doesn't contain anything gross or dead, just a beautiful plastic—well, rubber—woman that I blew up myself." She rolled her eyes at Shelly's gasp. "I've got several like this and they're all flawless in body, complexion, hair quality and fashion style. I get to have liaisons with spectacular-looking women," Natalie said dreamily. "I feel so much better when I'm with them, so confident, and my Pickle loves it when they join in too."

"Pickle?" Shelly's voice hit a new high note.

Natalie grinned. "A lot of people use these, you'd be surprised. And if Reuben wants to take you to court for sexual malpractice or something, I have a lawyer who has definitely heard and seen worse. Besides, he is bound to confidentiality." Natalie giggled. "He'd better be after what we did in Niagara Falls."

Shelly frowned. "I read somewhere that in Jewish theory, if a wife has an affair the husband is obligated to get divorced, but these days divorce is for wives without enough to do to keep them busy."

Natalie snorted her derision. "You can shove theory you know where. That rule is for orthodox women—by the way, I can still hear all that bacon oinking around in your stomach." She shook her head firmly. "Anyway, this doesn't qualify as an affair, Shel. The way I see it, if you stay unsatisfied, there won't be a marriage to save anyway."

Shelly slowly nodded. Nobody seemed to be watching and the box was safely within the confines of the trunk. "Okay, you can open the damn coffin," she said. "My curiosity is killing me and this is just for fun, right? A rubber woman?"

"A love doll."

"To play with. And it wouldn't be an affair, right?"

"Right. You're going to use it and enjoy it." Natalie beamed at her. "Would I give you something you wouldn't enjoy? Be like me— just pretend you're in one of those bordello scenes in a film like *Henry and June*, with many different women to choose from, and enjoy it."

Shelly watched, not sure what to expect, as Natalie unlatched the box, then gasped. "Oh my God! I have never!"

"Isn't she beautiful?" They looked at the love doll in silence for a long moment, then Natalie closed both box and trunk, and opened the door for Shelly. "She's a top-of-the-line model. And you will use her, I can tell." Glancing at Shelly, Natalie grinned. "You're excited."

Returning from their Saturday outing, two lucky ladies were greeted by the sounds of two shabby, snoring creatures. Shelly snorted. "Lucky us."

"Lucky indeed," said Natalie. "We can stash your new friend."

They brought the gift in through the back door and tiptoed into Shelly's room, past the bed where Cohen was snoring. He didn't even stir as they stashed it at the back of the closet. Shelly's new hobby would give him much more than he could ever hope to handle.

PITY

Cohen was filled with excitement over his trip to London. His dear friend, Costas, on the other hand, was not. Now a financial bigwig, Costas was a busy man who enjoyed forcing small elastic bands around large rolls of money he had "really" earned. "Not like the old days, my friend," he'd say, waving his wad of bills in emphasis. He also liked hanging out at cigar bars frequented by people that Cohen saw as being creepy CEOs and Wall Street stuffed shirts.

Costas took him to his favorite bar once, and only once, before heading off to a work-related social gathering. As they entered, Cohen hung by his shoulder and tugged at his sleeve. "Look at these people, Costas," he hissed. "They're not my type of people at all. I don't like them."

"Well, I do, and they're certainly my type," Costas said, nodding at people as he settled at the bar. "Lighten up, Reuben. This is a hangout for some of London's top movers and shakers."

Cohen sat moodily over his lime-flavored light draft, glowering at the suits who were busy moving and shaking, and drinking green martinis. He knew what they were like. They were all show, people who wouldn't think twice about shredding questionable accounting records or cheating on their wives with hookers. He sank lower and lower over the bar, eyeing all the showy belt buckles and platinum pimp rings, cringing at the raucous voices and staccato laughter.

"It's going to be tough trying to get a good chunk of change from the insurance company on this one, mate," Costas said. Leaning back on the bar, he swooshed another gulp of premium ale around in his mouth and belched. "I mean, c'mon, getting hit on the head by a silly pot has caused you all this harm?" He snorted. "How much can you milk a head injury? You look alright to me."

Cohen didn't say anything, just put his pint between his palms before squeezing the glass. He lifted it to his lips and swallowed the last of the beer. His fatigued and injured head just didn't have enough energy to allow him to explain what he was going through.

A group of Costas' friends stopped by. After rapid introductions, Cohen got up and wobbled over to the washroom, feeling as unsteady as a newborn foal. Behind him, he heard the laughter of Costas and his loud business friends. He seemed to hear Cassandra's encouraging voice: "Only with hard work and patience will your balance get better, Reuben." *Let them laugh, those pricks.*

In front of a urinal at the end of the row, he squeezed the damp support bar on the wall and braced himself. The wet tile floor was slick for even a stable pair of feet and he was afraid of slipping. He blinked and the whole room blurred beyond his tears.

Returning from the washroom with tear-stained eyes, Reuben discovered that Costas had left. An unpaid check rested under his empty glass. "Thanks for the ale," it read. "See you back at the flat."

Cohen shook his head over how much his friend had changed. The free-spirited Toronto swinger and fun-loving guy had become a tight-assed London foreign business consultant always involved with some kind of big financial deal. He was also a prick. Cohen, meanwhile, spent his holiday taking twice-daily trips to the William Hill outlet in Hampstead to place his bets on soccer matches. Then he'd head to the Flask Tavern to down pints of beer flushed from the kegs and peer through clouds of smoke to watch soccer matches on the wide-screen pub television (including Liverpool vs. Manchester, Southampton vs. Leeds, and one ferocious Birmingham vs. Aston Villa game). He solved dining problems by simply having kidney pie for lunch and dinner every night, on his own. Cohen's spare time was spent at the cricket pavilion, downing a few as he tried to decipher what the hell was going on. That was enough to amuse him and keep Costas out of his fucking hair.

The day he was due to leave, he was heading for Hampstead when it occurred to him that Shelly would be sure to ask, "What about the culture? The history? Buckingham Palace and Madame Tussaud's? Harrods — oh, Harrods! Did you get me anything from there?"

Cohen just wanted to go home, so he reluctantly did what any London tourist did: bought postcards and wrote an assortment of lies. Then he gamely hunted up the free pass that Costas had given him. "So you can appreciate the beautifully painted portraits of queens, kings, dignitaries, media personalities and many other important individuals," Costas had told him.

"Sorry, Costas," Cohen had said, hesitantly accepting the pass. "I don't really know art, politics or other stuff that good, but I'll see if I have time to check out some free faces."

Now, with Shelly and her impending questions on his mind, he finally ventured forth to the National Portrait Gallery. The first face he gawked at in the gallery was a portrait of Queen Victoria that hung in the Victorian Exhibit Room. He stared at it for several minutes and concluded that she did nothing for him intellectually, artistically or even sexually. He had decided she was just another blue-blooded bitch with no boobs when a tall woman stepped in front of him. She wore a short plaid skirt and knee socks. Cohen smiled, expecting to see a beautiful lass, but when she turned around, she was an old one, all weathered and wrinkled.

The old lass began lecturing, in time-honored tradition, to no one in particular. "Attention, please," she shouted at the air, flinging up her arms. "That's her, the beautiful Queen Victoria when she was only eighteen years old. This is after her coronation. She is wearing a very long dress."

Cohen tried to interrupt her with a smoker's cough but his erstwhile professor paid no attention. "She is sitting on a large throne. She is in a church. She is wearing a scarf across her body."

"You're so well spoken," said Cohen, rolling his eyes at her.

She barely gave him a glance. "She is in full light. God's light; it gave her the power to rule so well. She reigned in Great Britain for sixty-three years."

"So knowledgeable," Cohen interrupted, rolling his eyes again.

This time she glared at him before continuing. "A collection as rich as this cannot be taken in at a single gulp without causing mental indigestion. You must feast slowly and digest a little at a time."

He pointed at the next portrait. "Who's the fat bitch beside her?"

"Oh, don't be silly, dear!" said the wrinkled professor. "That is our beloved Queen Victoria as well."

Cohen felt as if he was missing something. He stood speechless but only for a second. "A lot older and uglier queen. Why isn't she smiling?"

"She had nothing to smile about," the old lass said sadly. "After her husband died she went into a terrible state of grieving, and wore mourning clothes for the rest of her life. She was a very sorrowful widow." She leaned towards Cohen in concern. "You look shaken. Are you alright, my little learner?"

This new portrait was having a profound effect on Cohen; he felt as if his head was swelling. "Her eyes," he said. "They're dead black. Like the rest of her. Dead. Black. This picture is scaring the shit out of me." He swung around and bumped into two security guards.

"Excuse me, sir," said the larger of the two, blocking his way.

Cohen squinted from one to the other. The second guard looked quite frail and a tad scared, and stood as if he was bracing himself for an unexpected reaction from a lunatic.

"Sir, you are causing quite a concern, standing here talking to yourself," said the large guard, shaking a disciplinary finger in Cohen's face. "You are creating quite a disturbance, and if you keep talking out loud to yourself, we...well, I," he looked at his partner, "will have to escort you out of here."

Cohen just smiled bashfully. The guards nodded and moved on, in the apparent belief that he understood their authoritative request. He didn't. He gave himself a shake and started limping quickly towards the next room, muttering, "There has to be some hotter lookers in this gallery."

The wrinkled lass laughed. "Stay and digest, child," she called out after him. "The bright colors of this room will soon make your tummy quiver with gaiety. The contents of this great gallery should be sipped, not gobbled. You're gobbling! Gobbling!"

Hurrying forward, Cohen looked back to see her absentmindedly rubbing her crotch and gazing intently at Queen Victoria.

The gobbler moved on, every step accompanied by a piercing squeak as the rubber sole of his right shoe came into contact with the layers of varnish that veiled the beautiful hardwood floors. His loud, limping progress through rooms of timeless elegance engendered amused tittering from curious tourists and enraged murmurings from the London proper. Aristocratic wrinkles tightened with anger. One art lover shrieked at him, "You are interfering with the enjoyment and analysis of these exquisite portraits."

Cohen stuck his tongue out at her and then, to honor his new commitment to art and maintain a civil relationship with his gazing counterparts, decided to do the right thing. He removed both of his new shoes, tied them together in a crude knot, swung them around his neck, and stretched his wool socks up to his knees, and the National Portrait Gallery returned to its tranquility.

Silently and aimlessly gliding around in his woolen footwear, Cohen came to a sliding stop. A hot teen with long blond hair and a light sweater was entering the Britain 1960 to Present exhibit room. Cohen had a flash of memory, young girls — puck bunnies — leaning over the boards, coming on to hockey players in the hope that sleeping with the good-looking ones would gain them a reputation of being hot. Cohen smiled. He shed his woolen skates and, with socks and shoes in hand, followed her in.

The display focused on 1960s pop, fashion art and film by some of the leading photographers of that era, including photographs by David Bailey, featuring his iconic studies of Jane Birkin, Michael Caine and Mick Jagger. The puck bunny was staring in awe at a black and white portrait called "Mick Jagger in Eskimo Parka." Cohen padded barefoot across the room to stand beside her. "Isn't he something?" he asked. "Wouldn't you love to rub noses with him?"

She answered at gunfire speed, without taking her eyes off Mick. "Well, one great thing about Mick is that he's really hot! He looked adorable in the sixties, he was sexy in the seventies, and he was still pretty hot in the eighties, not that I was around, and he's still very sexy, even now. I love him so much!" she said, clasping her hands in front of her lush bosom. "I just rented *Bent* last weekend. I can't say I think he makes a pretty woman, but I wouldn't like it if he did. He drives me crazy! I've never had a real man yet but when I do he'll be all Mick. With school starting soon, maybe there will be a guy just like him in one of my classes this year." The teen gasped with hope.

Sticking out his lips, Cohen said in a bad English accent, "*I Can't Get No Satisfaction* but I would love to get some *Sticky Fingers* with you, my little *Honky Tonk Woman*."

She let out an adolescent giggle and skipped away. Cohen stood frozen in place but his mind followed her.

The puck bunny breathed a heavy sigh and kissed him on the cheek, and they skipped off hand in hand, out of the gallery and onto a double-decker bus to her parents' flat in West London. Once there, the thin walls of her bedroom shook with Bill Wyman's deep bass chords. Concert posters, shirts, ticket stubs, snapshots of pissed teens, beer caps and roach clips littered every surface of her room.

Cohen leaped onto her sagging single bed and stood there, balanced precariously. He swung his hips in sexy gyrations while lip-synching to the Rolling Stones' *Just A Shot Away*. His lone, now topless, audience member was standing by the bed, shrieking with excitement. He reached down and pulled her up on stage. She reached out and her ring-clad fingers extended into his messy blond hair and swam down to his skull as she lunged forward.

Cohen's eyelids twitched, weighted down with fatigue. Bone weary, he awoke to the unpleasant feeling of bright beams of light irritating his eyes. He was barefoot and clinging to an overhead strap of the tube as it sped through a tunnel. Shoes dangled from his shoulders. Socks were stuffed in his pockets. Harsh fluorescent lights flashed colors from rows of advertising signs into his eyes.

His head spun in confusion. There was no puck bunny, no rock show sex. His own stubby fingers were sifting through his hair. Slowly, memory surfaced: he had stumbled into the train after almost missing his connection to the Piccadilly Line, covered in filth after tripping over his own feet and crashing down a long and narrow flight of stairs in the underground.

Cohen rested his double chin on his collarbone, feeling the slow *thump thump thump* of a sunken heart, and said to himself, *I want you back, my puck bunny, my tight-ass teen. How disappointing to realize that you're nothing but an irresistible aspect of my imagination.*

He turned his head a little to catch a blurred glimpse of a swish of letters slowly coming into focus as the train slowed to a stop. The station wall read "Belsize Park." This was Cohen's stop. Somehow he was on his way back to Costas' home.

London Explorer
CANADIAN TOURIST SURVIVES FALLING
THE EQUIVALENT OF SIX STORIES DOWN
UNDERGROUND STAIRWAY

London—A Toronto, Ontario, man survived a twenty-metre plunge down a slippery underground stairway early Tuesday morning, say emergency officials.

The man, Reuben Cohen, was whistling at a group of schoolgirls when he disappeared down the flight of stairs, said Fire Department Capt. Dave Point. "The man was intoxicated with infatuation when he fell," security officers said.

It took the rescue team an hour to place a harness and rope around the fallen man. Cohen screamed in pain when he was struck several times by concrete steps while being hoisted to the surface, said Point.

"But he remained conscious and did well for the situation he was in," said Russell Kooper, a rescue technician. "He was breathing well, he was talking to us and he wanted something to eat. So those are three good signs that he will soon be fine. He just needed to get his wits about him."

"The man's heavy build helped him from being

knocked unconscious," said Point.

The man, who fell the equivalent of six stories, suffered only minor injuries. "Just a few bruises," said Point. "He's a tough mate, that Canadian boy! He can play on my midday rugby team any day."

Cohen arrived at Costas' flat a bruised and battered man. London was no place for him. Before getting back on the tube for Heathrow with his luggage, he showered, changed into clean clothes and borrowed just a touch of his friend's cologne. He left a pot of flowers on the front step as a farewell gift. Holding the dirty pot against his clean, pale blue shirt while writing a good-bye note — "Thanks and see ya" — was a mistake. Drainage holes in the pot's base allowed spots of black soil to pitchfork themselves onto his shirt.

"A pot with holes in the bottom? Why the fuck does a pot need holes in the bottom?" he shouted to himself. "Why am I always dirty in this United Kingdom!"

Cohen just wanted to go home.

On the tube for the last time, he felt like a squished sardine. His luggage hung from his shoulder; a folded map of the tube line with routes highlighted that led to the airport, and a lined piece of paper with a written description of his route, were in one front pocket of his jeans. Lots of single pound notes to buy more tickets, if needed, were in the other front pocket. Gum, candy, and a racing form were shoved in his back pocket. A plastic grocery bag was twisted around his finger, holding a bottle of water and a chicken sandwich from the deli near Costas' place, plus just a little Pindol to settle his nerves if needed.

Swaying clumsily with the jouncing of the train, he moodily comforted himself by mentally describing his journey to Shelly:

As soon as I entered Belsize Park station, things started going wrong. It was a huge maze and I lost my way. Shelly, you wouldn't believe all the fucking little tricks. Like...like why does the Northbound Line travel southbound too? And why are there mul...mult...so many ways to one place? Why do the stations have so many entrances and exits? I keep getting lost.

The eksa...escalators look like huge dinosaurs, hungry dinosaurs. And London is always fucking wet, so the floors are always slippery.

Some ticket machines only take coins and five-pound notes. Some only take ten- and twenty-pound notes, and you can't tell. Some machines don't even have change. A red sign above the machine says if it has change, but it doesn't always.

And there's all the goddamned choices for tickets. Do I want to go one place or lots of places. Do I want a one-way ticket or am I coming back to Costas' place. Or should I get a travel card to go around a bunch of different zones, or maybe just a two-zone ticket, or even just a one-zone ticket. It's too much, Shelly. I wish you were here. I asked one of the fucking Underground cashiers, "If I leave a zone but come back to it do I still only pay for two zones?"

"Well, sir," he told me, "I think you must refer to your guide and reference book. I have too many customers to serve." I don't think he knew the answer. Asshole.

I waited twenty-five minutes on the Belsize Park main level and then took an elevator (they call it a lift) to my platform level, and finally found the Northbound Line going south, if you can believe it. I watched for Leicester Square Station to arrive. I was sure I'd missed it. I had to stand because I couldn't even find a seat.

A calm pigeon that also could not find a seat waited calmly at the train doors in front of me. It appeared to know where it was going because as soon as the doors opened it flew out and con...confuhdd...was sure of itself as it made its way to another line. I limped out behind it, lost and needing to get to Heathrow.

"Taxi please."

I just want to go home.

ZOOLOGY

Cohen, safely buckled in his seat, thought that the crew on this flight had to be the ugliest in the history of air travel. They looked like circus monkeys serving foil-covered trays. Dinner was chicken in swirls of gelled fat with dried-up rice. Dessert was something that looked (and tasted) like a pink coaster encircled by stale coconut granola. Weak tea or coffee was available if the suffering passenger was not yet experiencing the delights of gastronomic distress. Cohen had already downed two glasses of red wine and two Pindol. The medication did not mix well with the alcohol.

A heavyset flight attendant pounded down the plane's narrow aisle and knocked Cohen's elbow. "I am not a wicket in a fucking cricket match!" he screamed at her.

The attendant — *clumsy ugly stewardess* — stopped and turned to look at him with apology on her simian face. The only (and erotic) oddness of her wobbling chins was their resemblance to chimpanzee tits. He stared at them, captivated. Hypnotized. Reality spun and fell away. His bleary eyes shifted to her thick bosom. In a haze he deciphered her nametag: 'FATSO,' it said in bright red letters. He stirred in his seat, alone but for the luscious FATSO.

"My apologies," she said timidly. "I am unlovely at times, I am. You are, of course, not a wicket, but your bold and handsome physical features do resemble one of the most famous cricketers of all time: N. J. A. Foster. It's because of your eyes and excess weight, of course."

"No fucking way, mate. He was a fat-ass too?" Cohen said.

"In 1927," she said, "he captained a Mal…a Mal plus an Asian… Malaysian side which beat an Australian team boasting five test players. Five. He batted for more than one whole hour." She giggled. "My father still has two balls."

Cohen carefully fondled his crotch to make sure that he did too.

"He displays them on his mantel beside a big picture of me," gloated FATSO. "He caught one while he was eating a shish kebab during the game. Reacting quickly, he placed the skewer in his mouth when the ball was heading directly towards him and made a basket with his two hands. He caught it: a real Kookaburra cricket ball." She giggled again. "His balls are signed by N. J. A. Foster himself. The other one he bought at the souvenir stand. Every man wants two balls."

FATSO's large mouth conveyed a bewildering variety of sexual meanings to Cohen's addled mind. He closed his eyes and rode each one like a string of train cars moving through the night and into his consciousness. A warm glow spread throughout his body.

"Would you be so very kind as to autograph me, Mr. Foster? Do you mind if I call you Mr. Foster?" the heavyset creature asked. A willing Cohen, swelling with obese sexual excitement, let his cricket fan escort him down to the compact washroom at the back of the plane. They went in and locked the door behind them, sliding the panel to a red "OCCUPIED."

"Is that your real name?" asked Cohen, intrigued by the big nametag balancing like a tightrope performer on her left breast.

"Wouldn't you like to know?" she said, and bent forward to whisper into his ear, "I need you to put your mark on me. Start autographing my body."

Cohen licked his lips and smiled.

With one quick exhale of minty breath, FATSO ripped off her uniform blouse to display enormous breasts crowned with puffy nipples. Wedged between them were several paintbrushes, all at attention and awaiting Cohen's artistic hand.

"Oh, Mr. Foster! This is such a turn on. Sign my breasts. Sign my belly with my very own paint." With a great heave, FATSO balanced on the counter and placed her stiletto-clad feet on either side of the sink. She looked meaningfully at him and then at the wet palette of her vagina. Without hesitation Cohen dipped one thick brush between her legs and began to decorate the canvas of her breasts and belly with wild brush strokes of genius.

Although they were squeezed into a space that felt no bigger than a large shoebox, Cohen's brushes found a way to speak. Before long, this cultured master of paint had completed a beautiful full body portrait, in early Renaissance style, of the great Mehrab Hassain Opee — a renowned cricket player from the Bangladesh Tigers (complete with the focused expression he always wore when batting).

Overjoyed with her gorgeous latex-painted body, FATSO cried, "Oh, Mr. Foster, you are a man of many talents." In an act of full appreciation, she smothered him with her blubbery breasts and then with her thick red lips.

Moments later, the artist came vaguely close to quoting Renoir when he finally retrieved enough air to speak. Laborious words escaped his blotched lips, translated into a misplaced mutter of mimicry: "I never think I have finished a cricket player until I think I can pinch him."

The new N. J. A. Foster was finished. All Cohen could see now were splotches of red. The red made him think of Shelly — maybe she would enjoy a fling with FATSO. Oh yes! Two overeaters cooking up sparks of fat passion in the tiny washroom, munching on each other and submerging spooned tongues into layered skin.

"Hey, bud! Do you want a great ride in a great car?" A gravelly male voice splintered Cohen's fantasy. Somehow he was standing on a sidewalk with his luggage beside him. An unshaven beast of a man loomed up in front of him, looking like a tramp who had just awoken from a long night in a cardboard box.

"Wha...wha...where's FATSO? Where'm I?"

"At the airport, of course, and I bet you're lookin' for a way home." The shaggy beast stood over Cohen's bags. "My name is Jerry. Just call me Cheap Jerry. I'm not cheap, I just do this part time, y'know. I've got a great car. You see the old Caddy with a little rust, third in line?" He flung out his arm in a wide sweep and proudly exclaimed,

"That's mine and I'll give you a ride for a great price. How 'bout it?"

Still intoxicated, Cohen was in awful shape. With gut-grinding stomach pain and the inevitable headache, he couldn't even ask a relevant question, but managed to slur something irrelevant, his words jumbled like a bowl of alphabet soup. "I chwas jhust onaplay...on a plane with...FATSO. How'd I...how'd I get here with you? Outside, beside a lih...limey...big car?"

"Who cares? You're here now. Get in! Let's go!" Jerry grabbed Cohen's bags and heaved them onto the backseat, and his fare after them. Eight cylinders roared as the old black Caddy bolted out of the taxi line and raced towards the exit with contemptuous disregard for other vehicles.

The limousine had everything: a television with a CD player; a selection of newspapers and girlie magazines, a stocked bar with a full supply of cocktail accessories, including fancy stir sticks, slices of lemon and lime and bright red cherries. There was even a ratty but thickly cushioned footstool. Cohen rested his aching leg on it.

From the rearview mirror hung an air freshener in the shape and color of a cartoon lioness. Cohen blinked. *Jerry was expressing his sexual feelings in lion language to Shelly, who drooled over Jerry's fat pork as she imprinted him with love bites on his belly.* Cohen dabbed his sweaty brow with his sleeve.

Jerry caught him staring at the air freshener. "That's Simba, the lioness in *The Lion King*. Isn't she beautiful? Doesn't she smell great?"

"Oh sche's beautiful all right. For a lion. But I can't schmell schit," Cohen answered.

Jerry leaned back to offer him a handshake. Unfortunately, this gesture was too much for a very intoxicated man who was just returning home from another country. Cohen just stared at him without comprehension. Jerry slowly withdrew his hand and, with a quick look in the rearview mirror at his passenger, said, "Hey, man, sorry about back there at the airport, y'know? I wasn't thinking straight because I'm in a serious physical crisis and I don't usually look so grubby. The thing is, I got really drunk last night after learning that my wife of two years has fallen in love. She ran away with another guy, a Toronto Blue Jay's field photographer. Now I can't even go to the games anymore. I'll kill him."

Cohen merely blinked at him.

"Can you believe women?" Jerry asked. "They're all the same. When the going's good, they're there, but when it's not, they look for someone whose way is going good." He smacked the steering wheel. "She says I'm flawed, no longer a wonderful physical specimen. But more important than that, she says I've lost my sensitivity, my caring nature." He snorted. "A man at my age should be a little more concerned with important things, you know: bills, the market, sports, stuff like that. Hell, it's a woman's job to always look good. Right? Am I right?"

Cohen nodded like he understood. He didn't. "I shknow what you mean, man, I shknow," he drunkenly sympathized, and thrust out his chest like a real man. "Perhaps you chshould change girls and change tah...teh...teams too while you're at it. The Yankees kick ass."

The Caddy swerved into the next lane and Cohen landed on the floor. "Just get me home pleesh," he pleaded. "I think I got a lady in my bed."

As they raced along the dark and almost empty highway without a word until Jerry asked, "Could you run some lines with me?"

"Run what?" Cohen whined from the floor. "I can't even chshtay sheated."

"Don't mind the theater talk. I live for the stage, and now I've got the chance of a lifetime. No more driving for others if I get this part. I'll be driven to the theater."

"Wha' the fuck?" said Cohen.

"Day after tomorrow," Jerry said over his shoulder, "I've got an audition for a role in a musical, a spoof of *The Lion King*. It's called *The Hungry Henchman*. Chance of a lifetime, man," he repeated, thumping on the steering wheel. "I got a chance to be the warthog. Well, actually, the character is a spoof called Pabulum the kosher pig."

Jerry waited, expecting an enthused response. Cohen failed to give it. "Don't you have dreams, man? Don't you fantasize?"

"I schure do," Cohen said from the floor, "but not about being a kosher pig."

"Please just help me out, man. I helped you out at the airport, didn't I?" Without waiting for Cohen's approval, Jerry hit the play button on his CD player. Over the musical intro, he shouted, "This is the theme song, *Hanukkah Matata*—you know, *Don't Worry!* You play Kreplach the Hasidic rascal, which is the spoof version of Timon the meerkat. Kreplach is a dough and meat mixture eaten before Yom Kippur, y'know. I'm not sure what it has to do with meerkats but it sure does sound yummy." He threw Cohen a bunch of loose sheet music with Kreplach's lyrics highlighted. The pages fell on his gut. "Okay now, I'll be Pabulum the kosher pig.

"And don't worry, just have fun. I do. I even changed the words to the chorus a bit, you know, to add some Jewish flavor and show my diversity as an actor. Years ago, apparently, the director of this musical spoof converted to Judaism, something about getting put into his father-in-law's will. If he stayed Christian, he was going to die poor, so he did what any good Christian would do—turned Jewish." Jerry threw back his head and laughed. "I'm just trying to get him to like me more than any of the other guys trying to be kosher pigs."

Jerry waited for his cue and then, with music blaring, burst into song in full kosher pig dialect, all the while using the steering wheel as a bongo drum. Cohen, still on the floor, laughed out loud. He thought he must be having some sort of weird nightmare.

Hanukkah Matata!
What a wonderful eight days—or is it seven?—Oy Vey!
Hanukkah Matata! Ain't no Passover craze
It means no worries or unsalted lox for the rest of your days
It's our tip-free philosophy.

"Your turn, Kreplach," belched Pubulum. Kreplach was too drunk. He forgot to sing.

"This is really fun," screeched Jerry. "I am so happy you decided to help me out, even though you're not. Do I sound like Pumba the warthog—I mean, Pabulum the kosher pig, or what?" Pabulum/Jerry zigzagged through traffic oblivious to blaring horns and shouted obscenities.

"Get mmmmmmmme the fuck hommmmmmme," Kreplach/

Cohen mumbled. "The fuuuuck hoooommmmme, you loooooooney-tune wild pig!"

"Just a few more lines and we'll be there, buddy!" said the swine.

A few minutes later, Kreplach was wrenched head first out of the cab by Pabulum. The drunken rascal of a passenger promptly vomited on Pabulum's hooves and squawked, "Go to hell, you crazy kosher pig."

The swine threw out his passenger's bags, slammed the car door, scooped a fifty-dollar bill from Kreplach's wallet and took off. Kreplach went to sleep on the street where he'd fallen. When he came to, it was already daylight. Still befuddled, he managed to jam his key into the front lock, twisted it clockwise, and tackled open the door. There was no squeak. Someone must have fixed it.

Shelly was not sleeping.

PART SIX

September

Excerpt from diary entry — Shelly Cohen

The trick in life, I believe, is to accept and deal with what you have been given. You may not like what you get, but sometimes you have to consider it a gift. This "gift" I have received is going to take a lot of considering. I must sustain direction and a positive outlook. Perhaps it is finally time for me to actually have some fun.

TUNA ROLL

The first sounds to reach Cohen's ears were shouts of erotic pleasure from behind his bedroom door. These shouts sounded very peculiar. *She has someone else in there, the bitch*, he thought. He tiptoed along the hall and set one of his dumbo ears against the wood.

"Get going! Get off on me! You want me to lick what? Bend over, bend over!" were the teasing orders shouted in a mechanical female voice that sounded kind of like Shelly's.

"Enough!" Cohen shouted. He crashed open the door. And stopped, mouth open, eyes bulging. What he saw was way, way beyond explanation. He thumped his head with the heel of his hand. It was still there. "Shelly, what the fuck is that thingamajig...sex addition...fake female gadgee...gadja...toy...thing-a-majig?" Cohen cried out in incomprehensible blasts.

In front of his eyes was a life-sized, trash-talking mannequin. On his bed. Straddling his wife.

A red-faced Shelly snatched the covers and pulled them up over her and the sex toy, shrieking, "You scared me. You're not supposed to be here."

"I am so. What is that thing?"

"Oh my God! I got mixed up with the time zones."

For the first time in their marriage, Cohen was temporarily speechless. A brief flash of memory swam through his head and he groped his way along a fond recollection now enclosed by gloom. Cold, murky waters sloshed through the layers of his memory and enclosed his mind. What once was, was no more. Now his beautiful bed was a dump site, debris pitched into the sea. He swam along the wreckage that was his marriage and his spouse, and dropped deeper into the darkness, seeking a more attractive refuge. He remembered how much he had loved his wife before The Pot Mishap. Once upon a time they had shared everything: triumphs, thoughts and bodies. These days, the only things he shared with her were frustration and anxiety. Now he opened his eyes and frowned, unable to even remember what a beautiful woman Shelly had been.

"Oh, Reuben," Shelly moaned. "This is Ting Titta." She sat up, fumbling in the doll's long hair. "You can record your very own voice into the tape recorder in the back of her head. Isn't modern technology incredible?" she said, showing Reuben the little tape recorder. "She's running out of energy. Do we have any Triple-A batteries in the house? I have to program her to say more of what I feel. I think I'll record her to say, 'Fuck off Reuben!' Ha ha!"

"You know, Shelly, I don't fucking believe this. Even for a guy who has seen it all, this...this is something else. You're screwing a doll, a doll that talks." Cohen shook his head. The doll was the size of a woman, with an erotically molded mouth, flowing hair, voluptuous breasts with full nipples, slender waist and soft hands with painted nails. It even smelled good. He wanted to fuck the new intruder. "This is very weird, Shelly. How does she get inside of you? Screw you? She has no...no thing...no ding-a-ling!" Cohen glared at his wife and her synthetic lover. "Where did you get this thing, you stupid fat cow?" In a fury he often said things he would later regret. This time was no exception. "You know what you are? You're a cheating, fucking bitch. A cheating fucking bitch, plain and simple. Next thing I know, I'll find you in one of those porno booths in Times Square."

Shelly yanked the sheet higher and growled, "Now you listen here, Reuben, you unemployed, disabled fat-ass. This is not cheating. Her name is Ting Titta and she penetrates me with emotion. Natalie tells me there are many more types of these women to explore, and I will! I'll explore them all. She says that Pickle likes love dolls and that he has improved sexually. You should be like him."

"You're cheating!" yelled Cohen.

"No I'm not! I am using my creative imagination. You should try it. I need more attention and this presents me with possibilities that you don't offer anymore." Shelly glared at him, as if daring him to respond. He didn't.

Her look softened. "C'mon, Reuben!" she urged him. "Learn to play with fantasy, don't be afraid of it. Think of all the great creative types, artists, sculptors and musicians, and painters like Picasso and Dali. They all had great imaginations, and they weren't afraid to use their imaginations to accomplish all sorts of things. Don't you know this? Don't be such a stupid man."

"Stupid man, stupid man," retorted poor, mocked Cohen. He wished he had the courage to square his shoulders, look her in the eye and say in his own defense: "*I just got back from London, Shelly. London, England. I was overseas. I'm filled with culture and paintings and stuff. I even got a table for three at the Walthamstow Stadium for Dog Racing with no reservation,*" he'd say, impressing her with his improvised English accent. "*That's in East London. And three is an odd number. There are not many tables for three anymore. Not unless you're a somebody. They referred to me as an International Guest. International, Shelly.*"

And then he'd taunt her: "*Have you ever been on the left side of a car? I mean not driving, no. With someone else driving on the other side, not the right side. Well, it is the right side but to us it's the wrong side. I was. I now have international flavor. Do you?*" he would ask.

But he didn't say any of that. Instead, he curled up on the floor like a disobedient dog and cried, "You're right. I should read more litt...litter...litter and a rat...you know books and stuff." He rubbed his eyes and straightened as a thought occurred to him. "Picasso was never with a rubber woman," he shouted. "For God sakes, Shelly, what can a rubber woman do to you that I can't?"

Shelly raised her chin like a cocksure trial lawyer. "It's not real, Reuben—the fucking thing isn't even alive. But I'll tell you, I give her my own voice and she talks to me. It's more than sex, it's an emotional journey. We women look at sex much differently than you men do. It's about emotion, Reuben. Not just fucking. Emotion!"

A flush of anger shot through Cohen's body. He shouted, "If you want to play this way it's going to get ugly. It's going to get real ugly and real messy. It will stink, Shelly, really stink. I can play this game too."

"Ooohhh, Reuben, I'm shaking!" Shelly stretched and adjusted the bed sheet, then eyed him thoughtfully. "On a serious note, it's a good thing you're home. You got a call about a doctor's appointment, just after you left." She paused, her sarcasm giving way to a look of mild concern. "Lo and behold, I think the appointment is for today. I forgot to write it down."

"Doctor? Today? On a Saturday? Fuck!"

"He's squeezing you in or something." Shelly scooped her watch off her bedside table and peered at it. "Shit, it's one o'clock already! It's a good thing you're home. I told Pickle all about it and he should be coming to pick you up any minute now."

"You're telling me now about a doctor appointment today that you confa...confer...said yes to a couple of weeks ago?" Cohen asked, flabbergasted. "I just got home from England," he said, and then, trying to impress his wife with his new sense of independence, added, "That's in Europe, you know."

"Big fucking deal, you got on a plane," Shelly muttered under her breath. Then she ordered, "Go and wait for Pickle so I can play without being disturbed. And close the door behind you."

He slunk out of the room and waited on the other side of the door. A moment of silence passed and then Ting Titta spoke: "What women really want from men is confidence."

He stormed down the stairs, followed by the mechanical Shelly voice: "Personal confidence is the trump card."

"If you want confidence, I'll show you confidence," he muttered as he headed out, slamming the door behind him. Then he stopped short. Through black clouds of exhaust in front of his house, Cohen could just make out the shape of a shabby station wagon.

"Hey, Reuben! Let's go! I'm ready for ya." Cohen could hear the familiar sound of Norm's hoarse voice over the toothless roar of the engine, but couldn't see him though the clouds of pollution. "Come closer to the curb," ordered the distant voice.

Cohen waved exhaust smoke away from him, and reached out to a vibrating strip of rusted metal. Peering through the filthy passenger window, he saw lights blinking intermittently like a UFO. He gestured for Pickle-the-alien to lower the window.

"Just scream," Norm shouted. "The passenger window doesn't go down. Come to think of it, neither does the driver's."

Cohen bellowed, "Where did you get this piece of shit? What happened to the slick BMW?"

Norm screeched open the door, and eased out of the driver's seat. "Would you rather walk?" He patted the car roof. "The heater only operates on low, there is no music because the radio was stripped. Brake fluid's leaking, and when I do a left there's a weird noise. The doors don't lock, Reuben, and I'm sure there are a few more surprises I haven't found. But I tell ya, buddy, these are just minor inconveniences—I don't need my wife's car anymore. I'm independent." Norm raised his right arm like a victorious fighter. "I bought this baby with Scratch N' Win Bonus money. I'm sure to win more scratches and when I do, I'll trade her in and buy something really special like an expensive station wagon."

"And you have that dog collar that I gave you hanging from the rearview mirror." Cohen smiled. "It's blinking."

"In a strange sort of way, it gives a disco feel to the vehicle. I bet the ladies will love it. Maybe my Natalie will wear her hotpants if I take her to the Quick Shake and Burger drive-thru in this thing."

"Natalie still wears hotpants?"

Norm just smiled and pressed the button on the collar. "I'm being attacked. I'm being attacked. Help. Help," cried the mechanical voice. "Isn't this great," said Norm. "It'll reduce my chances of ever being murdered and it looks so much better than those cheap dice things. Plus, it's a memento to honor Scratch. I was a good owner."

"You are where I want to be!" Cohen jerked the passenger door open and hopped in. When Norm was settled behind the wheel, Cohen patted the dash. "Let's move out."

As the car lurched forward, exhaust billowed, but once they picked up speed the black cloud trailed behind for other poor suckers to deal with.

"Hey, buddy, how was England?" asked Norm.

"Soccer. And beer," said Cohen. "And rain."

"Any hot babes?"

Cohen scowled as the image of Shelly and her plastic lover flashed through his mind. "I don't want to talk about it."

Norm shrugged. "Okay. Whatever."

Cohen leaned back in his seat. "Hey, Pickle? When I get all the money from my settlement, I'll buy you a nicer car so you can be even more in deep...depend...you know, what you said before."

"Independent?" Norm offered.

"Yes, that's it." Cohen nodded happily. Then he noticed that Norm was wearing gloves. "What are those things for?"

"Just think of all the hands that have touched this wheel, and all the things those hands have touched—toilets, money, girls, escalator railings, doorknobs, their own crotches and armpits." Norm's voice rose to a shout. "Dirty bastards! Because of them I could make myself sick, plus I don't want to pass on germs to my buddy. That's you, Reuben!"

"Don't get sick," yelled Cohen.

Norm wiggled his leather fingers for him. "I won't. I bought these racing gloves—genuine alligator skin and cow leather. I'm protected, and I'll look good driving this piece of shit. I know that my wife is a vegetarian and she's concerned about animal rights and stuff like that, but these gloves were bought for humane reasons." Norm laughed as he defended the innocence of his fashion accessories. "The alligator was sick and it was going to die anyways. That's what they told me."

Cohen laughed. The car jittered down the street. This time, Dr. Snaidearman, the neuropyschiatrist, was waiting.

DEAR AFTER DOE

"I'm really sorry I couldn't see you sooner," Dr. Snaidearman told Cohen as they sat in his office. "It was very hard for us to squeeze you in what with the mistake Dr. Stephan's office made, my busy schedule and you going on a little holiday, so it was best to see you now. Better later than never." He giggled.

Cohen frowned at him. "How did you know about me taking a holiday?"

"Dr. Stephan told me of his recommendation. I think it was a good idea." He giggled again. "How was London? Tallyho, old chap."

"How did you know I was in London?" Cohen asked, hunching in his chair.

"My secretary called your wife a long time ago to see if she'd heard from you and to book the appointment. I felt bad about the error. She told me you hadn't called yet but said if you were dead, she would have heard." The doctor tapped a pen against his desk blotter. "With whom were you lodging there, my good boy?"

"I guess nothing is secret anymore," Cohen whispered.

"Excuse me?" The doctor leaned forward to eye his patient, then leaned back again. "Don't worry about a thing. I'm the right doctor this time, I'm the real Dr. Snaidearman. Not the neurologist but the neuropsychiatrist. You're with a dear, not a doe." He eyed Cohen as if hoping for a round of applause. When it wasn't forthcoming, he swiveled around and, hanging up some x-rays to view, explained the images to Cohen.

"Your MRIs conclude that the left hemisphere of your brain has been damaged, and this has created a severe serotonin imbalance. I recognize that you have language, memory and emotional control problems. But there are some benefits that will also manifest. Until this injury, your left side suppressed the creative instincts of your right side. Because of the injury, your right side is enhanced." He gave Cohen a delighted look.

Cohen was confused.

"The damage you sustained will have awakened the artist within. Don't worry," Dr. Snaidearman assured him. "I have treated several patients with frontal dementia before; one was my Uncle Oswald. There is no doubt in my mind that your mind can drastically improve and be truly creative. For the next little while, I want to add one more thing to your existing list, and in a few months we'll reassess. Let's see−" He flipped through the file on his desk. "I see that you are taking Pindol for your blood pressure. Then you've got Fluoxetine, an antidepressant that actually delays orgasms. It's a popular drug with many of my patients. Trazodone, another antidepressant, balances your neurotransmitters. Then you've got Carbamazepine, an anticonvulsant." He closed the file and leaned back in his chair with a reassuring smile, "Don't worry, your insurance company takes care of it until your accident benefit litigation is settled and you get some money."

"What about after that?"

"Then you'll be responsible for buying all your medication."

"Won't it cost a lot?" asked a panicked Cohen. "I can't afford all this shit!"

"Right now you're covered," said the doctor, "so don't worry. I'm going to add Vitamin B_5 to your cocktail mix. Happily, Vitamin B_5 is available over the counter so I don't need to write a prescription for you. It will be used to release energy from the food you eat and improve tissue generation. It will be good for you, Reuben, but," the doctor warned, "don't take too many at once. One a day will suffice."

Cohen was confused. He nodded as if he understood. He didn't.

"Now, Vitamin B_5 does have some side effects, Reuben," the doctor admitted. "It will likely push large gaseous bubbles out of your

system with great regularity. In other words, you'll be farting a lot."
He laughed.

Cohen laughed back at him. "Oh well, I'm a stink-ass already."

"Yes, Reuben, we must do something about that too someday. Another side effect is a possible increase of libido."

"What's that?"

In a soft voice, the doctor explained, "It's the drive for sex. This vitamin may produce a mysterious testicular secretion that will awaken your sexual arousal, your desire to explore the unknown. Any woman you find physically attractive will increase your desire to even greater heights. In other words, you may want to screw anything." The doctor giggled again. "Excuse me for the terrible language."

"I already do want to screw everything," Cohen shouted.

The doctor held up his hand for calmness. "No matter how much a mind like yours has been traumatized it can be readily converted, with the right medications and vitamin supplements, of course, into a source of sexual power."

"It already is," Cohen interrupted. "Fuck this. What's the point?"

"To get better, Reuben," the doctor said. "Would you rather have a few temporary side effects or a permanent serotonin imbalance? C'mon now, think!"

Cohen had discovered that he often couldn't understand what doctors were saying because of the all the big words. But it was clear to him that this doctor seemed to be making a sincere effort to put things in terms that his patient could understand.

The doctor said softly, "The side effects will awaken your desire to create new life, God help us."

Cohen could only stare at him in consternation.

"Sex will be the substance of your dreams whether awake or asleep."

"It already is." Cohen shook his head and cried, "Fuck this."

Dr. Snaidearman had some final instructions for him. "If your balls become tremendously swollen and hard, I want you to relieve the pressure. Sexual self-gratification is more than acceptable. If you are deprived of the normal outlet, then you must choke the chicken, let your backbone slide, yank the spank, as they say."

"But I already do all that playing with myself stuff," confessed a confused Cohen.

"You won't be taking this forever, but, while you are, choke, Reuben," the doctor urged. "Choke! In fact, if you stretch your erectile organ several times a day, its length can be appreciably increased." Dr. Snaidearman's mouth expanded in a smile so wide that it almost swallowed his face. "Wouldn't it be great to have a longer penis? Longer than it is now, at least?"

"It would be a dream," answered Cohen.

"Perhaps your penis could grow as long as Pinocchio's nose." Dr. Snaidearman giggled and the giggle bounced around the room as patient and doctor looked at each other, excited at the idea. The doctor smiled. "If you feel you're acting strangely or have uncontrollable impulses, come and see me. Or we can have dinner together. I know a great little Thai place." He tittered. "Sometimes I just won't come in to the office if I don't feel like working. I may call in sick, you know, fake the scratchy cough. In that case, I have an emergency number you can call."

He took a book of matches from his pants pocket and wrote the number down inside the leaf before handing it to Cohen: 1-888-269-OSRP. "It's the Obsessive Sex Recovery Program. Call for help if you need it. It's like a social club for adults with invisible disabilities such as Attention Deficit Disorder and Asperger's Syndrome, except that OSRP is strictly for those suffering from the addiction to sex. That is an invisible disability as well. An obsession with sex can only harm your well-being."

Dr. Snaidearman laid his arm across Cohen's shoulder as he ushered him out the door. "They meet once a week for social activities and fun. Some very sexy people will be there, Reuben, but please be aware of those who don't share a desire to stop sexually addictive behaviors. Some individuals only go there to meet vulnerable people." With a flirtatious grin, Dr. Snaidearman gave Cohen's shoulder a little squeeze as he said good-bye.

"Good-bye, doctor," murmured Cohen. He swiveled around as the walls faded in and out. In front of him was a door. He cleared his throat, finger-combed his hair and walked into the room. The meeting was already in progress and nobody looked at him as he took a chair in the circle.

The OSRP meeting facilitator cleared his throat. "Why don't you start us off, Miss Paisher. Have you made any headway since our last meeting?"

Miss Paisher blushed. "You did suggest last week that I must never, ever talk with strangers. So I don't." Ripping off her satin blouse to expose her lacy black bra, she proudly exclaimed, "I fuck the bastards instead. Afterwards I have coffee with them. Make sure we know each other a bit, y'know? Then I fuck them again, but this time I'm making love to someone I know. That's my new motto: 'Fuck a stranger and then make love to a friend.'"

The meeting facilitator looked confused. All the men at the OSRP meeting stood up to give Miss Paisher a well-deserved ovation.

"Enough, gentlemen, enough!" ordered the facilitator, then he looked at an excited Reuben Cohen. "Our new member has a question for you. According to my seating plan, I'm calling on Reuben Cohen."

Blushing a romantic red, Cohen faced Miss Paisher. "I just wanted to let you know that I know of a great coffee shop around the corner and was wondering if you would join me after the meeting today?"

"Mr. Cohen? Mr. Cohen! You have to leave. The doctor needs his office, you can't just sit here." Cohen blinked at the doctor's receptionist, who was shaking his shoulder. "Dr. Snaidearman said it was okay if you sat here while he went out for coffee, but he's coming back any minute now."

"Okay, okay," mumbled a confused Cohen, "I'm going."

The young woman patted his shoulder. "Dr. Snaidearman left you a sample of Vitamin B$_5$ to tide you over until you get to a drugstore."

Cohen shoved the box in his pocket and stumbled out. Norm was waiting for him, with UFO lights blinking. They were off to their regular spot. Or so Norm thought.

Excerpt from journal entry—Reuben Cohen

Now that I've talk to Dr. Snaidearman I am so happy that I decided to subscribe to a wonderful selection of pornographic magazines just after I returned home from the hospital. Pickle's barber told me about the magazine. They play poker.

I find myself flipping through the pages compulsively each night. I become down or not feeling too up if I don't flip. Now I have anxiety attacks when fantasizing about the woman in the pictures.

Excerpt from Progressive Doctor Report
Compiled by Dr. A. B. Snaidearman

Reuben Cohen's anxiety levels and pleaser personality together with his need to present in an intact fashion have continually presented challenges for his rehab team. This is exacerbated by his determination to resume his normal activities, despite the associated fatigue and heightened stress which impact his judgment.

Reuben's ability to positively respond in a focused, constructive and candid manner in his psychological sessions will determine the ability to provide him with the correct combination of medication necessary for him to function at his optimal level.

HEAD FIRST

Shelly set Ting Titta aside and went to work putting the final feminine touches on her new love nest. Natalie had told her to give it a continental flavor and Shelly would soon find out what her friend meant by that. Natalie was only an hour away and today they wouldn't be going out for brunch.

Shelly's first step in bedroom renovation was clearing out all the unwanted trash. Thus, Reuben's shit, as she called it, had to go. With a few quick swipes, she emptied his dresser drawers. Several pairs of underwear, all of them stained, odd socks, and undershirts reeking of BO were laid across Shelly's arm. The dumping had begun.

A violent heaving of all his clothes into the spare room that Reuben now called his office, and all was just about clear. "Reuben doesn't even have a job anymore. Why does he need an office, anyway?" she grumbled, refusing to let herself remember how they'd planned to make it into a nursery. She grabbed an empty box and headed back to the bedroom.

The other useless shit was gathered together — including racing forms, an old Champion Horses calendar, a bunch of sports magazines (most of them back issues of *Care and Training of Your Greyhound*, because one of Reuben's dreams was to own his very own racing dog and call him "Kill the Rabbit"), a Looney Tunes Pez dispenser (Shelly sucked out a few stale Pez), an empty piggy bank and a bowl of hardened mini donuts — and dumped in the trash.

In the now tidier room, Shelly created an Asian atmosphere that tickled her senses: soft desert colors were contrasted with Chinese-red pillows that sank into the plush depths of a pink goose-down duvet. Mellow candlelight glowed and spicy incense smoldered in brass holders all around the room. A massive green and purple Wandering Jew plant hung in one corner and the delicate yet crisp notes of a Chinese hammered dulcimer filled the room like frenetic and multi-toned raindrops. As a final touch, she hung a sign from the bedroom doorknob. It looked like a neatly handwritten place card at a Japanese wedding reception:

HENTAISEIYOKU

which, according to Shelly's research, was the Japanese phonetic pronunciation for "Abnormal Sexuality." She stepped back to eye the overall effect and frowned. The Wandering Jew plant reminded her of the unsightly clumps of a derelict's tangled hair. A moment later it was banished to the front porch.

Freshly bathed and clad in sexy lingerie, Shelly was admiring her zebra-patterned toenails when an exuberant knock sounded on the front door. Shelly leaped up. Natalie had arrived with her new friends. Many new friends. Cohen would be sleeping elsewhere for a while. A long while.

AIR ASIA

Shelly and Natalie lay on the duvet, preparing for their adventure. "I'll give you a foot massage," offered Natalie, wanting to get a better look at Shelly's striped toenails. "Where did you find this wild paint? I'm tired of painting my nails red, although digging my ten little knives into Pickle's fat ass is apparently somewhat cruel and definitely fascinating." She laughed.

"Funnily enough, they're decals from the zoo gift shop. Can you believe it?" Shelly wiggled her toes, trying hard to get the image of Pickle's butt cheeks out of her mind's eye. "A few months ago, Reuben wanted to go and see the monkeys, such a childish thing."

"That is so cruel!" Natalie batted at the foot. "You support the zoo? You eat meat and you support the zoo. That's disgusting."

Shelly yawned. "It's my decision what I consume and whom I visit behind bars."

Natalie grimaced. "Please tell me if those poor animals you paid money to visit were licking and biting those cage bars. Or maybe they were eating their own feces or self-mutilating?"

"Don't be ridiculous."

"Caged animals are deprived of family and mates. They have no opportunity to run, to soar in the sky, to swing through the trees or roam over long distances. They have nothing to do and don't need to use their intelligence, if they have any left. And you paid to see that?"

Shelly stuck out her tongue.

"Those animals are just like Reuben, aren't they?" Natalie's sharp tone finally sliced Shelly's ego.

She sat up. "You're a fucking hypocrite. You may be foolish enough to not eat meat, but you wear what encased it!" Shelly's words exploded as she pointed at Natalie's boots. "You have dead animal skin wrapped around your ankles, don't you, you hypocrite!"

Natalie sniffed and pointed the toes of her elegant footwear. "These are elephant skin boots and I wear them for humane reasons, something to do with Zimbabwe or somewhere like that. The poor elephants were too sick or too old; they were going to die anyways. And, really, could there be anything sexier than the outfits designed for female blow-up doll enthusiasts? Think of the choices! Elephant skin boots are just the beginning. Think of the accessories — the dead animal skin miniskirts! Lacy leather lingerie!"

Shelly stared at her, confused.

Natalie pursed her lips and said primly, "I only started wearing these boots to honor such beautiful, warm and fat circus beasts, but now I think they are a sexy fashion accessory. Need I say more?" She frowned. "And speaking of warm and fat, we've only got a couple of hours before Reuben and Pickle show up." She snickered. "Thank God they haven't come back yet, you would have been in serious shit."

"Fuck 'em! I've got nothing to hide!" Shelly leaped to her feet and started dancing around the room singing, out of tune and without knowing most of the words, her own improvised version of the old Helen Reddy hit:

> **I am woman with sexy zebra toes,**
> **Hear me roar 'cause the rest of me is like a lion**
> **And there's so much of me I'm**
> **too big to not pay attention to,**
> **And I'm not gonna go back an'**
> **pretend everything's fine**
> **'Cause I've listened to it all before**
> **From the doctors and the therapists and Reuben**
> **And I've been down there**
> **And it hurt, dammit!**

Natalie, inspired by the improvised lyrics, jumped up on the bed and danced along.

No one's ever gonna
Keep me hurtin' no more
Not Reuben
Not the doctors
Nobody!

Natalie raced out of the room and returned a few minutes later with a wooden box that was considerably smaller than the one Ting Titta had come in. Shelly ran barefoot to retrieve a hammer from Reuben's so-called office while Natalie lugged in the air tank from the trunk of her BMW, a small upright device that looked like it was designed for a scuba diver.

By then Shelly had returned, out of breath. "You brought the tank," she said. "Thank God. I actually thought I'd have to blow them up myself."

Natalie laughed. "You'd be an idiot to try and blow these things up by mouth. You'd be exhausted and dehydrated in minutes."

Shelley waved the hammer overhead, dancing around the room like a stripper ready for the runway, wiggling her butt in time with the beat of the music. Then she smashed open the box lid and turned it upside down, scattering balls of compressed rubber across the floor. She eyed the tank. "How do you work that thing?"

"Watch the magic." Natalie picked up one of the compressed rubber balls and attached it to the valve. The tantalizing and colorful face of a Japanese woman began to grow, right in front of their eyes.

"Oooh, that IS magic." Shelly laughed in excitement. "This is taking my breath away. She looks like Ting Titta but Ting didn't start out as a rubber ball, I got the whole lady."

"Think of these balls as embryonic Ting Tittas," Natalie instructed. "For your first fetish air experience, I inflated Ting Titta because I was excited for you to get started right away. But we must work for our pleasure and today you'll learn the basics you need to put kinky things into proper perspective."

"I could get my own air tank." Shelly giggled as the airflow began disentangling the entire rubber body of the Japanese woman. "She's got breasts, a Virginia and everything. She's beautiful."

Natalie shared her plan. "I know you like diversity but don't hack off more than you can chew. For your new experience I stayed with Asia: China, Korea, Thailand, Japan, Malaysia, Indonesia and Vietnam. I had a funny feeling you'd like Ting Titta so I stuck with her cultural flavor, but these are a little different: they don't talk. Those tape recorder ones are very expensive. Consider Ting Titta a special gift." Natalie detached the now inflated doll and handed her to Shelly, who placed her carefully on the bed.

Natalie grabbed another ball and attached it to the tank valve. "You see here, Shel, the little Japanese one needs only a volume of, say, thirty cubic feet. This aluminum 6061-T6 tank is ideal for taking on small women like those from Asia but when we get to Europe we're going to need something with a lot of inflating power. I like to fill these babies until they're tight and hard and about to burst. I find it a turn on to see how I can blow up a doll all by myself."

Shelly stepped closer and, with every thrust of air now entering the face of the emerging rubber Chinese woman, grew more intense. As facial features grew tighter they started pressing against Shelly's body. "Your lips articulate elaborately against the underside of my breasts," she murmured to it. "Your tiny nose brushing lightly over my hard nipples and chest is driving me crazy."

After a while the second doll was fully inflated. Natalie threw her against the bedroom wall and tossed the Japanese airhead after her. "Just leave them be—I love to watch them bounce around. Wait till we pile up the rest of them, it'll look like an oxygen orgy." She motioned Shelly to the tank. "And now it's your turn."

The novice blower got the hang of it right away, with some basic verbal instructions.

"The sound of another doll being inflated by a tank does not turn me on at all. And your music sucks." Natalie waved at the stereo. "It's a real mood killer. I'd rather listen to yodeling chipmunks or what's-his-name, Lawrence Welk." She snatched a CD, her favorite Asian soundtrack, from her purse and shoved it into the CD player.

"This is Volume Three by Asia to Far. Listen for the remarkable acoustic rhythms and the focus on drums, guitar and bass." She hit Play and stood in silence, a look of serenity spreading over her face as she murmured. "This soundtrack features compositions by the great Sam Lee. Believe it or not, there is some unique rapping from Joust in here as well. The deep beat pulses right into your erogenous zones...ah bliss! Your heart rate will increase, adrenaline and endorphins will flow." She shuddered. "Remember that in Asia people are very bashful about kissing, so you have to get them hot in other ways, like sexy music!"

Shelly was too engrossed in the emerging new doll to do anything more than nod, barely noticing when Natalie ran out of the room. A moment later she was back in the bedroom almost lost in spheres of brightly colored Chang Mia parasols. "Are these not gorgeous? To hide in the shade when you get too hot, and it's too hot in Asia, baby." Natalie jiggled with laughter. "And now it's time for you to start having fun." Striking a dramatic pose, she added, "You know how to whistle, don't you? You just put your lips together and blow."

INHALE, EXHALE

"You're going to get dizzy and faint, man," the owner of the Wet Your Whistle Sex Shop, a Grateful Dead Deadhead, told Cohen. He was trying to dissuade this customer from remaining in the doll section. He had other thoughts and more important things to do. Like constructing a fragile house of playing cards. "Like I said, the guy's coming in to fix the air tank tomorrow. You should wait till then."

Cohen just kept blowing.

Deadhead shook his head. "Just don't get all excited by being surrounded by sex stuff. I really don't want your huffing and puffing to blow my house down. This is my treat for the day. Yesterday I ate twelve edible condoms, all lemon flavored—so lively is the lemon, such zest! And all thanks to that Columbus guy, you know, that guy who discovered stuff."

Cohen nodded. He actually knew about the guy that Deadhead was talking about.

"On his second voyage," the sex shop owner informed Cohen, "Columbus planted lemon trees in Haiti which led to abundant lemon crops within twenty years. That harvest got all the future settlers into lemons. Dig it, man? Oh, the lemon! So many delicious ways to use them sexually.

"But for my treat today, I am constructing a house of naked women." Deadhead shuffled the deck. Each card bore a photo of a nude woman provocatively posed. As they bunny-hopped through Deadhead's long fingers, the cards gave an illusion of motion to the figures, much like the animated frames of a cartoon.

An excited Cohen leaned on the counter to watch the action. "It's like watching a quick porno film," he laughed. "It's a hint of a movie. Get me some buttered popcorn!"

"This is my deck of Naughty Boy's Poker Cards. A whole deck for only $24.95 — want one instead of a blow-up doll?"

"No."

"Well, watch how you blow. Extra pressure on your eyes will have a bad effect on your vision and you could go blind for life, man." Deadhead took a long drag from his hand-rolled cigarette and proposed a tempting diversion. "I've got some radical stash under the cash if you want to trip out."

Cohen declined the offer. "My eyes have been bugging me my whole life, anyway," he said as Deadhead's heavy exhale of smoke crashed down his three balanced cards.

"Fuck, man! That was my first foundation! Building a house with nude babe cards is one of the toughest things I've ever tried to do. I could work better if you weren't standing so damn close to me." Looking down his nose at Cohen as he rebuilt, he suggested, "There's an energetic orgy of other sex toys, man. Fancy rainbow vibrators, dildos, S&M stuff, lubricants, ticklers, safe sex goods, all sorts of stuff — do you hear what I'm saying? There's a lot more to choose from than male sex dolls. But if that's what you get off on, man, just watch how you blow," warned the card master. He exhaled again and the three cards crashed down again. "Fuck!" he shouted. "I'll never get this house of babes built with you here."

Cohen hurriedly moved aside and started blowing furiously.

"I guess my house of babes will have to wait. After all, you are the customer." Deadhead came out from behind the counter and began dancing dreamily to the music that was playing. Flower power stuff, he called it. "Listen to my words — don't force the air or you'll just drown in the backflow, man! Get my drift? You've got to remind yourself to give it some time. A smooth river of air will provide a sure path to heaven — don't push the river!

"Don't try to fill the skinny man all at once, fat man! Do as nature has intended: take it slow and blow with emotion. You'll get more out of it that way. Don't shit-kick your lungs, man.

**You'll be gone, gone, gone
cause you'll be sittin' on top of the world.**

You hear me, man?"

Cohen took a deep breath, not to find more air to blow, but to speak. He wished he had the courage to square his shoulders, stare Deadhead right in the eyes and say: *Just shut the fuck up, go back to your house of babes and don't sing anymore. Poor nine-fingered Jerry Garcia would be rolling in his grave if he heard you. I've paid for these dolls and I want to take them home alive. If my wife wants women, I want men.*

But he didn't say any of that. Instead, he curled up like a chastised dog, flattened his ears as he blew, and listened to Deadhead sing as he swirled and danced around.

**Been a hard day and I don't know what to do
Wait a minute baby, this could happen to you
Gimme some lovin'
Gimme some lovin'.**

Cohen's cheeks were swelling and he felt as if his eyeballs might pop. The sex shop owner shook his head and said, "You never know if a doll is going to explode, man. Wearing glasses is recommended to protect your eyes." Deadhead took a jump shot, and a pair of dusty shop glasses strung themselves around Cohen's neck. "Two points, man! Put them over your eyes! Saved these from grade nine shop class, the only class where I got fifty. Made my Pop a rad ashtray and next day he died on the sofa with his hand on a burning Camel cigarette and the ashtray on his gut beside the remote and some Cheezies. He was watchin' a Hawaii Five-O replay—'Book 'em, Dano!' Pop was cremated but the ashtray didn't burn. I still have it."

Deadhead resumed his card house construction and Cohen kept blowing. Eventually the card house was three stories high and Cohen had flopped back on the floor wheezing, with two partly inflated love dolls lounging on the floor beside him. Deadhead turned on his heel and waved a hand towards the smog of cigar smoke outside the window. "Your friend's been out there a long time, man. Is he gonna wait until you're done blowin'? How come he won't even come in?"

Cohen, disoriented, out of breath and sweating profusely, sat up with his head between his knees and gasped, "That's my part-time friend, Pickle. He works for me, but now he thinks I'm gay and he's not into gay guy stuff. But I'm not gay, I'm just out for rav...rev... revenge. Pickle said if I was blowing up women dolls, things would be different. He'd res...respect me then."

"Even if you're not gay, you're still gonna get an ass itch sitting on cement, man," Deadhead warned him. "In two hours you've got Big Joe and Construction Man inflated, sort of, but you still got Black Guy, She-Male, Julian Rock Star, Nasty Boy, Party Pal, and Red, White and Blue Doll to go and I don't think you're gonna make it, man. It's already four and we close at six on Saturdays. You've been blowin' here since two."

Death don't have no mercy in this land.

Two hours later, eight love dolls, some with sagging muscles and others with no muscles at all, lay on the floor in front of a very exhausted and bewildered fetish seeker. "You know, man," said Deadhead, "I'll just tie a hitch knot around your love dolls so you can get them home easy."

"I'm not going far," Cohen wheezed. "I'm just taking them to my buddy's car and then we're going right home. Wait until my wife sees me with these things."

"Why didn't you just blow them up at home then, man? I bet you would've had a pump that works there. You were crazy to try and blow them all up by yourself. I bet your lungs will be shit-kicked for the next while and I could have got my babe house finished if you had left sooner."

Cohen struggled to his feet. "You don't understand. I've got to burst in on Shelly with these things ready to go! I've gotta show her up! I gotta show her I mean business!"

"Settle down, man. Let me help you get outta here." In a matter of minutes, Deadhead had attached four dolls to each of two separate lengths of cord, then he knotted the ends together to make a long loop. Cohen placed it around his neck. Deadhead stepped back, screaming with laughter. "With your fat-man boobs, you look like a flabby dominatrix with a cape of men."

Cohen, wearing his cape of love dolls, stumbled out of the sex shop, worn out, dizzy and dehydrated. He had persistent sharp pains throughout his body. Behind him, Deadhead slammed the door and swung the sign to read "Sorry — Closed."

There was no sign of Norm.

"Pickle, where are you? You were supposed to wait for me so I could put these guys in the trunk of your crappy car!" Cohen could not lift his head nor even swing his arms past his gut. He toddled along the busy street, screaming, "Pickle, you hom…homo…pho… homophobic bastard, I'm not gay. These aren't even real men. C'mon, Pickle, pick me up! Pick me up!" He stumbled and caught his balance, barely, with weary effort. "Fucking dirty, rotten, filthy, stinking, buddy asshole! I don't know my way home, man!"

Cohen was cotton-mouth thirsty. Only once before had he been this thirsty — after downing two gallons of bubble gum ice cream to impress the Real Men Gang at Zachary Goldman's ninth birthday party. All that ice cream had blasted his body with salt, sugar and fat. He'd been sick for days but, after that, finally, a gang member.

Now, trudging homeward, or so he hoped, his every step was impeded by rubber love dolls hanging from his neck, which made for a long and arduous journey of one small step after another. Cohen was afraid to enter any kind of establishment that might be able to provide him with water. He feared ridicule and harassment. Mostly he feared being seduced by gay men. Cohen refused to need water that badly. He was in trouble.

PART SEVEN

September

Excerpt from Speech-Language Pathology
Assessment and Progress Report
Compiled by Yanna Harrington

After repeated analysis, Reuben Cohen has presented consistent speech problems subsequent to his head injury. These include difficulties with:

- · awareness
- · attention to detail
- · handling large volumes of information
- · short-term memory
- · word finding
- · verbal fluency
- · explaining things clearly
- · exaggeration.

He was observed to be somewhat impulsive in conversation, with his intonation suggesting assumption of listener's knowledge.

Excerpt from Progressive Doctor Report
Compiled by Dr. A. B. Snaidearman

CHANGES IN BEHAVIOR AND SOCIAL SKILLS
Client: Reuben Cohen

· Difficult for him to "keep up" in social
  situations
· Frequently exhibits inappropriate emotional
  responses
· Exhibits frequent impulsive behavior
· Frequently displays inappropriate behavior
· Frequently exhibits inappropriate sexual
  responses
· Exhibits childish behavior
· Presents as being overtly self-centered
· Experiences frequent personality and mood
  fluctuations
· Complains of experiencing increased
  difficulties with interpersonal relationships.

SEASONED
STEREOSCOPY

For a dehydrated, hallucinating Cohen with his cape of semi-inflated love dolls, the streets were spattered with gay men trying to capture a lover for the evening. Weak and homophobic, he was easy prey for hunters seeking a savory single homophile. Lounging outside gay clubs, "Red in tooth and nail polish," they spotted the haggard and bedraggled Cohen and prepared to pounce. With the dim St. George streetlights reflecting off the bodies that dangled from his neck, he was like a tender venison roast steaming in sweet cider sauce tempting hungry carnivores to come and taste the meat.

Candied Cohen had been exhibiting the physical characteristics of a deer for a quite a while now. On their first post-Pot Mishap date, to celebrate his improvement (Cohen wanted to prove he still had the ability to treat his wife), he and Shelly went for a two-for-one cabbage roll and the all-you-can-eat sauerkraut special at Mars Deli. Then they picked up a large bag of jelly beans from a corner store and strolled hand in hand to Cheap Ticket Night at the Revue Movie Theater. Playing at 7:30, *Bwana Devil*, the first feature film in 3-D, had filmgoers excited and critics astounded. It was a no-brainer melodrama about rampaging lions that preyed on railway builders and it scared the hell out of everybody. On screen, as the train rounded the corner and headed straight for the theatre, the viewing audience, faces full of buttered popcorn, jumped out of their seats and rushed to the exit, screaming. All but Reuben Cohen. He didn't even flinch.

After such a bizarre spectacle of nonperception, Shelly pleaded with him to seek medical help, so Cohen forced himself to make an appointment with an optometrist.

"Mr. Cohen, I have bad news," said kindly Dr. Freidman, bracing himself. "The test results are conclusive: you do not have normal depth perception. Oy Vey! My poor boy." Dr. Freidman patted Cohen's shoulder. "You have good peripheral vision but you do not have 3-D vision. It is very strange. Although it is not possible for a person to have this, you have it. You see like a deer. It's a disorder called stereoscopy. Will you need treatment? You will need treatment. And maybe glasses." Dr. Freidman laughed. "I could get you extra thick ones so you could see double. You know how the song goes—'Two girls for every booooyyy'!" Dr. Freidman laughed again.

Cohen didn't laugh. Every man needs to hang onto at least one set of hangups from childhood, and Cohen was no exception.

As an optically challenged child, life for Reuben Cohen had been fuzzy all around, so he got glasses, but his parents hadn't let him choose his own frames. He wanted designer glasses: metal frames with spring hinges; they bought him the cheapest frames in the store: hideous purple plastic frames with thick bifocal lenses. Reuben called them his purple puke goggles.

Every morning, as soon as he reached the playground area at school (he had to see where he was going), Reuben would hide his goggles in the bushes. Then Daniel Gooerevich saw him with his glasses on and told the whole class what a homo Reuben was. Kids started asking if he wanted help finding his way home (he really only needed help finding his glasses hidden, so he thought, in the bushes by the monkey bars), but they just wanted to laugh at him. They called him names when they saw him wearing glasses, names like "Four-Eyed Homo" and "Thick Lens Loser."

So Reuben hadn't worn his glasses at all anymore. He had trouble focusing on things. He suffered headaches from the light. He blinked, he squinted, he got tired, but, best of all, with no glasses, he wasn't called names. Still, refusing to wear glasses as a child may have hurt his vision for good.

Excerpt from journal entry — Reuben Cohen

As I got older, I got used to not seeing good. Plus, I blame my favorite actor at the time, Mitchell Andrews, who had a few bit parts in that famous detective show, Mathitch. *Mitch got attention from the ladies. I thought I looked like him a little and tried to copy his hairstyle and the way he walked.*

In one show, he played this cool-looking bad ass who always hung out by the pool in the back yard of his L.A. mansion. He's smoking a Marlboro and downing a diet Fresca while smearing this hot babe's body with suntan lotion. Only she was not a hot babe at all. She was a HE. Mitch was smearing lotion on a guy's back! I felt sick, but things got worse. After rubbing this guy, Mitch put on a pair of plastic-framed glasses. My favorite actor was hotly rubbing another man — bad! And he wore ugly glasses — worse!

The next day I read about him in the paper.

Los Angles Explorer
MITCH ANDREWS COMES OUT

Los Angeles — TV's hottest commodity is living his life under the glare of the media spotlight by being one of the first openly gay actors to play a gay part in a television series.

I never had anything to do with him again. Damn gay Mitch Andrews with his plastic frames.

DEER HUNT

Decisions made as a young child came back to haunt Cohen. So did his undiagnosed but extant homophobia.

A routine night of face sitting, ass sniffing and armpit licking was to be quickly put on hold as gay deer hunters, up way past their bedtime, with hard muscles and swollen organs, drunk on tequila, and exhaling clouds of exotic air, clamored for the excitement of bad behavior. These gays were in need of a buck hunt. In the wee-wee hours of the morning, the big-game hunters, once intelligent and informed members of the community, became intoxicated by a chubby deer encircled by a necklace of humanlike figures with swaying rubber gonads.

Unable to distinguish between motionless background and motionless figures, the confused deer had only one choice: to rely on his quick ability to sense movement. Tonight, that was his only defense, but, tonight, that defense was not enough. "I need my sight," he gasped. "I need deer glasses."

He sniffed. Analysis of the wind detected danger. He sniffed again: exhilarating, provoking and soothing scents were close by. His keen sense of hearing picked up the imitation grunting of human bucks, warning him that something was amiss. The startled deer raised its tail and rushed off, but it was too late. Nervous, and befuddled by severe stereoscopy, the prey spun wildly through urban woodlands, trying desperately to scare off his pursuers. It did not work.

One of the hunters told his team, "This sexy creature with the oh-so-lovely cape seems to think he's a fucking deer or something." Trapping him inside a circle of clasped hands, like in a children's game, the hunters attacked with guided missiles of poetic song.

We want your sweet soft kiss
We want a taste of bliss
We want to dive and swim
On your sweet and beautiful skin.

The evening hours slipped beneath the sun. Drag queens in bar windows were no longer the life of the party. Moans and groans of after-hours activity turned to yawns. Empty tequila bottles watched for the sun's reappearance, waiting for it to open lovers' eyelids. Sleepy hugs tightened with refusal to begin a new day.

The serenity of dawn in Toronto's gay district evaporated with the arrival of Shelly Cohen. Brake pads squealed; like a racehorse breaking from the gate, she exited a Diamond taxi. Heavy earrings dangled and jumped as Shelly's shouts of disbelief stirred up the entire community: "Oh, my dear God! I found you, Reuben. My darling stallion!" Adorning his cheeks with bright red lipstick, Shelly sobbed.

Reuben's eyes opened after his long sleep. Light-footed men and women (enjoying warm bagels smothered in garlic cream cheese and topped with salted lox) skipped around them, laughing long and hard. One threw them some loose change and told them to take a shower.

"It's time to go, Reuben. I'm getting you out of here and back home. Take my hand," Shelly said gently, assisting her husband. He reached out, but instead of Shelly's hand he grabbed a hard billy club.

A large beat cop loomed over him. "It's guys like you who we've got to keep moving. You think the street is your hotel for the night, don't ya? If you don't want trouble, get on your way." The billy club jabbed into his ribs as the authoritative figure added, "And take those things off of your neck. You are very, very strange. Man, oh man."

Battered and bruised, a cold and hungry Cohen-the-stray struggled to his feet and stumbled off, deflated love dolls drooping from around his neck. He was trying to find his way back home.

Moments later he collapsed.

LASSIE GO HOME

Later that morning, Cohen awoke to a severe decline in his physical ability. Cool gusts of wind and morning rain danced on his face. He struggled to his feet and drooped over the closest fire hydrant, feeling like a gloveless prizefighter who'd been tossed out of the ring, like a battered Jersey Joe Walcott after a beating from Rocky Marciano. Marijuana had left him with the munchies and periods of strangely altered vision. Only his sense of smell remained intact after his night of high-pitched songs, screams and shouts from partying gays, dykes and drag queens.

He had to get home. Like a lost dog searching for his home, he limped down the puddle-filled morning streets, his world reduced to pungent odors. Familiar smells moved him forward. Whiffs of familiar yet long forgotten "Shelly sex sweat" — her rarely used perfume — gave him a small degree of sensory pleasure. However, one particular smell disgusted him, so compelling that he could hardly think of anything else. This odor had its own smell-face, a handsome Asian face that played through his mind like an out of control movie reel: an evocative and evil Sushi chef starring in "Chop Chop Chunky Shelly." With California rolls for eyes and teeth like fat brown rice, he rolled Shelly chunks tightly between shreds of seaweed-colored bed sheets.

Last night's deer hunters followed his paw prints through empty downtown streets, urging him to "keep staggering on." He stumbled forward, muttering under his breath. *Even gay men and women suffering with slamming hangovers know I need to get home to save Shelly from the evil Sushi chef.*

The gay community that Cohen wanted so badly to leave provided a safe haven for individuals of diverse sexual practices. It was a popular melting pot that gave individuals an opportunity to claim spaces and distinct personas of their own. One colorful silken-haired character had developed a crush on Cohen while watching the hunt through binoculars. Silken-haired began singing the theme song from *Lassie* as the anonymous object of his affections stumbled down the street. Quickly realizing that his neighbors also knew this melody, the choir director was inspired to coin a chorus. Spirited gay men and women, and those in between, sang together to encourage the lost soul:

> *One still night among the silent hills,*
> *I learned a secret that I will share with you.*
> *In the hush, I heard the whippoorwills reveal,*
> *The Secret of the Silent Hills.*
> *Not a secret men scheme and plot for,*
> *Only true words, we should not forget.*
> *'Love can cure the world of all its ills.'*
> *And that's the Secret of the Silent Hills.*

Then, as one, they added a final chorus:

> *Make it home*
> *Make it home*
> *You bitch*

THIRSTY

"What the hell happened to you?" The words bounced off Cohen's eardrums and rattled around in his head before finally reaching his brain. The voice sounded a lot like his neighbor Herman.

"And what the hell are those things?" A gum boot entered his range of vision. The toe nudged a deflated love doll. "You've been getting pretty weird but this takes the cake."

Blood from Cohen's hands and knees decorated his own front porch. This did not bother him in the slightest. He was just happy to have finally made it home and was so thirsty that he began licking the only water available. Thanks to Herman's tendency to overwater, puddles had collected around a pot that held a fat Wandering Jew plant. When Cohen had licked the last few drops, he looked at the healthy plant. It reminded the dizzy wanderer of a woman who had let down her damp curly hair in an attempt to unwind.

"The bedroom would be a better place for a Wandering Jew," he croaked. "It's a romantic little devil."

"Maybe so," the old man answered, "but if I were you I'd get the hell out of this neighborhood and come back looking like a human being. You're gonna cause a scene."

"I am a wandering Jew," said Cohen. He lifted his head with effort and squinted at Herman. "I'll wander no more."

Herman shook his head. "You know the old bags around here. They'll be calling the cops on you. You're not a pretty sight."

"Oh, Herman," Cohen cried. "Don't be stupid."

"Me stupid?" Herman snorted. He jabbed a gum-booted toe at the deflated Construction Man. "You wanna be gay, well, that's your business, but you start acting plumb crazy and the cops'll take you to the loony bin. Get inside your house. Now!" Herman stomped his feet. "Get inside, Reuben! I hear sirens—the loony bin's coming."

Cohen didn't hear any sirens. He began smacking his tender head against the front door, barking, "Shelly, Shelly, Shelly."

The door swayed open ever so slightly. Cohen fell inside and stumbled up the stairs to the bedroom. Hearing howls like he had never heard before, he pricked up his ears. Seeing images like he had never seen before, he bared his teeth.

FISHY CONTINENTS

Little carved boats were floating in a moat that encircled what used to be Shelly and Reuben's bed. Filled with raw fish, they went around and around and around. The bed was now a sushi bar and an evil sushi chef was busy dipping Shelly's toes into a dish of wasabi.

"You Japanese men certainly do amuse with your cuisine-type erotica." Shelly sighed as she pointed her toes towards the chef's face.

"Shut up," ordered the sushi chef who then proceeded to suck each seasoned toe as if it was a delicate slice of tender tuna. Gazing into Shelly's eyes, he stroked her bright red gills and leaned over her sniffing. "You smell good and fresh," he said over the burble of a Zen water fountain. "My delight has just begun."

Cohen watched, horrorstruck, as the sushi chef eased a large cutting board underneath Shelly and started cutting her into small, neat slices with a very sharp knife. *Chop chop.* Holding morsels of chunky Shelly in his left hand and a ball of rice in his right, the evil sushi chef pressed the two together. Then he dropped the sushi into his mouth one by one and chased them with warm saki, swallowing in explosive ecstasy. Before Cohen's eyes, Shelly, helplessly submissive to each bite, disappeared into the chef's body.

Cohen barked, "What the fuck? What the fuck!" He lunged forward and banged into the closed bedroom door, smashing it with his head again and again until it finally opened under the repeated blows. "It's not just dolls anymore, it's a real guy this time. A real Japanese sushi chef. Why, Shelly, why?" he cried, falling into the room. "What have I done to deserve this?"

Shelly propped herself up on her elbows and stared at the Cohen-dog with his dangling rubber collar. "What sushi chef? Are you nuts? After all this time you're just a bunch of loose marbles, aren't you? What's the matter with you, Reuben? You know I play with dolls. Love dolls with no brains. No brains, just like you." Shelly squeezed Ting Titta's inflated head in front of her husband's bulging eyes before throwing the doll onto the floor. "I would never cheat on you. This is fantasy, not cheating! I'm not actually doing it with anyone. I'm just trading fantasies of flesh and latex, you fucking idiot."

She leaned over the bed to pick up a compressed rubber ball, a doll that had yet to be inflated, and hurled it at Cohen's head. "I am exploring Asia, such a beautiful continent. Let me explore—let me fantasize," she exclaimed, flinging her arms up in a dramatic pose like a would-be starlet. Then she focused and her arms drooped as she finally noticed the condition of her stray. "You're bleeding, Reuben! What happened to you? You're all swollen up. And what the fuck do you have tied around your neck?"

"These?" Cohen crouched down and patted the dirty and deflated men around his neck. "Just call me the guy who…who sailed the ocean of blue in the nineteen hundreds. Cus…Chris… Co…Colombo, that guy, you know, who went to this place and did that thing. Oh these damn words. I can't find my damn fucking words."

Shelly just stared at him with a look he didn't want to see. He turned his head and saw something beside him that looked vaguely like the defunct air tank at the Wet Your Whistle Sex Shop. He shoved a parasol aside and lunged for it.

"Hey, where do you think you're going with that!" Shelly yelled. He didn't answer, just dragged the tank down the hall to his chaotic office and slammed the door. It swung open again.

"Reuben! Get back here with that!"

After slamming his door a number of times, trying to close it, he screamed, "Leave me the fuck alone! I'm exploring, Shelly. I'm exploring America, all of America, north, south, east and west, and maybe a few more. I'm even going to New York City. That's right, downtown America." He slammed the door again, still screaming.

"Let me have something too. Excuse me while I introduce myself to one of my many new friends. His name is She-Male. Just exploring, Shelly. Exploring!"

News of Christopher Columbus' discoveries had spread throughout Europe and stirred the adventuresome spirit of mankind. News of Reuben Cohen's discoveries stayed idle and stirred the adventuresome spirit of only Reuben Cohen.

WAFER SLICED

Separated by little more than a hallway and a few sheets of drywall, both Cohen and Shelly remained motionless in their separate solitudes. Neither knew what to do. Never before had either considered taking fantasies into reality, but they had, and were now beginning to suffer the consequences.

After using the air tank with extreme difficulty, Cohen stood gasping in the middle of the room. All around him, strewn over furniture and piles of clothing and sprawled across the dusty floor, were semi- inflated and aroused American men.

All the materials in the office combined to produce an odor so awful it was as rank as the Coolers' dressing room after another late night hockey loss. Cohen's office had smelled bad before Shelly's redecorating but this was downright awful.

Shelly, on the other hand, was in a sweetly scented Asian paradise surrounded by rubber women lounging on the floor in various states of inflation. She lifted Ting Titta off the floor and exposed her microphone. She tried to speak and couldn't. She licked her lips and tried again, but with Reuben across the hall she couldn't give voice to her fantasies. *There must be another way to achieve sexual pleasure*, she told herself. Her fantasies, better in latex than in life, now had an unwanted intruder: reality. She felt too inhibited to indulge in heavy petting and emoting with Ting Titta and her other Asian playmates. Verbalizing when alone was permissible. To do it with her crazy husband within earshot was impossible.

Motivated primarily by fear, Cohen didn't have a clue how to sexually approach a barely inflated male love doll. He examined the confusing genitalia of the pouting She-Male doll as he unzipped himself, moaning in frustration. "This damn thing is impenetrable."

Rubbing himself against the doll, he tried to imagine that the exotic creature was real. Ignoring the protruding evidence of She-Male's maleness, he focused on the doll's feminine qualities. "Those boobs, that mouth," he crooned. In trying to woo this inflated hermaphrodite, Cohen suffered emotional trauma. Aware that arousal would cause him uncontrollable audible pleasure, he froze. His queer wife was in the adjoining room and would hear him.

Ever since Natalie had introduced her to the latex joys of Ting Titta, Shelly had been relying on the tangible and audible in her fantasy life. Could she change? Could she get images and words in her head by imagination alone? Could she reach climax with only imagination? With Reuben within hearing range and inhibitions cramping her style, she had to try. Closing her eyes she focused on fantasy. Nothing. She tried again. Then it came to her. Knocking Ting Titta to the floor, she sat up. It was time to use her last tangible resource: a pen. She rummaged around in her night table and came up with a silver pen with a stubby sausage shape. Was she so bad an erotic writer that she couldn't get herself off? No! Georgian College had made a big mistake in firing Midnight Mazzalma.

In truth, had life been different, what would have really gotten Shelly off would be making notes of a different sort, notes about her children: dentist appointments and soccer games, romances and best friends, favorite foods. And the secret fears, hopes and dreams of her kids would have filled the pages of her journal.

Deflating male love dolls just did not get Cohen excited; not even She-Male did it for him no matter how hard he tried or how badly he wanted to get even with his wife. Only mental images of real live women sufficed. He fell back onto his soft chair like a crash test dummy, hoping that his frail memory could come up with at least one of the women he had previously fantasized about. Placing his feet firmly on the floor, he shut his eyes to make his mind a *camera obscura*, a portable darkroom.

Nothing.

He could not recall his Polish Kishka Queen; his South African Yannaphrodite; Valerie, the Goddess of Hot Yoga; the tight-ass Mick Jagger fan; FATSO, the cricket-loving flight attendant — all were gone. His head injury had now shut them out.

Cohen had once considered taking actual photos of every face he wanted to remember so he could have tangible images, but the idea had seemed weirdly inappropriate and boring to him. Photographed faces were only frozen two-dimensional depictions. Also, he kept forgetting to carry his camera.

An image developed by the mind's eye had endless potential; unfortunately, for someone with Cohen's disability, remembering was the chore. His hands turned into fists, his jaw tightened. His blood pressure rose as fast as a boy from his seat at the end of a Sunday School class. His eyes flew open, his tension exploded in a scream.

Nothing.

Leaping to his feet, he grabbed the semi-inflated She-Male. Using the doll as a shield, he rushed at the window. The impact cracked the glass. He hit it again. The glass shattered. With this violent maneuver, Cohen cruelly murdered the innocent erotic toy. Knife-edged pieces of broken glass pierced the skin of the once vibrant dysfunctional doll and penetrated its main artery: the air-valve. Wrapping She-Male's lifeless skin around his fists, Cohen-the-murderer smashed the jagged edges of glass until there was space enough for him to squeeze his obese body through.

He plummeted to the ground. Dazed and bloodied, he struggled to his feet and, in a frenzy, staggered down the street towards the Fresh Deli.

The silver sausage pen allowed Shelly to explore the once hidden layers of her own mind. Her most satisfying sexual fantasies were now going into a journal. So absorbed was she in her pleasurable pursuit that the sound of shattering glass went unnoticed. As her writing progressed, she began to express her most secret feelings. Before long she started to hear a voice: her voice. Her OWN voice. This new voice was not like the monotone announcements at the airport; it was the voice of a real person and it brought her words to life. She felt powerful, like Erica Jong.

For the first time ever, Shelly was hearing her own voice in her own writing, and it was rich and beautiful. Confident that others would never read her journal, she spoke the truth. Her truth.

> Oh, Asia, beautiful Asia. You brought me Ting Titta, who talks to me in my own words. She's a poet with a tinny voice. Ting Titta and the others have brought me out of myself, freed my inhibitions, looked at me without demands, without expectations.
>
> Oh, Ting Titta, blast me with love. Love me in my sadness. How your mechanical voice has extended my sexual limits, my creative limits. How did I remain closeted all this time, how did I deny myself such pleasure?
>
> First there was Ting Titta with her words, which were my words, and now this! Oh, you graceful swirls of ink on paper, you silent yet eloquent voicings of my thoughts – how I yearn for you. How I long to immerse myself in you.

 Quiet, almost silent, sex had now transpired for Shelly; she was letting loose without the fear of being heard, without the need for dolls. This art of writing was wilder and potentially far more erotic and cognitively demanding than any inflatable lover. Pen and paper were now her keys to paradise. She was becoming aroused between the sheets of her personal journal.

She cleared her bed, shoving everything aside but her pen, paper and true feelings, propped herself up with pillows, wrapped herself up in a blanket, and started to write. She was writing her way to the discovery of a new self, a better self. Writing was her lost partner and she loved her, loved her with blue ink.

"Gone? How can she be gone? Don't tell me she went back to Poland," a distressed Cohen told the cashier at the Fresh Deli. "I need her, I've got to put her back in my head, I've got to see her."

The cashier, a heavyset middle-aged woman, leaned over the counter. "You're the roast beef and cheese on poppy seed bagel. You I remember. Here every day, but not for long while, yes? Does Katarzyna know you?" The woman shook her head decisively. "No, she does not. I am Agnieszka, her mother. She tell me everything but nothing about strange bloody man in her life!"

Cohen wiped his hand across his face. It came away streaked with blood. "She does know me, I took her many places."

"Hey, Agnes, who is this crazy guy?" a customer yelled from a side table. Another joined in: "Call the police."

Agnieszka leaned forward to eye Cohen closely. "Katarzyna never mention you. Never. She has man in Poland. His name is Alfons. He will beat you." Agnieszka shook her head. "You look like already you have been beaten. You are a mess."

Cohen looked down at his bloody shirt and the scratches on his hands and arms. He was confused.

"We can't even enjoy our meal," barked a regular. "You gonna get him out of here or are we gonna have to leave?" Another regular, Adalbert, shouted for Agnieszka's husband: "Ignancy—we need you. Get out here! Quick!"

Ignancy appeared with the force of an angry cowboy entering a saloon. He was a thin man and about seven feet tall, with long black hair and sad eyes that didn't soften his hard image in the slightest. Even with chocolate stains and Hawaiian sprinkles all over his otherwise white apron, he looked menacing.

Adalbert was saying, "If the bloody man doesn't get out of here, I go somewhere else, even somewhere not owned by Polish family."

"Yeah, yeah," the other regulars chorused.

"Out! Out of my deli," shouted Ignancy. He strode to the front counter, waving a stainless steel spatula like a sword. "You bother my Agnieszka and my friends, and you really bother my good friend Adalbert. You must respect older Polish man. He fought in World War Two," Ignancy growled, pointing the spatula at Cohen. "You're the roast beef and cheese on poppy seed bagel man. We laugh at you." Ignancy snickered. "You bother me, you bother my customers. And you are not clean, all blood and dirty. You must leave my deli."

"Beat him, Ignancy. Beat him good," Agnieszka urged. "He say he dated Katarzyna."

"No more roast beef and cheese for you," Ignancy said firmly, looking down his long nose at Cohen. "Strange man like you causes trouble. Better go and not return." Ignancy tossed back his long black hair and grabbed Cohen, dragging him out the door while Agnieszka yelled again, "Beat him! Beat him!"

"Don't you at least have any personal belongings of Katz…ass? So I could try to pit…pic…imagine her?" Cohen desperately stuttered as he was dragged outside. Everything seemed to be moving in slow motion and, as Ignancy tossed him onto the sidewalk, it occurred to Cohen that it was quite odd Ignancy wasn't wearing a hairnet. It seemed to him that restaurant regulations would require Ignancy to wear a hairnet like he himself had worn at Murphy's Seafood Shack. Or maybe Ignancy was breaking Canadian restaurant sanitation regulations and, if so, this would have to be reported.

Behind them, Adalbert and his friends, recognizing Ignancy's heroics, stood up and sang the Polish national anthem. Through the cacophony of Polish lyrics, only Cohen could hear himself crying as he fell to the ground. The memory of his Polish Kishka Queen replaced thoughts of hairnets. "I need her image, that's all," he blubbered, dabbing his freshly-scoured elbows with his stained shirt.

Shelly's streams of fantasy came to an abrupt halt. She could not write anymore. She was out of ink. "Get out of my fucking way," she yelled at the love dolls as she scurried around her room, desperately searching for any kind of writing utensil.

Before long, every parasol and doll had been kicked aside, every cupboard door flung open, and every dresser drawer ripped from its casing and flung against the wall. Picture frames and lamps shattered, spraying shards of glass. In full spate, she lost her balance and slammed face down onto the wooden floor. She cried in frustration. She cried out in physical pain.

In a state of panic (which was now his usual condition), Cohen chose to enter his house the same way he had left: through the window of his office. When exiting, he had fallen. Now he had to climb. He looked around wildly before spying a ladder leaning against the side of Herman's house. He dragged it into his own yard, propped it up against the ledge below the broken window, and started to climb. By the time he reached the twelfth rung, he knew he was in trouble. The angle was too steep, nearly vertical, and the ground at the foot of the ladder was soft.

The ladder started to slide sideways. To save his life, Cohen had to make a move far beyond his confidence. As the ladder toppled, he grabbed the window ledge in a move any contortionist would be proud of. From her front yard, Hilda Greenberg cheered, but Cohen still had one more move to make. A grunting upward thrust with both arms allowed his fat stomach to rest on the windowsill. With feet scrabbling at the siding, Cohen took a deep breath and pushed off, diving headfirst into his office.

But he'd forgotten the broken window glass. As it scraped his beefy borders, Cohen cried in pain. His audience cried out in despair.

FIGHT NIGHT

In one corner of Cohen's office, bent over and in severe pain, was Shelly "The Asian Blower" Cohen, weighing in at one hundred and fifty-two pounds with a record of zero and one, hailing from Belleville, Ontario. Bruised like a beaten banana, staggering already and wearing absolutely nothing, she seemed concerned about only one thing: the horrendous appearance of her opponent.

In the other corner of Cohen's office, also bent over and in severe pain, was Reuben "The Polish Pretender" Cohen, weighing in at two hundred and twenty pounds with a record of zero and four, hailing from Toronto, Ontario. Bleeding like a stuck pig, wearing ripped clothing and entering the ring tonight through a smashed window, he too seemed to be concerned about only one thing: the horrendous appearance of his opponent.

"Well, Howard, I'll tell ya. Both winless fighters look terrible. In her last bout only moments ago, Shelly the Asian Blower went down hard onto a hardwood floor while looking for a writing utensil. Can you believe that? A complete loss of muscle control had her unconscious for quite a while but, funny enough, the bell saved her. Loud noises made during the ring appearance of her stressed opponent awoke her just in time."

"George, I have never seen a fighter in poorer condition than Reuben the Polish Pretender. He looks like he is on his way to the slaughterhouse for the second time. In his last fight he went down and hit his head on the canvas, but that canvas was made out of cement. Can you believe it? He has suffered serious injury before and tonight just may be another horrible whipping.

"Here we go, fight fans, these boxers are ready to fight with words. Listen for those one-liners."

Round 1:

The fighters are in the center of the office. They clinch, both looking for openings. The Asian Blower is the first to come out swinging with a line of impact, landing a wild left: "I feel that you go too fast and never want to have foreplay with sex."

"A great shot using the 'you' statement has made the Polish Pretender feel like all the blame is on him. I think he's hurt."

Cohen misses with a wild right: "I feel we might enjoy taking our time and using more foreplay. I've got so much to learn and I'd love your help. Will you assist me?"

"Dumb...dumb, Howard. Using the 'I' focuses on the way he feels. 'I' language incorporates an open-ended question. An opening, Howard! Shelly's taking too much time to think here when she could have nailed him with a yes or no answer."

"You're right, George, and now they're simply clinching with questions. Let's listen."

"What the hell happened to you, Reuben? You're all cut up!" the Asian Blower asks while attempting a quick straight noun shot to the Polish Pretender's flabby solar plexus. Absorbing the blow, the Polish Pretender answers with a weak jab and another clinch: "She's gone, gone back to her homeland! I need her image. What do I think about now? I need someone to remember, a picture to remember, someone real to fantasize about."

"Who are you talking about? Who is gone?" asks the Asian Blower, raising her arms to protect her face from emotional damage.

The Pretender cautiously jabs with quick shots: "Just a girl, a foreign girl I fantasize about, but it's just fantasy. I'm using my creative imagination like you told me to!"

"Can you believe that, Howard? In a fight with words the Pretender states his feelings honestly. What a mistake! He tells his opponent personal information and now the Blower looks hurt but I'm telling you, Howard, she's not emotionally devastated. She's such a curious and tough sport."

More words from the Pretender back the Blower into the corner when he comes in with a three-punch combination of questions: "What the hell happened to you, Shelly? Your face? Your whole damn body?" groans the Pretender as he throws another wild right hook and misses.

"George, these two are trading 'em with thirty-five seconds left."

The Polish Pretender jabs again: "You have more black spots on you than a damn Dalmas...Dalmatian!"

The Asian Blower, avoiding a left hook by crouching down, replies with an uppercut: "There is nothing left. No ink! No ink! Don't you ever write in bed or do you just eat hard mini donuts? A simple pen, that's all I needed to express my fantasies. Ever since The Pot Mishap you just don't do it for me anymore, Reuben. I get my real pleasure through my OWN voice. I need ink!"

"Did you hear that, Howard? The Blower answers with honesty too. Oh, my! She needs to learn to hurt the opponent. She needs to edit her thoughts before she speaks."

The bell sounds to end the first round.

Shelly's Corner: "C'mon, stop your gabbin'. Tell him what you really need," instructs the Asian Blower's corner man while squeezing water over her face. "Work on that cut-up ego with your words. Your words! Put an exclamation mark through his body!

"He's a fat-ass who's got a lot to learn about fantasy, so teach him. Isn't it time to share? Nothing is sexier than talking about pleasure to the man you once loved. Nothing! Share with him what turns your crank. The right words at the right time will start your fire. Use an inflection, strengthen your words. Burn him! Watch that hook!"

Reuben's Corner: "If she has to write about it you're just not doin' it right. Let her ask for what she wants, an' tell her what you like as well. Role-play, man, role-PLAY! Move your feet and stick to the body. Imagine that you're so full of passion you're climbing the ropes! Listen to her stories, man!" shouts the Polish Pretender's cut man. "Remember, she's a bleeder. Watch that aphasia; say your individual let-ter sounds, don't blend the sounds together. You'll remember the words better that way."

Round 2:

Even before the bell sounds to begin the second round, the Blower and the Pretender are clinched nose to nose in the center of the office. Instead of following orders from their respective corners, both boxers come out swinging pickup lines. The feeling-out process has ended and each starts trying to subdue the other into submission.

The crowd begins to boo. Those who paid big bucks for ringside seats are not getting their money's worth because this form of clinch-ing is boring to watch, but the true fighting fans are staying put. "You never know what could happen with these two," says an old-timer.

Sure enough, with their facades of dignity intact, the verbal bat-tery starts. The Asian Blower throws the first line to begin the round. "Those boxing boots are very becummmmming on you…and if I was on you I would be cumming too."

The crowd roars.

"Great use of a pun, Howard. Great use!"

"The Polish Pretender smiled, but he's clearly shaken, George, and has a cut over his right eye."

"You gotta come back with one!" his corner shouts.

"Ahhh," mutters the Polish Pretender. He eventually throws out a senile shot: "Did you just smile or did the sun come out?" His corner hides their collective face in shame.

"Blood is flowing down the Pretender's face, George. He's bleed-ing badly. He missed with that wild right."

"That's not a pun, you idiot!" shouts the Pretender's cut man. "I'm not sure what it is, but it's not a pun!"

The crowd hisses in disappointment and the Asian Blower hits him square on the jaw with a jab joke. "Are you tired? Because you've been running through my mind all day," puts the Pretender into a dizzy spell. He is on the ropes and swinging wildly, trying to punch back with a weak: "Do you believe in erections at first sight or do I have to walk…walk by you again?"

Even the Asian Blower laughs at that inept attempt, while the Pretender just becomes more disoriented by her fighting ability.

Shelly's corner: "Alright, Blower, one more big one and he's out. What I want you to do in this round is initiate sex without throwing a word. Forget about giving him unfamiliar words to think about; make him use his eyes to create a picture, respond with smiles and laughs."

Pulling a large plastic Wet Your Whistle Sex Shop bag out from under a pile of towels behind Shelly's corner, her cut man gives her instructions. "Put on this G-string and these stockings and garter belt, and you won't have to do a thing. It's time to let your man know how much you fancy him. He'll be out before he can say his own name."

Shelly slips the sexy garments over her naked body before the bell for the third, and final, round is heard.

Reuben's Corner: "We're in big trouble."

The ring doctor looks at the cut above Cohen's eye.

Round 3:

The referee signals for the fight to continue. One quick blurred glance at the Blower's ass cheeks, separated only by a G-string, and, without a word, the Pretender tumbles to the canvas, his head crashing down with a heavy thud. Blood flows freely from his face in the closing seconds of the round. He is either very horny or out cold. The referee counts down: One–two–three…four… five…six…seven-eight-nine-ten-OUT!

Rubbing oil into the palms of her hands to warm it up and lighting candles while the Polish Pretender's favorite tune (the theme song from *Lassie*) plays over the speakers, the victorious Asian Blower starts to give her knocked-out opponent a back rub with pronouns.

All the ring lights were out. The crowd had disappeared. Shelly had disappeared. Cohen was alone—in his office, in ripped clothing and covered in blood. He called Shelly's name. Nothing. She was gone from the arena.

Excerpt from Progressive Doctor Report
Compiled by Dr. C. F. Stephan

Reuben's attention skills have improved immensely. Initially he was unable to process a continuous series of information accurately if it required even a slightly complex evaluation. Now he is able to do the same task with moderate success and is progressing to more challenging attention tasks.

Excerpt from diary entry — Shelly Cohen

I can't seem to park things, you know? I need to do it with my stress. I need to not have to keep paying attention to all this shit. I can't stand it. I need to be able to put it aside like you park a car and only drive it when you need to. I keep trying to park my problems and deal with them when they need to be dealt with. It's not working.

I don't feel healthy. How about me getting some attention? Don't I deserve it?

PART EIGHT

October to November

MALFUNCTION

On the table, folded into a tight paper square, sat a clipping torn from a week-old newspaper. Cohen unfolded it and smoothed it out. A grainy photo of a blond woman smiled at him from the page. Below it were blurred words that had once been just a meaningless jumble but had now clarified into a heartrending obituary.

> **COHEN, Shelly Sooter**
>
> Suddenly, after a parachute malfunction at the Parachute School of Authorville, Ontario. Once beloved wife of head-injured Reuben Cohen, godmother to the late Scratch and vicious Kyle-Bob, and friend to Pickle and Natalie Berofsky. Friends may call at the Deep Breath Chapel, 2585 Bloor Street West, on October 15. Cremation to follow.
>
> For those who wish, donations to the Parachute School of Authorville Safety Division would be appreciated. Roast beef and cheese bagel sandwiches will be served at the newly managed Fresh Deli (their new slogan is: "These New Owners Wear Nets") at 2885 Bloor Street West, following cremation, if you feel like it.

Two wilting sympathy bouquets that had been sent by courier now rested on the counter beside the day-old donut rack. One card read "With respect from Dr. Stephan" and the other, "With respect from Dr. Snaidearman." Ironically, they had the same message:

> So sorry for your loss. I am available for a scheduled appointment when you are ready to see me. Please be advised that after your insurance company has agreed on a settlement, YOU will be responsible for prompt payment of all medical bills incurred on your behalf. Perhaps a financial advisor should be appointed to keep your medical expenses in order. Best regards and good luck. See you when your grieving is complete.

Among the few mourners at the Fresh Deli were Cassandra Baker, Yanna Harrington, a disheveled Pickle, and Kyle-Bob who was locked in a travel cage. Natalie, who was not there, was going through a horrible period of mourning. The capricious Scratch 'N Win worm had turned and they lost everything, even the BMW. After selling their furniture and condominium, they had just enough left to purchase a handful of Scratch 'N Win tickets and a used mobile home in a trailer park in South Florida. Natalie had headed off early to catch a few rays and meet some of the clan.

"Shelly would have understood," she had told Cohen before scooting away in Pickle's used car. "And I don't want any of her crap. It would just bring back too many sad memories, and none of her clothes would fit me now anyways. I'm down to a size two and, at the rate she was going, Shelly wouldn't have been able to get anywhere near even a size sixteen."

Luckily for Pickle, the Greyhound bus to Florida didn't leave until that evening. "It's a long trip," he told Cohen. "Kyle–Bob should be okay, he seems happier when Natalie's not around. He knows I'll kick him if he gets yapping, but I hope I don't die like that Ratso Rizzo guy did in *Midnight Cowboy*." Pickle laughed. "Did you ever see that movie? Ratso was kinda like you, but a little slow. It's a good movie, drugs and sex and stuff. Maybe you'll rent it when you feel better." He awkwardly patted Cohen's shoulder. "But I do feel bad, buddy. And I know Natalie does too." Kyle–Bob growled at Cohen from behind the bars of his travel cage.

"It was a nice service and all," said Pickle. The bagel sandwiches had disappeared and Pickle had nothing left to do but say goodbye. "If you're ever in Fla...Fluh...Florida, look us up under the name Broomfield. We had to change our last name 'cause the tax man may come looking. Not that we have anything now." Pickle paused, searching for something more to say, and then absently scratched his crotch. "I hope things work out for ya," were the only words he could find. He clapped Cohen on the back, hefted Kyle-Bob's travel cage, and walked away until he was just a dull blur in Cohen's eyes.

Next to offer her condolences was Cassandra. "I never met your wife, Reuben. She was always at work when I arrived, but I'm sure she was a great lady if she made you happy." In truth, Cassandra was scared for Cohen's well-being; she knew how important having a wife had been for him. Not only did he need her company, but he needed someone to look after him and help with his many cognitive challenges and affairs. "I feel terrible, Reuben. Anything I can do to help, just let me know."

Fatigued and frustrated from only fantasizing about this black beauty for such a long time, Cohen decided to take advantage of his emotional state. *Females are good at sympathy and feeling sorry for ya and stuff.* Mopping improvised tears (thanks to a glass of water left on a nearby table) with his sleeve, Cohen opened up his can of sexual desire and spilled the beans. "Well, as a matter of fact, Cassandra—" Cohen took a deep breath and prayed to Aphrodite for luck.

The sympathetic therapist was enthused about offering help. "Yes, Reuben? Yes?"

"Cassandra, if you really care about me, you would remove your blouse, take off your triple-D bra and make your lusciously dark watermelon tits, each with a cherry on top, do an authentic Zulu dance in front of my face."

She stared at him, shocked, and began to cry, but maintained enough energy to calmly say, "I treated you like a real person, Reuben, as I do all my clients who need help. Therapy for injured individuals is my life's work. I listened to you, I encouraged you, I had hope for you, and now you turn into some kind of perverted beast? You are not who

I thought you were, Reuben Cohen. Not in the sleet…sleet…slightest."

Then, instead of physical punishment, such as a swift kick to his balls, the angry physiotherapist simply turned her back and icily walked away until she became a dull blur in Cohen's eyes.

The subject of his next "bean spill" sat in a corner, sipping coffee. As he neared, her pale image became clearer until he could make out a few recognizable characteristics. Blinking under freshly improvised tears (thanks to the water fountain outside the men's washroom), he concluded that the red hair and wide horse mouth could only belong to his speech therapist, Yanna Harrington.

Seeing his flooded eyes, she told him, "Tears are an ex…excell… very good way to express pain. Cry, Reuben, cry! It's so healthy for you at this time." Articulating her words carefully, the speech therapist continued, "I understand that you are going through a myriad of emotions in your grieving experience."

Cohen nodded as if he understood. He didn't.

"You have the right to feel sad."

Cohen nodded again, enthusiastically. "Oh yes, Yanna. I am sad. I've been crying all day and…and then…then some more of the days before today. That means I've been crying for quite a long time, not just now."

Yanna looked discouraged. "You are in a state of mourning, Reuben, but you must use your articulation and sentence structure techniques to find words the way I've been teaching you. Please. Also, it will make me look good when others hear you and find out who I am, and then I'll get more clients and make more money. Maybe I'll make enough to go on a new African wildlife adventure."

"What if nobody asks why I speak so good?"

"Tell them who I am anyway. I love positive acknowledgement." Yanna took a handful of business cards from her purse and gave them to Cohen. "Give these cards out to anyone who doesn't speak well."

DOMINATE YOUR WORDS WITH ME
YANNA HARRINGTON — SPEECH PATHOLOGIST
"SOUNDING GOOD NEVER FELT SO GOOD"
CALL ME AT 5-SPEECH TODAY!

He ignored her, his attention drawn elsewhere, and her cards fell to the floor as he lunged at something that excited him: a gold basket sitting on an empty chair. "You've got a nifty little gifty for me? A surprise? For me, poor Reuben Cohen? The new widower?"

Yanna, on her knees picking up her scattered business cards, answered testily, "Well, Reuben, now it's not a surprise since you've already seen it, so, yes, please accept my gift."

She stood up, shoving the cards back in her purse, and then picked up the gift basket. Holding it in the manner of a bikini-wearing car model (knees slightly bent towards the resting basket, ass tucked inward, arms pointing toward the gift with a long, tantalizing gesture of her long red fingernails) she smiled and described his prize. "It's a basket filled with scrumptious cookies. Chocolate-dipped vanilla, double fudge squares and classic chocolate chip. I thought this would cheer you up. I know how you love your treats."

He had already begun to drool.

"My husband can't eat them, he's a di...dia...abetic," said Yanna.

"You're married?" He stared at her in surprise. "You never told me that!"

"Why, of course not, Reuben. It's a matter of principle. You and I have a patient-therapist relationship, that's all. I don't share intimate personal details with you and I don't wear a wedding ring, it irritates my skin."

He frowned. "But I want to share with you, just some of you. Let me have some of what your husband has when he gets home. Out of all your qualities it's only your exotic accent and horse-shaped mouth that really turn me on. I'll share those with your husband anytime."

"And I want to share a couple of my qualities with you too, Reuben," Yanna said patiently. "I want to share my knowledge of language and my love of helping the unfortunate, and that's all. You get to share these two qualities with me once a week. Isn't that enough?"

There was no better time than the present. *Females*, he thought to himself, *are good with sympathy when feeling sorry for ya and stuff.*

Taking a deep breath, Cohen prayed to Cupid for luck and said, "Well, as a matter of fact, Yanna, I want to listen to you moan. Since I met you, I've dreamed of hearing you moan with sexual articulation while you place your nipples in my mouth and rub against me. I want to lift your naked ass off that ventriloquist stool and tie your arms to your shower rod. Then I want you to give me oral sex with that huge horse mouth of yours, that huge South African horse mouth. I want my genitals to be your snake and eggs, your fucking oral stimulation. I want to be the main course of your erotic feast and when you're finished you'll talk dirty to me in that sexy South African accent of yours."

Staring at him in shock, Yanna started to cry, yet still maintained enough strength to articulate her words in a calm, professional tone. "Perhaps the wisest advice I can offer you is to baste yourself with suntan oil and then go and burn in hell. I didn't fail you, Reuben Cohen, you failed yourself. I was there to help you. I was real with you. You were never real with me. You deserve to be wiped off the face of the earth! Goodbye, Mr. Cohen." Her calm, professional speech finished, Yanna slapped Cohen's cheek with angry force.

He stumbled backwards, hands to his face. Yanna set a handful of cards on the table. "Don't forget to give out my business cards," she told him. She started walking away, then turned and came back towards him with outstretched hand. He shrank backwards, petrified that she was going to hit him again, but she just scooped up her cookie basket and walked away until she became a blur in Cohen's eyes.

PARATROOPER

Cohen kept the obituary with him as a keepsake. He thought this act of
sentimentality would glorify him as a widower. Although unable to
remember much about Shelly except for her once marvelous body and
thick bush of blond hair, he yearned for the stupendous nights of raw
sex they'd had in the good old days. As he shifted in his chair, staring
at the printed page the black pigment of the newsprint wavered and
became blotches of dark clouds.

> *In the late hours of June 16, 1944, a tiny plane flew
> over the sandy terrain of Normandy. Far below, the
> weather was cold and blustery and the air was filled with
> the roar of heavy gunfire. Shelly Cohen, an unproven
> talent from the First Canadian Parachute Battalion, was
> called upon to clear the way for the land troops that
> would soon arrive.*
>
> *Her orders were to secure the drop zone by destroying
> the bridges at Varaville where the River Dive meets its
> tributaries. In full battle gear, with knife, toggle rope,
> anal stimulator, large vibrator and tubes of extra
> lubrication, Shelly received further instructions.*
>
> *Battle sounds impeded the clarity of the instructions
> from her superior officer, Captain Jean van Vegas. "Give
> a good blowing to the Germans and make sure to take out
> their heads," was what she thought she heard him say.*
>
> *The brave female paratrooper dropped into the war
> zone where she was beset by heavy enemy ejaculations.*

She fought to the best of her ability but was soon captured. Her role as sex slave did not allow her to see daylight again.

Shelly Cohen did, however, meet her ordered objectives. While she was giving oral pleasure to enemy troops, the rest of her country's allies were able to sneak in through German lines. Eventually the enemy had to use the withdrawal method. The skies began to clear.

Excerpt from journal entry — Reuben Cohen

> When I was twelve (it was even before my Bar
> Mitzvah), my grandmother caught me jerking off in the
> family hammock. She said I needed electric shock therapy
> and a penis enlargement.
>
> "Oy Vey! Such a little penis. It's like a small and
> squeezed piece of kishka! Where's the gravy?" she said.
> Then she added, "Young minds should not think like
> yours. You'll burn in hell for this. You're twisted like
> Satan. Satan has turned you towards lust."
>
> I've always found women hard to deal with. Still do.
> Every time I look at one I see myself fucking her. Fucking
> her any way, any how, any time. Fuck! Fuck! Fuck!
>
> I blame my mother. She would strip for me to the
> sound of Nat King Cole. Yeah, she was lonely. My father
> was always out delivering mourning hats to Shiva
> houses and French-kissing with all the lonely widows.
>
> I didn't argue when my hot mom stripped for me. She
> was so happy pretending she was someone else and I
> would pretend she was a movie star or someone not real.
> I lied to my friends about what a great body she had.
> They said, "What a lucky baby you must have been to
> suck milk from real boobs. All of our moms had
> implants." They followed me home every day, wanting to
> see real mom tits, but she never stripped for them. I was
> her only customer, nonpaying of course.

I don't think Dr. Snaidearman knows half the trouble I'm in. I
am deeply, madly and absolutely insane about women. All types, sizes,
shapes and colors. The damn Pot Mishap really messed me up and
now all the pills and shit makes me crazy.

These doctors just don't understand about head injuries. They
say something that's ig...ig...stupid because they don't understand,

and if I try to tell them, they don't get it. They make me crazy. So many things just don't show up on medical tests, like the way I'm feeling sexually and my real desires and fantasies.

Head injuries are poorly understood. Especially mine. I can't always go by what a doctor might tell me but I don't argue because I don't want them to think that I am not cop...copperay...doing stuff right. These fucking words.

I have been through so many ups and downs battling this fucking injury. The Reuben Cohen who existed before this injury has changed. On the outside, I've only got a limp and a few scars but inside I'm not the same person I once knew and was proud of. Not at all. My hurt can't be seen.

These doctors are stuh...strah...people I don't know in white coats who have entered my life. I didn't invite them in and now they are sending me confusing messages.

Will I be okay or won't I? "Everything will be alright, Reuben," they tell me again and again. Alright my ass! I'm sick, sicker than ever. I'm going out of my mind!

SETTLE FOR THE BUFFET

The morning of the mediation, it took only minutes for Cohen to become a tear-drenched lump. The image projected at the start of his lawyer's PowerPoint presentation displayed a handsome Reuben wearing a black tailor-made suit with a black satin tie, and accepting a Professional Chef Diploma that looked like a warranty for a kitchen appliance (it was just one of many presented to the class of excited new chefs on graduation from the Culinary Arts Program). Underneath his proud smile, the bright words "The Old Reuben Cohen" stretched across the screen. Other images followed.

The first series of pictures showed Reuben and Shelly kissing and hugging. The next showed them dressed up for Halloween, Reuben as the racehorse with jockey Shelly whipping and riding him. It was a beautiful memory that could not be easily forgotten, even by Cohen. Tears welled up in his eyes.

"Oh, those halcyon days before the accident," said his well-rehearsed lawyer to the defense team.

Cohen couldn't take seeing any more, he had lost so much. "That damn pot," he yelped. "That damn pot!"

"Perhaps you should take Mr. Cohen out of here," his lawyer told the junior associate assisting him. "There will be more things that I don't think he should see."

Like an injured athlete, Cohen limped out of the mediation room, leaning on the strong shoulder of his lawyer's assistant, his face wet with tears. His lawyer smiled. Insurance adjusters and their lawyers didn't dare show a glimpse of emotion.

The assistant led him to a soft-cushioned sofa in the empty meeting room next door. Cohen stretched out, glanced at the Business section of the *Globe and Mail* newspaper and quickly became agitated. All the stock listings, prices and acronyms confused him. Business was none of Reuben Cohen's business. He dropped the newspaper and manufactured a series of hair-raising coughs that he hoped would act as a friendly reminder to the loud legal parties to keep the noise down. *Remember me, The Pot Mishap victim?* he thought at them. *I need to sleep.*

A few hours later, the assistant tapped him on the shoulder. "Wake up, Reuben. It's time for a bite to eat." Lunchtime had been reached, but a settlement had not. Further presentations, arguments and deliberations would continue after lunch.

Another conference room had been set up with a buffet. Cohen stumbled in and cautiously filled a plate, and he watched, amazed at the sight of Mr. Rose, the insurance lawyer representing Murphy's Seafood Shack, squeezing soft cheddar cheese into the mouse holes of Swiss cheese. His fingers looked like half-smoked cigars. Mr. Rose (the fattest and hairiest insurance adjuster at the mediation) didn't even bother with a plate. While one hand shoved meat and cheese into his mouth, the other hand busily collected more. Everyone else was at the far end of the buffet table, eating decorously. Keeping a safe distance from Mr. Rose protected their designer suits from the food particles blasting out of his mouth. External appearances were so important.

Internal appearances were another thing. *All lawyers are greedy*, thought Cohen, *especially the rich ones*. Most of them tried to hide it. The successful ones concealed their greed behind carefully call... calti ...cultiv...learned social skills and the ability to bend the truth and play word games. Cohen knew this because Pickle had told him. "Watch out for those guys," Pickle had yelled over the noise of his rust bucket. "Your own lawyer's okay because the more you get, the more he gets, but the other guys only pretend to give a shit."

Pickle was right, Cohen decided, except about Mr. Rose, who clearly didn't care who witnessed his greed.

"At the last mediation I attended," Mr. Rose said to the room in general through a spray of cracker crumbs, "they didn't even supply food. Hell, they only had these skimpy little crackers and some kind of lame dip. That's not real food, and I can't bargain on an empty stomach. A he-man of a lawyer needs a he-man of a meal." Mr. Rose licked his fingers and chuckled. "Even if this is just lousy cold cuts with assortments, it's still a feast. I think my clients are in luck today."

Cohen's lawyer smiled. "Dig in, you wouldn't want it to go to waste," he told Mr. Rose. "And don't forget the dessert."

Burping softly, Mr. Rose headed for an array of beige-crusted pecan butter tarts, their shells filled with brown goo and dusted with powdered sugar and mint leaves. He sighed, licked his fingers again, and announced, "When it comes to sweets, mediations produce the most incredible specimens." He snatched a tart from the table and chomped into its sweet center, pulverizing the nuts with caveman molars. Grunting in pleasure, he stared straight into the cold eyes of the only female lawyer present as he dipped his fat tongue into the center of the tart, then shoved it into his mouth and licked his lips. "Ah, if my ex-wife could only see me now. I'm as happy as Saint Nick on Boxing Day!" He gave a hearty chuckle and then, in one swift maneuver, like a plague of hungry birds attacking fruit from a plum tree, his fingers picked the dessert table clean of pecan butter tarts. "Let's get to work, shall we? Let's go settle this thing."

Cohen snagged a fudge brownie and added it to his laden plate, after which he returned to his sofa where he stuffed himself and then immediately dozed off. He slept throughout the afternoon.

After lengthy arguing, negotiating, dealing, compromising and bluffing, the parties involved in this intense poker match finally agreed on a settlement, right after the insurance representatives for Murphy's Seafood Shack realized that the opposition was holding a much stronger hand. They swallowed their pride, threw down their cards, and accepted ninety percent responsibility for negligence in The Pot Mishap.

FISCAL RESPONSIBILITY

The head office of Baxter Financial Consultants was located in an immense building that resembled a giant monochromatic Rubiks Cube,
just like all the other buildings around it. *From a hot air balloon,* thought
Cohen, *Toronto must look like an array of gray and black puzzle pieces.* He
had left home three hours early to make it in time for his appointment
to discuss the options surrounding his financial settlement. Now he
looked at his watch and smiled: he was right on time. He squinted at
the office directory in the lobby until his eyes came to rest on:

BAXTER FINANCIAL CONSULTANTS   SUITE 502

In the reception area of Suite 502, a man was stretched out on
the larger of two sofas. He looked dead, but there was no real bad
smell so Cohen supposed he wasn't. Nobody else was around, so he
figured the man must be Mr. Bobby Baxter. Deciding that Mr. Baxter
might want to ruffle and preen his financial feathers after he woke
up, Cohen perched on a chair and reviewed his own financial savvy
and portfolio. This didn't take very long; he had neither. Any kind of
financial lingo confused him, and acronyms like RSPs and GICs and
the NASDAQ meant only one thing to him: BS for BullSHIT.

Cohen moved to the vacant sofa and watched the man for a few
minutes, but he got bored. A pen and a pad of paper rested on the
magazine table. He grabbed them and decided to make a wish list of
the things he desperately wanted to buy when he got his settlement.

When I'm Rich

- A pair of designer look-gooder glasses
- A return airfare to Poland
- An Indianapolis Colts football jersey for Herman next door
- A Green Bay Packer football jersey for Hilda my other next door neighbor
  Hilda is not beside Herman, Hilda is beside me. So I'm in the middle of both of them
- A bunch of flowers to Cassandra to apologize
- Another bunch of flowers to Yara to apologize
- A car for Pickle, If I can find him.
- A few extra sexy female escorts delivered daily. He He He
- Fresh poppy seed bagles. I'll get the beef muscle!

He was tapping his pen against his teeth, trying hard to think of other expensive stuff, when he noticed the man was staring at him. "You must be staring at me for some reason. You are Mr. Bobby Baxter, are you not?" Cohen politely asked the awakened corpse.

"Well, I ain't Bill Gates. If I was, do you think I'd be sleeping here waiting for you?" Mr. Baxter sat up, scrubbing a hand through his thin hair. "Mind if I have a smoke?" he asked perfunctorily. Taking a hand-rolled cigarette from behind his left ear, he fired up his lighter.

"Go right ahead," Cohen said, belatedly granting permission as Mr. Baxter inhaled. Cohen shoved his wish list in his pocket, then drummed on his pad of paper while the air quickly filled with smoke. He frowned. "Kinda small in here, isn't it, Mr. Baxter? I was expecting something a little fancier, being in the financial district, downtown and all. My dead wife worked for the Royal Bank. It was a much nicer building."

Mr. Baxter pulled a face. "You think it's small now? Just wait until my daughters get back, we'll be crammed in here like sardines." He laughed as he tapped his cigarette ash into a plant pot. "We're not a huge conglomerate like the bank your wife worked for. They take you for everything they can. You're not safe going with banks anymore." He leaned back and eyed Cohen. "The two ladies in my life have caught the decorating bug again and hired a couple of painters to paint my office walls a cream color — fuck! They were pumpkin orange, I liked that. Now the place stinks so we have to conduct business in here today. Don't worry. I'll have you back here when the paint's dry and you'll see my office. It's a hell of a lot nicer than this little room. It's no Royal Bank, but it's nice."

Cohen perked up. "Did you just say that you have daughters?"

"Oh yes! Two beautiful girls, all mine now. My wife skipped town with my ex-partner years ago." Mr. Baxter flicked ashes at the plant again. "Floyd and I were good friends until he screwed my wife. I kicked his ass out of the office, and now it's a family business, just me and my daughters." He pulled a pamphlet from his wrinkled pants pocket, coughed to clear his throat, and read:

For more than eight years my daughters and I have been providing plaintiffs with meaningful financial alternatives. Whether you settle your claim in a lump sum cash settlement or a structured settlement we encourage you to call on us.

The door swung open and in strutted two young women: Mr. Baxter's daughters, each holding a thick stack of files and balancing a large cup of steaming coffee.

"Yes, yes, yes!" Cohen shouted like a cheerleader at a high school pep rally. Mr. Baxter eyed him. Cohen smiled. Mr. Baxter lit another cigarette and introduced them.

"Oh, Daddy, stop smoking," ordered Betty-Anne, the elder daughter, waggling her dangling chin. "You know it's not allowed." She squeezed her fat rump into a space beside Cohen, then placed her stack of files and coffee neatly on the magazine table. Cohen felt uncomfortable. Not only was Betty-Anne hogging sofa space but she didn't even have any appealing body parts for him to look at.

"Do you want us to die from secondhand smoke?" asked Holly, Baxter's witty, big-breasted daughter. She delicately directed her firm ass cheeks towards a narrow patch of sofa cushion on Cohen's other side. He was squished between the sisters, but at least he was now visually amused.

Holly crossed her legs and in the process booted Cohen in the shin with her stiletto heel.

"Fuck!" he roared, "that hurt."

Holly hastily swung around; her face and what was visible of her ample chest flushed an attractive strawberry red as she whispered, "Sorry."

Cohen swallowed. Mr. Baxter's younger daughter was gorgeous. Every body part was sumptuous. Except for her feet. They were huge. Clydesdale huge.

Holly placed her files and coffee cup on the floor. Seconds later she shifted and the coffee spilled, spattering the hem of Cohen's pants.

"Thank God it's not all over the files this time," her father lightly scolded her. She jumped up to grab a tissue and got Cohen in the ankle. He grunted in pain. It didn't take him long to decide that she felt insecure about her feet. She wore powder blue stilettos in an obvious attempt to beautify her canoes. It didn't work. At all.

"Be careful, honey," said Mr. Baxter. He waited until Holly was finished her cleanup and then, with another cigarette dangling from his lips, he crossed his hands on his lap and said, "Now that we are all comfortable, let's hear what you suggest, girls."

Mr. Baxter and Holly looked at Betty-Anne. She took a leisurely drink of coffee, then set her cup aside. "Well, gentlemen," she said confidently, "after reviewing the value of Mr. Cohen's financial settlement, Holly and I have determined that he will be much better off with a structured settlement rather than a lump sum payment."

Cohen didn't like the sound of that.

Holly jammed the sodden cleanup tissues into her empty coffee cup and picked up her notes. She drew in a deep breath, expanding her two best assets, much to Cohen's delight, and spoke her mind. "The lump sum is tax free; however, once it is invested, the income earned is taxable to Mr. Cohen, possibly leaving him with less money to spend." She took another deep and visually stimulating breath. "According to Mr. Cohen's history, financial background, and market knowledge, we cannot foresee him successfully managing his own investments." She glanced at Cohen and smiled as if to soften her words. "We at Baxter Financial have determined that a structured settlement is the best solution for Mr. Cohen."

"Do my girls know their stuff or what?" Mr. Baxter asked a bewildered Cohen.

Cohen nodded as if he understood. He didn't. He stared blankly at them, one after the other, and then shouted, "Am I getting all of my money now and in cash?"

Betty-Anne tsk-tsked and Holly took another very deep breath. "Mr. Cohen, you can't just have one very large sum of money," said Mr. Baxter. "This money is a fair amount, but it has to last for your lifetime. All your needs, everything for the rest of your life, will come from this."

"I want my money now — all of it! I want to be rich, now!" Cohen burst upwards from the feminine confines of the sofa. He laughed and proceeded to dance around the room. "Rich! Now!"

"Stop dancing and listen to me!" Mr. Baxter screamed, chasing a joyous and limping Cohen around the room as his daughters watched, mouths agape. Cohen climbed over the furniture like a circus monkey. Mr. Baxter grabbed him and wrestled him onto the sofa, which forced the dancing animal to remain still for a moment.

"People with your type of injury lose money very quickly," gasped Mr. Baxter, keeping a firm grip on Cohen. "If you blow this money, help will be hard to find. With a structured settlement you get a fixed monthly income perfectly suited to your needs. Didn't you hear Holly?"

"Sure," Cohen said. In truth, he had just been watching her breathe in and out.

Mr. Baxter sat beside Cohen on the sofa, still holding him down. His grip might have looked friendly, but it felt like a straitjacket. "Now, Mr. Cohen," said Mr. Baxter, "I am going to ask you the most important question you will be asked today. You need to listen carefully." He paused. It felt to Cohen as if the whole room paused, even the walls. Finally Mr. Baxter said, "What are your needs, Mr. Cohen?"

"I need to inj...enju...enjo...have fun! Every day!" Cohen struck his hands together. "I made a list of the things I want now," he said, handing Mr. Baxter his crumpled wish list. "I wrote it when you were sleeping." Mr. Baxter didn't even look at the list. It slipped from his fingers and onto the floor.

"I'm going to make more wish lists. Lots of them," exclaimed Cohen. "Fuck structure! Give me the whole damn wad. Keep your taxes. I want the money. I want to spend it before I die, and that could be any time."

"Exactly," said Mr. Baxter. "It could be any time. I recommend that you name a beneficiary, someone you could give your money to if you die. Who would that be?" Mr. Baxter snaked a hand into his pocket and retrieved a metal cigarette case. Flipping it open, he sucked another rollie into his mouth like a vacuum, and lit it.

"My friend Pickle's dog Scratch was murdered! Shit!" Cohen fell silent for a brief moment, then burst out, "Hold your horses! On second thought, give it to my Polish Kishka Queen. She is a piece of Polish perfection. Her name is Kat...Katz...Kat-ass-something. She lives in Poland, it isn't that big of a country. You could find her," he said. "It's on my list. I want a plane ticket to go and visit her."

"Is she better looking than me?" asked Holly.

Cohen shrugged. "Not better looking. Just different. A different sort of thing. She's forah...foreen...you know, from another place...not here." He stared at his financial advisors. They were busy looking at one another, not at him. Betty-Anne was whispering to Holly, who didn't look half as attractive anymore what with her big and clumsy feet, and Mr. Baxter was surrounded by a cloud of noxious cigarette smoke that was irritating Cohen's throat and making his mouth feel like an ashtray. He lost his patience, and angrily jumped up. "I'll phone in my bank info tomorrow. I want direct deposit, you know? Make sure the money goes in there, the whole damn thing." He stormed towards the exit.

"Wait a minute, Mr. Cohen," Mr. Baxter called out. "We have some papers you need to sign."

A hand touched Cohen's arm. Unfortunately, his imagination was as rich as he wanted to be. He swung around to face them. "Do you three musketeers actually think you can stop me from leaving this so-called office?" He sneered. Reality slipped aside and allowed him to execute a masterful karate move to escape his tormentors. But it was too late. They gang tackled their prisoner before he could reach the door. Holly held him down with her enormous breasts while Betty-Anne shoved documents in his face. This took forever.

The tortuous team battled him with simple explanations that lasted for hours and hours, filling his head with details of exactly how much money would be going where. Cohen suffered in silence, sprawled out on the floor. They had tied him to the legs of a sofa with the straps of Holly's giant bra, silenced him with a thick wrapping of packing tape, and administered two trigger-point injections of an hypnotic sedative. When all was said and done, a glazed-over Cohen had verbally agreed to a structured settlement.

"I promise that you will have enough for your underlying needs and interests," said Mr. Baxter. "I guarantee it. A large sum of money will be put into an annuity which will provide for all medical costs, including drugs and any kind of therapy you need, for life. And you could have a housekeeper come in twice a week."

Cohen liked that last bit. He even put his own ad in the Help Wanted section of a weekly newsletter called *What's Up* that could be found every Friday night under the wipers of parked cars near bars and strip joints.

MONEY FOR YOUR $ERVICE

Tall, slim, blond and busty housekeeper needed for a handsome, financially secure man suffering from a whole lot of problems. Must be able to cook a little, clean a little and give good massages with no restrictions when requested by her employer. Must look good in a bikini and have a nice tan.

Serious Inquiries Only

Please call (905) 231-8P94 and ask for me. I'm Reuben.

SMALL STEPS FIRST

Unlike a dog bewildered by the creature staring back at him from the bathroom mirror, Cohen knew exactly what his reflection was: a big disappointment. He wished that all the mirrors were covered like in a Shiva house where mourners would sit on hard, low benches and not be able to see themselves. He did not want to see himself. He was not the man he used to be. He needed to make a new life for himself. He needed to give himself a new image. Staring at the fat, gray-faced creature in the mirror, Cohen decided to take action.

Money would cater to his needs. A physically strong body would laugh at such abuse, and welcome even more gluttony. Exercise would simply prolong his enjoyment of newfound personal wealth.

This was a new Reuben Cohen. A new Reuben Cohen with new dreams, a new Reuben Cohen who could hurt himself and yet rebound from his excesses. A Reuben Cohen who could endure any pain to achieve his goal: to live an obsessive lifestyle. To eat. To drink. To live off of life's delicious merriment.

An hour later he was at the local gym. An enthusiastic young man there set him up with a program called "A Week to a Better You." The young man showed him around the gym, expounding on the benefits of the program. "For the next seven days," he said, "you will devote yourself to exercise. You'll increase your strength and stimulate your endorphins. This will reduce stress and fight off depression. It'll be great, you'll see. You'll eat the right things and build up your strength."

Cohen went upstairs and chose a Stairmaster Turati C525i Pro Climber. He set it to a forgiving hydraulic resistance, wedged his feet into the pedals, entered numerical lies (Age: 82, Weight: 155) into the Stairmaster's computer to set his desired pace, and gripped the handlebars. That was the easy part. Maintaining a fluid pace was the hard part. His feet paddled up and down, up and down. His legs ached, his muscles burned. A memory flashed through him of how, as a budding adolescent many years ago, his legs had failed him.

Reuben's greatest achievement at the age of ten was becoming a member of the Real Men Gang. Their clubhouse was in the attic of their favorite store, Charlie's Confectionary, high above the smog-filled adult world below. It had become THE hangout. Charlie Barker, the store's seventy-six-year-old owner, turned a blind eye to who was cutting classes or skipping detentions. He didn't care.

At the back of the candy store was where the real highs were. (Deep breath.) Candy of all kinds. Best of all were the old fashioned licorice pipes. Eating a pretend pipe with red clusters at the tip gave the illusion of smoking. Placing the red tip of a pipe in your mouth was a devilish thing to do and astounded some of the younger kids on the playground who didn't yet have the guts to even buy licorice pipes. (Deeper breath.) Smoking satisfaction for those youngsters came in the form of Popeye Cigarettes.

One afternoon, Nyman, leader of the Real Men Gang, raced up the stairs yelling, "Holy shit! Here comes Miss Jacobs." (Pounding heart.) Not only was Nyman taller than the other boys, but he was tough. He even wore a black pirate's patch over his left eye for no reason other than to look cool. Nyman was very tough.

"Let's go, we gotta get out of here!" Nyman yelled. "I locked the door. That'll hold her off for a few minutes." He scanned the crowd of adolescent gangsters until he saw his lieutenant. "Lipshits, what's our escape route?" (Very deep breath.)

Miss Jacobs, their teacher, was wildly pounding on the door. Even old Charlie Barker was scared of her. With his hands over his ears and peaked cap yanked down to keep him from looking, Charlie vanished into his storage room and softly shut the door behind him.

"Let me in! Let me in, you bunch of rotten apples! You miscreants!" Miss Jacobs screamed. "The principal will hear about this." (Enraged throbbing of heart.)

Lipshits signaled and Nyman gave the high sign (the swear finger) for the escape. Everyone slipped out, skittering down the back fire escape, and then drifted away like leaves in the wind. Almost everyone, that is. Only one unlucky, and unfit, gang member had to suffer the consequences of getting caught. (Banging of heart.) Already out of breath, this guy was in trouble.

Cohen's pace slowed to that of an aged, arthritic horse. His face was creased with wrinkles of doubt and hesitation. Drops of sweat rained onto his gut.

All week, Cohen devoted himself to creating his brand new image. After seven days, twelve minutes a day, of working on his physical well-being and strength conditioning and…and nothing. An entire seven days consuming the right blend of nutrients for his body to function better and — nothing. An entire seven days replacing chocolate and candy for tasteless chicken and fish and — nothing. He had not lost any weight in a whole week; he hated every miserable minute of exercise and he felt just like shit.

"Time's up, mister! I'm booked on this treadmill now. Get off," ordered a large tank of a woman who was aiming to shed some of her excess plating. Without saying a word, Cohen jumped off the machine and left. This concluded his "Week to a Better You."

He called Mr. Baxter and demanded all his money up front. "Screw structure," he told him. Happily for Cohen, although financial advisors regularly disagree with their clients' sometimes ridiculous requests, they have no choice but to comply. It is, after all, the clients' money.

Reuben Cohen was now solely responsible for managing all his own financial affairs, including medical expenses. From the onset, decisions had been, primarily, his own; now they would be made wholly without guidance, unless he hired someone. He never would.

HOLIDAY

After more than a year of post-Pot-Mishap anger and living with the aftermath of a traumatic brain injury: dealing with regret, fear, anger and immense sexual desire every day, Cohen was far from being the real Reuben Cohen. He was no longer a hardworking and promising chef for one of Ontario's most prestigious seafood houses, no longer a jock who could snap a puck high into the net past a frustrated goalie, no longer a fun-loving guy out for a beer with his teammates after a game. No longer a caring, passionate husband. No longer a determined individual achieving goals that he set for himself.

He wasn't those people anymore. He had broken with everything. His look on life had changed and he had to rebuild. He had left his self-confidence and his ability to positively present himself far behind, along with his former sexuality and his emotional stability. His brain, exhausted from its ongoing attempts to heal itself, needed a break. With depleted self-esteem, and constant worry about how others saw him, Cohen needed to escape from the truth. Fantasy was so much simpler than hard work. It was an easy way to avoid the pain of being alone, and he was afraid to be alone. He had been hurt enough and just couldn't bear it anymore.

Fantasy had two simple rules. First, he had to build it. Second, he had to reach it. Like an alarmed hermit crab, Cohen liked to hide out in his chosen crustaceous shell that protected him from the constant attacks of reality. No one meeting Cohen in this disguise thought he was stupid, learning disabled, fat, lazy, sexually incompetent or ugly. In his fantasy shell, they all loved him. They all needed him in their lives. They were all passionately intimate with him and hungry to taste his oyster.

Alone in his crowded and still bloodstained office, he tried to imagine one, just one, female image that could accompany him on his journey. Pleading with his injured head to show him that image, if only for a little while, he squeezed his eyes shut. With his emotions packed and running, fabricated images began to seep into his mind and slowly clarified into fairyland focus. Perhaps his exotic Kishka Queen would be his first stopover, or, on second thought, a journey to Africa to visit Cassandra, his luh…lushuh…luscious physiotherapist, was a sexual supposition. And, of course, jolly old England always had succulent treats on its menus. Even prim and proper royalty might be a fun nut to crack, or perhaps the Mile High Club would be worth the price of admission. It would be sweet to play hide-the-salami with a thirsty flight att…attend…babe.

Wherever he decided to go, Cohen was appreciated, and when he returned from his mental holiday, reality was always a little easier to handle.

POP QUIZ

A loud and irritating noise eventually penetrated layers of foggy sleep. Cohen rubbed his eyes and listened. Someone was knocking. He rolled off his comfy red sofa and shambled to the door.

"Pickle! What are you doing here?"

"Let me in, let me in," Pickle rasped, squeezing through the doorway. "It's fuckin' cold out there."

"But this isn't Hot Yoga day."

"I know, I know. You don't have a doctor's appointment either." Pickle rubbed his hands and looked around. "Geez, Reuben, this place is a pigsty."

"It's not so bad," said Cohen. "It's, y'know, homey."

"I hear ya, just like the days back when, right?" Pickle moved a bowl of greasy mini donuts off the easy chair and sat down. "I came over because I had an idea. Well, Natalie did." He lifted a business card out of his wallet and handed it to Cohen. "This woman there on the card, Bryna King, she booked our Las Vegas wedding, arranged the whole thing, and it was something. You saw the DVD, right?" he asked, and shrugged when Cohen shook his head. "Well, anyway, this Bryna ain't much of a looker but she's got a great ass. Call her if you feel like taking a real trip," he waved the card away as Cohen tried to hand it back. "If you call, you do. If you don't, you don't. But I've got more. You can keep that one. You're a nobody until you have somebody's business card."

"Okay, but I don't want to trip...tra..."

"Travel," said Pickle. "But you could go places and meet some beautiful babes. You're holed up here day in day out. It's no way to live and now you're rich ya gotta treat yourself, man. You could meet hot babes."

"Yeah," Cohen said excitedly. "Hot babes on hot beaches!"

Tightly sandwiched between Wong's Tattoo Parlor on one side and The Broken Nut Dollar or Less Food Market and Erotic Art Gallery on the other was BK Travel. BK stood for Bryna King, of course.

Cohen, chewing on a pepperoni stick lifted from The Broken Nut Dollar or Less Food Market and Erotic Art Gallery, fingered Bryna's business card and thought of how important Pickle had looked just giving it to him. He stuck it back in his pocket and walked straight into BK Travel. One quick glance revealed a place that looked more like a wasteland than a work space. Three orange cabinets, heavily dented, stood against the wall with stacks of folders teetering on top. Paper coffee cups were strewn around an overflowing wastebasket.

Smiling brightly, Cohen said hello to the only person there, a middle-aged woman wearing a flagrantly red wig. She was clad entirely in black from neck to toe except for a leopard-spotted miniskirt, and she looked like a black cat wearing a hairpiece. Her lush bosom looked as if it had been squeezed out of a tube. Cohen wondered if her panties were black. Or lacy. Or both. Or maybe not there at all.

Her desk was covered by a thick layer of paper. *She must be really important and busy*, he thought, impressed. Unfortunately, she was sitting behind the desk, which meant that he couldn't see her ass.

"You must be Bryna King, my travel agent." It sounded good. Cohen stretched out his pepperoni-greased hand to greet her.

Ignoring the hand, Bryna simpered, "It is so nice to finally put a face to the voice." She gestured to a chair and he sat down. She smiled. "You mentioned when you called that you want to meet women."

"Yes."

"You said you are retired and have lots of time on your hands—you want to explore women from various countries. I think diversity would be fun."

"Yes. Can you find me some fun places to go to? Pickle said you could."

Bryna smiled. "I could put an exciting package together for you, but first, I want to show you a new option. One that will expand your horizons. If I can find the damn thing." She stood up.

Cohen tensed with excitement; he was finally going to catch a glimpse of her ass.

Bryna began rummaging through one of the filing cabinets. Her ass cheeks looked very much like Cassandra's, he decided, although he knew they probably weren't black. Still, from what he could make out, they looked firm and smooth and had just enough jiggle for fun times. Of course, with the miniskirt in the way, stare as hard as he might, he could not make out the exact cheek proportions, but he was happy enough with what he could imagine. This ass could accommodate any dream of punishment and pleasure. Cohen licked his lips at the thought of it all and leaned forward. Bryna flicked him a sideways glance and then quickly sat down, as if she knew what he was thinking.

As she shuffled through the stacks of paper on her desk, Cohen caught glimpses of letters, pamphlets, film-processing envelopes, pink Post-it notes and strips of Kleenex tissue.

"Aha! Here it is," she shouted, sounding as triumphant as a detective who had just found the missing weapon in a murder case. She held up a brightly colored pamphlet. "Holiday PreDestination! I think you'll really enjoy yourself here, Reuben. May I call you Reuben?" She scanned the pages before passing it to Cohen. "They have functions every Friday. It will help you decide where you want to go," she said, watching as Cohen stood up with the pamphlet almost touching his nose, his eyes glued to the pictures. She sighed and sat him back down.

"For every assembly, I invite all the single clients in my database. I anticipate selling more double vacation packages this way!" She beamed at him. "Whether you are looking for a life partner or just someone to hang out with, at Holiday PreDestination you could well find what you're looking for, Reuben," she said, selling like a telemarketer.

Cohen held his breath, confused and unsure.

She patted his hand. "It's fun and safe, and anonymous unless you decide to take it a step further." She giggled. "I hope you do take it further because that means more commissions for me.

"There's a gathering this Friday night at Uncle Albert's Downtown Grill. The directions to it are on the back of the pamphlet. Just fill out this questionnaire and I'll match you with women who have similar interests. And come in a suit. The better you look, the better chance you have of meeting that someone special. Remember, Reuben —first impressions are so very important."

"I'll be there!" he shouted, full of innocent hope and still squinting at the pamphlet's blurred and provocative pictures.

Bryna nodded thoughtfully and said to herself: *the travel agent gods have smiled on me today. This guy is a complete loser, such a shortsighted, overweight, bewildered man. He'll have to go to at least a thousand speed dating sessions to meet a girl who likes him. Fifty bucks a gathering and I get back ten percent a shot, so if he goes a thousand times that's…*she punched the numbers in her pocket calculator. *That's—oh my travel gods!* She looked at the number with a grin. *That's a helluva lot of money.*

"Time to fill out the questionnaire," she said smoothly, handing over the appropriate paper. "You can sit on my soft chair. Do you have enough light? Do you have enough room? Can I get you something to drink, Reuben?"

"I'm not thirsty but I would like a chocolate bar."

"There's a variety store just next door. I'll be back in a jiffy with your treat—any particular kind?"

"Anything but a Mr. Big," Cohen said, and started the laborious task of answering the questions on the paper.

Holiday PreDestination Dating Questionnaire

See how your dating attitudes compare with other singles. Fill in the blanks with an answer that best describes your personality for each question.

Name: Reuben Cohen

Sex: Yes

I would most likely be dating someone:
Who does not look as bad as my wife did. Not as fat. More attracting.

I would be least interested in dating:
Somebody who does not go goes all the way! You know, a home run in sex

When would I use the term "boyfriend" or "girlfriend":
Right away. I don't want to wait for sex

After a first date I would expect: want to be perfect
Oral sex at least. I want to go inside.

Of all the conversation killers the worst one would be:
Celebruting - celery - celebut - the non sex thing

On a first date I would prefer to wear:
Nothing - you know - nude no clothes

Thank you for your honesty and we hope that you find your perfect match.

TABLE NUMBER FIFTY-FOUR

Pickle pulled up in front of Uncle Albert's Downtown Grill. "You got everything?" he asked Cohen for the third time.

Cohen patted his pocket. "Pencils, my invitation, and the sca…scare…"

"Scorecard," said Pickle. "You've got to write down the names of any hot babes you want to date. And don't forget to call a cab BE-FORE you leave."

Cohen just nodded as he exited the car. Standing in a cloud of exhaust fumes, he eyed the place. Tall potted evergreens flanked a wide glass door. He tugged at his tie that Pickle had knotted for him and stepped onto the red carpet. A waiting valet held the door open for him.

This place is high end, he thought, and when he stepped through the door he was sure of it. A smiling hostess was in the lobby, greeting everyone and ushering them through another doorway. Cohen smiled and for the first time felt real excitement at the evening ahead. *She looks like a high-class hooker, and she smells good too. This place really is high end.*

Outward appearances were deceiving. Inside, the place had the atmosphere of an arcade. Several large plasma screens showed Wile E. Coyote and Roadrunner doing what they did, in an unending cycle. A CD jukebox played the latest hits. Scattered about the room were dartboards, arcade games, and popcorn machines. Any remaining wall space was filled with photos of rock stars; at the sight of a

Mick Jagger photo, Cohen started humming *Just A Shot Away* and wondered why. The ceilings were high enough, he decided, that you could hang yourself and not be noticed for a long time.

A potpourri of over a hundred well-groomed singles were crunched into Uncle Albert's, offering a variety of hues from cubicle pale to saddle tan. Cohen found it hard to believe that all these pretty people hadn't yet decided where to take their vacation.

Cohen was dressed to the nines in his one and only suit, a slick polyester number, with a carelessly knotted floral tie and a dirty white shirt. The entire wardrobe Cohen had haggled down to $6.50 from $7.00 at the Jewish Family Services Annual Holocaust Survivors Garage Sale. The wide brown bandage tied around his head to conceal "The Three" had been hunted out from under his sofa cushions. Now, all spiffed up and with splashes of Old Spice on his neck and thighs, he was ready.

The event coordinator stepped up to the bar; the squeal of his mike signaled for attention. "Welcome to tonight's special singles occasion. First, Uncle Albert's entire staff wishes to apologize for the teenybopper party atmosphere on the main level this evening. We are well aware it is not the frame of mind you need to be in. All of us here at the fabulous Uncle Albert's know that all of you are looking for romance, but — " he took several audible breaths as he looked around the room, "Bernard Goldberg has chosen Uncle Albert's for his Bar Mitzvah reception tomorrow night and, what with Bernard being the owner's nephew, it was impossible to decline his request."

The group moaned in disappointment and the event coordinator held up a delicate hand for silence. "Knowing this prior to tonight's singles event and how much work we had to do on the main level for Bernard, we have changed venues slightly. A private party room has been set up for your pleasure downstairs in one of our meeting rooms. And you're lucky. That's where our adequate but one-at-a-time bathrooms are located." He clapped his hands together and gestured to a door at the back of the room. "Okay, ladies and gentlemen, let's go."

Faces drooped and another group moan sounded, then slutty stilettos and lusting loafers (and a solitary pair of hopeful, albeit grubby, Hush Puppies) shuffled obediently down the steep stairs. The first singles to reach the bottom instantly broke into a round of applause. The narrow room had a country pub décor, with sixty numbered tables in a long line down the center. Background music, classic love songs, softened the mood for the partner seekers. "This is more like it," yelled a small Asian man looking for hot romance.

The event coordinator quickly pushed his way through the crowd to the bar at the end of the room. The squeal of a microphone again prefaced his announcement. "Here are the rules. Remember: you have only six minutes per table—use them wisely.

"Okay now, we have allocated two hours for you to meet twenty possible next loves or even that special soul mate. I don't think anyone has more than one of those! Don't ask for last names, phone numbers or dates during the event. Don't forget to use your scorecards. Start at the table number indicated on your invitation."

Bodies started to shuffle. He called for attention. "At the start of each six-minute session the bell will ring. That is the signal for you to begin. When the bell rings a second time, it is the signal to end your date. Then move it, lovers! Move on to the next table. All your table numbers are on your invitation."

Cohen stared at his card, numbers wavering as he blinked. The coordinator's voice faded in and out as he tried to listen, the words jumbling together. "What the fuck is going on here?" Cohen asked a woman wearing a cheerful "Need Help?—Ask Me!" button. This degree of multi-tasking was far beyond his cognitive abilities.

"Okay, er, Reuben," she said, looking at the top left corner of Cohen's invitation. "You start at table number thirty-four."

"What the fuck is going on?" he asked again. "Why all the…so much…so much…what's going on?"

"It's all right, sir. If you need any help, just ask me or any of the other assistants. I'm Judith Lynn," she said politely. "A lot of first-timers have a rough go at the start. I assume you're a first-timer?"

Cohen nodded. Judith Lynn ushered him to his starting point. Like a shy first-grader sitting across from his evil teacher on parents' night, Cohen began to sweat.

The bell rang. "What the fuck?" he muttered.

A triple-chinned young woman with a pony-tail and red-framed glasses sat across him at table thirty-four. She smiled and spoke rapidly. "My name is Janice as you can see by my nametag over my small left boob, my right one is bigger. I was named after my mother, not my real one, I was adopted. I go to church on Sundays and I love the snacks afterwards, I'm not a born-again or anything. (Deep breath.)

"I don't like bowling but it is kind of fun, I broke one hundred and ten for the first time. At the bowling alley where I bowl they have great Slushies. I wear a size-ten bowling shoe, I think they look cool. I love dogs but especially I love parrots and budgies, I used to have one but he flew away, I forgot to lock the cage door." (Deeper breath.) "I really like to go to movies and I love to watch television when I get home from a long day at CT, that's short for Canadian Tire, I'm a checkout girl. I love kids and want some one day, three boys kinda like the Three Stooges, three is my favorite number."

Her verbiage had allowed Cohen to do something very interesting: he did not listen to her. He simply stared. For five minutes and forty-six seconds, he stared at Janice's face and body, concentrating so hard that at the end of the session, when he closed his eyes he had a clear mental picture of her naked and on all fours.

Cohen blushed.

"Don't you have anything to tell me? We're probably short on time now but I'll listen," said Janice. She laughed. "Why do you have a bandage on your head? It looks funny."

The bell rang. After five minutes and fifty-six seconds of not listening to Janice's life story, all Cohen had time to say was, "What the fuck?"

"Move clockwise, Speed Daters," shouted the event coordinator. "Move on to your next possible true love."

"Speed dater? What the fuck is a speed dater?" A stunned Cohen asked the woman at his next table after Judith Lynn had guided him there. "I thought this was Holiday PreDestination."

"Your travel agent must be Bryna King, am I right?"

He checked the business card Pickle had given him, and nodded. The bell sounded for the next round.

"She's been known to mask the truth, that Bryna. She's afraid her single clients won't attend if they know what this really is, a fucking meat market. Capitalist bastards! Taking advantage of the lonely…but the clock is ticking and you may be my next Prince Charming, so let's begin. Sit down. I'm Christina, and this is Speed Dating."

"Dating? I don't need a date," said Cohen, obediently taking his seat. "All I need is a mental picture of dirty thoughts." Under the small table, Christina's legs were extended like the necks of hungry giraffes and the toes of her colorful boots bit into Cohen's pants as if they were soft leaves.

Christina was good-looking, very good-looking. To Cohen she looked like a blurry dark-haired Kim Basinger in *9 ½ Weeks* (one of his favorite movies because he liked the erotic scenes). Maybe this meeting would turn into a kinky relationship gone out of control.

As in the previous session, he was silent. It was difficult for him to endure the torture of a rapidly increasing lust for Christina, but he had to focus on creating a mental picture of this sex goddess. Her image was far more pleasing than that of many-chinned Janice. He memorized her face and then tilted his gaze down to the swell of her ample bosom.

He heard her say, "*I think you're delicious. I can imagine your large, ready-to-explode rocket on my naked body." Christina ran her tongue around her lips. "I'll do anything, baby! Bondage, ass plugs, ball or nipple torture, stilettos, caning, hot wax. Anything, baby! Open your mind to me. I am so attracted to you. You're such a bewildered, silent man, but don't you dare remove that bandage on your head. I bet there's something nasty under there.*"

Cohen blushed. Trying to build a mental image of a naked Christina was making him dizzy.

The bell rang. These six minutes had just flown by. Christina did not mark Cohen down on her scorecard. *She must have forgotten*, he thought, but as he stumbled from the table he heard her mumble to her next Speed Date, "That weirdo didn't say a word, just stared at me for the entire six minutes."

Every six minutes for the next two hours, Cohen shifted his fat ass from one chair to the next. In his mind, he was traveling from one tropical island to another, and the murmur of voices all around him became the rustling of palm trees and the sounds of the ocean. Then, for six minutes, he fixed his eyes on whatever woman sat across from him and never said a word.

Now and then a frustrated groan escaped the lips of a woman trying to get a response from him. He became known as "that weird silent guy in the polyester suit." Ironically, several women were turned on by his novel approach to Speed Dating and even considered writing his name in the "Very Possible" column of their scorecards. They never did.

Cohen left Uncle Albert's Downtown Grill a very tired, unhappy and still lonely man, no better off than when he arrived. From his twenty sessions, he could only recall a mental picture of the last woman he had visited, at table number fifty-four: a cute blonde with plump breasts accented by blueberry muffin crumbs clinging to her sweater. She wrote madly in a notebook and sipped a Caramel Macchiato all through their session. He could have sworn he'd been on that island before, but his memory had let him down again. *I'm sure I have seen that woman many times before. I know her face, but I can't rem...remb...think who she is.*

MONETARY MADNESS

Once The Pot Mishap mediation was over, Cohen had to pay for all of his therapy costs. He stopped going. He was responsible for his life-time supply of prescription medication too. He stopped taking them. To Cohen, the insurance settlement payout signaled the end of his brain injury. *Everything is over, I must be alright now,* he thought. *Anyway, it's just too damn expensive.*

This sense of closure allowed him to finally open another door that he was desperate to go through. With his new financial freedom, he would endeavor to find out who this new Reuben Cohen was and discover what he was capable of doing without medication to cloud the issue. He would strive to give his fluctuating personality a chance to develop.

> *Enough! Enough medication. Enough symptoms.*
> *Enough doctors. Enough testing. Enough questions.*
> *Enough trying to get back the past. It's gone. Enough!*
> *I want more! More striking and more colorful images*
> *of women. Women's naked bodies. Faces. Legs. Tits. Oh,*
> *I love tits! Give me culture! Women of different*
> *cults...looks...looking different...divers...diety* (these
> fucking words) *...diversity – yes! Women of diversity!*
> *For over a year I have suffered from the trapain...*
> *traman...tramotic....from all the pain of my head injury.*
> *I am tired of being told what to do and what to think and*

where to go and when to go there. I am tired of others making decides...decidan...decisions for me. But what do I know? Well, I know that I am different now.

I am doing my best to accept who I am. To accept my thinking thoughts and how it feels to have me now. To own ME after the accident.

I will make my own choices now and take raisins...raispon...responsibilities for my own life. I will respect me myself and love me. And know that things will turn out for the best the longer that I go in the long run.

I am going to live with the decisions of the owner of Reuben Cohen — that's me. And he. Who is really me will figure out who he is on his own. I will look forward now and not back to the past. Yes, forward!

Cohen's doctors received a stream of phone and email messages from concerned pharmacists who had become familiar with Cohen's routine over the past thirteen months, messages like:

Reuben Cohen has always picked up his medication from our Total Drugs location at 1712 Bloor St. West on the first of every month at 11:00 a.m. Even with his thought processes at times adversely affected, remembering to keep a regular regime of when and where he needed to pick up his medication was a characteristic of Mr. Cohen's that we here at the pharmacy really admired. But now his monthly attendance at our pharmacy has tapered off to a long absence. We have checked with our other locations. They have informed us that Mr. Cohen has not visited any of them either.

All of us here at Total Drugs are concerned for his well-being. Side effects of not taking his prescribed medications, although not life threatening, will be unpleasant for a man in his condition.

Please call us here at Total Drugs with any information you may have regarding his whereabouts.

And don't forget to remind your patients about the tremendous sale we're having this weekend. Buy a bottle of The New You Shampoo and receive a free bottle of Total Vitamins.

Sale runs until Sunday at 6:00 p.m. We hope that you received our coupons! See you there!

Since Cohen did not answer his phone and refused to try and read boring mail, it was impossible for his concerned medical team to track him down. If contact with him had been possible, his doctors would have tried to get him to comply with their wishes, for his own benefit, but they also knew that not taking medication was a personal decision. There was nothing they could do about it.

REUBEN REDUX

Reuben Cohen's life had taken him on many a sideways journey since The Pot Mishap, and he was not happy with the scenery en route. The old Reuben might have been content with reality; to the new Reuben it was a grim and unaccepting place. Mental holidays were no longer enough. He wanted more. And he wanted it every day.

Only one place offered him the visual stimuli and sexual freedom he quested after, but could not afford until now: his willingness to part with the remnants of his sanity and financial security would take him anywhere he wanted to go.

One icy day in late November, Reuben stepped out of the house for the last time and shut the door behind him—the door to the house that no longer meant home, now that the forgotten Shelly was gone. His jacket hung open. A stained T-shirt tried, and utterly failed, to cover a glorious expanse of belly. He limped down the sidewalk, past frozen flower beds and bedraggled plants, his scarred forehead exposed. A pair of prescription goggles was wrapped around his head. How he appeared to others didn't matter to him anymore. *They may think I'm gay but at least I can see*, he told himself. He was finally maturing.

A red-cheeked Hilda whistled through the fence. "Going on a trip, Cohen?" she asked, tipping seed into her bird feeder. Then she straightened. "Why on earth do you have a lunchbox tied to your hockey stick? It looks stupid."

Reuben ran his thumb along the taped shaft that rested on his shoulder. "It's my bindle stick."

Hilda snorted. "Mister Hobo, are you? And where are you going? Do hoboes have a Hockey Hall of Fame?"

Reuben remained calm as he limped out through the gate and approached her.

"Do you want something?" she asked, frowning.

He handed her his house keys. "Would you keep an eye on things? Pipes and...and stuff, y'know."

"I suppose." Hilda sounded surprised. "Where are you going?"

"Just taking an extended vacuum...vacant...going away for a while, that's all."

She eyed him, shaking her head. "You can't just go off looking like that. At least tuck in your shirt. Show some class."

Reuben shook his head. He refused. He said, "No."

"Turn around, Cohen," she demanded. He complied. She gasped. "I knew it. I knew it. I can see the crack of your ass. That's disgusting." She laughed out loud.

Reuben did not. "I'm so sorry you feel that way," he said, still facing away from her. "I don't think I'm dis...disgusting in the sly...slee... slightest," he said, and bent over, wiggling and clenching and unclenching his butt cheeks as if he was talking out of his ass. "I am Reuben Cohen's ass. Reuben Cohen's ass!" And his ass wiggled its cheeks right in front of Hilda Greenberg's God-loving wrinkled face.

Reuben then turned around and looked into her aged eyes, only to see many other eyes from his past looking directly back at him. "Not disgusting at all," he said to all the eyes. "Not disgusting in the sleet...light...sleet...in the slightest," he said. Then he turned his back on all the watching eyes and limped off down the street.

From the bindle stick over his left shoulder dangled his grub box, and inside it a homemade roast beef and cheese bagel sandwich kept company with Shelly's obituary and a thermos jammed with blank checks.

Reuben Cohen—the new and only Reuben Cohen—was finally on his way.